# The Faith of Ashish

Also by Kay Marshall Strom

The "Grace in Africa" Series
*The Call of Zulina*
*The Voyage of Promise*
*The Triumph of Grace*

# The Faith of Ashish

## Book 1 of the Blessings of India Series

### Kay Marshall Strom

a novel approach to faith

Nashville, Tennessee

*The Faith of Ashish*

ISBN-13: 978-1-4267-0908-1

Published by Abingdon Press, P.O. Box 801, Nashville, TN 37202

www.abingdonpress.com

Published in association with the Books & Such Literary Agency,
Janet Kobobel Grant,

5926 Sunhawk Drive, Santa Rosa, CA 95409
www.booksandsuch.biz.

Cover design by Anderson Design Group, Nashville, TN

Library of Congress Cataloging-in-Publication Data

Strom, Kay Marshall, 1943-
The faith of Ashish / Kay Marshall Strom.
  p. cm. — (Blessings in India series ; 1)
ISBN 978-1-4267-0908-1 (pbk. : alk. paper)
1. India—Fiction. I. Title.
PS3619.T773F35 2011
813'.6—dc22

2011008182

Printed in the United States of America

1 2 3 4 5 6 7 8 9 10 / 16 15 14 13 12 11

I gratefully dedicate this book to my many friends in India who continue to fight for the rights of Dalits—formally known as Untouchables. They are too numerous to name, but God knows each one.

A special debt of thanks to Kolakaluri Sam Paul. Several years ago I met Sam Paul in Ireland where he was speaking on present-day slavery as it exists in India. He told me, "You should write a book about the Dalits in India. Please, let people know about us."

I did, Sam.
Thank you so much for the challenge and inspiration.

# Acknowledgments

India in the twentieth century . . . what a panorama! What a story! I could never have dreamed of attempting such a work without the help and encouragement of so many knowledgable people.

First, I must thank Kolakaluri Sam Paul for planting the seed for this project. At the time, we were both in Ireland traveling with the movie *Amazing Grace*, and Sam Paul was speaking about major forms of slavery that still exist today. It was he who challenged me to write a book about the plight of India's Outcastes. Two years later, Barbara Scott, my editor at Abingdon Press at the time, watered that seed when she said, "Have you considered writing a trilogy set in India?" *Blessings in India* is the full-grown result.

I thank two organizations important to me: She Is Safe (SIS), formerly Sisters In Service, and Partners International, for introducing me to India and to so many wonderful people there. I especially appreciate Michele Rickett, president of SIS, and Cherylann Sammons, area director. We have spent many weeks together in many places!

During my trips to India, I have met so many wonderful people who have introduced me to this great country and bound me to it in unforgettable ways. I wish I could list them all. I especially appreciate Bishop Moses Swamidas who, through his writings and personal stories, opened up India's past to me. I also thank Dr. B. E. Vijayam, renowned Indian scientist whose innovative approaches have helped change the face of India in so many ways, and his wife, Mary. I thank P. T. George for the Indian understanding he has afforded me. I also so appreciate the help and advice of Jebaraj Devashayam.

Since he is himself a gifted writer, he has a particularly good eye for details and was able to point out cultural facts I never could have discovered on my own.

A warm and loving thank you to my best editor, my husband, Dan Kline. How I appreciate you. And I also thank my faithful reader/editor/friend, Kathy Force. What would I do without you?

# The Faith of Ashish

# 1

## South India

### March 1905

*A* small boy, his brown body sticky with sweat, stretched up on his tiptoes and grabbed an earthenware cup from the rim of the well. Water sloshed over the child's hands. The cup was already full—a fortunate thing, for the little one was too small to draw water by himself. He grasped the cup tightly in both hands and drank till it was empty.

Only then did the little one notice men running toward him. He didn't see the angry, snarling looks on their faces, though, because the glaring sun blinded him. The boy, his curiosity growing, rubbed his fists over his face and shaded his eyes.

A man rushed toward the boy. He raised a stick over his head and, without warning, smacked it down across the child's back. The little one screamed, "*Appa! Appa!*" but his father wasn't there to help him. The man cut the child's cries short with another blow, this one so hard it knocked the boy's breath out of him. When the little one managed to force his dark eyes open again, he saw still more men rushing toward him. He wanted to scream, but he couldn't. He could hardly catch a breath. Someone kicked him hard. Someone else pounded on him. Again and again and again.

"*Ap . . . pa!*" the tiny child gasped.

The next smack flung him hard against the side of the well, mercifully knocking him senseless. He didn't feel the rest of the blows.

When the men left, the boy lay still in a tiny crumpled heap.

## 2

*Y*ou know what you must do," Latha said.

Virat knew. Though it could cost him his life, he knew.

On the mat in the far corner of the hut, little Ashish moaned in pain. Virat could not bear to look at his son, so battered and broken. Instead, he busied himself with his dingy *mundu*. He untied the long strip of cotton from around his thin body and stretched it out as far as his arms would reach.

"I wove a new broom for today," Latha said to her husband.

"Put it in place. I am ready."

Latha held the long stems of the bundle of twigs firmly against her husband's back, and Virat rewrapped his *mundu* around both him and the bound ends. He pulled the cloth as tightly as possible in order to hold the broom in place. The garment must stay flat and smooth, though, with no folds. Untouchables were forbidden to wear folds. Caste rule. And caste rules must never be broken.

Even on this terrible day, Latha took care to adjust the jagged edges of the twig broom in such a way that they would not snag a hole in the worn cotton of Virat's only garment.

"Do the broom bristles hang down far enough?" Virat asked. "They must brush against the ground. Do they brush against the ground?"

Latha knew each crease on her husband's dark face, every cadence of his gentle voice. They had walked side by side through sorrow and disaster; they had journeyed together through want and despair. But never before had she detected the hoarse tremble of raw fear that now tinged his words. With all her might, Latha shoved at the broom. Jagged twigs clawed into her husband's bare back. Latha winced as blood ran down his brown skin, but Virat made no complaint.

Padding silently on calloused feet, Virat moved across the dirt floor to the sleeping mat he had dragged inside in order to protect his son from curious eyes. Damp locks of black hair framed the boy's swollen face. Virat reached out toward his child, but the broom on his back wouldn't let him bend down. So he stood stiff and straight, like a brown tree that cannot bend in the wind, and stared at his little one.

"Be a good boy," Virat whispered. "Remember, you are Ashish. Remember, you are a blessing. Always and forever, remember who you are."

When Virat left the hut, Latha did not follow behind him as required of a proper Indian wife. Instead, without apology, she walked by her husband's side.

"Now the cup," Virat said.

Latha plucked a dirty string from her husband's outstretched hand, looped it around his head, and carefully positioned it above his ears. She left the string loose, but tied the ends together in a knot. Virat slipped a flat tin cup over his mouth and pushed it securely in place under the string.

"Take it off!" Latha insisted. "Do not wear that awful thing here! This is our side of the village! *Our* house!"

"The new drum," Virat said through the tin cup. "Hand it to me."

As Latha fetched the drum, the door of the hut creaked open and little Ashish blinked out at the morning sun. Moving painfully, he shaded his bruised eyes and stared about him with a blank expression until he caught sight of his father—drum in hand, tin cup tied over his mouth, broom hanging down his back.

"*Appa?*" Ashish whispered.

Virat yanked the cup away from his face.

"Get back to the sleeping mat!" he ordered. "Now!"

"No, no, not so angry!" Latha pleaded. "Not today!"

Virat hadn't intended to be harsh with the boy. But the child had taken him by surprise. And once the words were out of his mouth, he couldn't take them back again, no matter how much he might wish it. Sadness flooded over Virat and washed away all the gentle things he would like to say, leaving him speechless. He couldn't think of one single word. So he simply shook his head and turned away.

With the drum tucked under his arm, the tin cup clutched in his hand, and the string still dangling over his ears, Virat called back to Latha, "Sacrifice the piglet to the village god. Implore the god to guide my steps. Plead with him to make a success of my journey."

Latha opened her mouth, but her words drowned in tears.

"Should I die, wife, take the boy and follow the road toward the mountains. It will lead you back to your father's house."

Virat, the Untouchable . . . Virat, the accursed . . . Virat, the despised outcaste . . . set his feet on the path that separated the familiar settlement of his lowly kind from the far side of the village, home to high caste warriors and kings and Brahmin priests.

And nothing would ever be the same again.

# 3

"I will work with you, *Appa*," Ashish had announced early on that fateful morning.

To the child, it was simply another day. Early each morning, Virat went out to scour the open spaces around the mud huts and up the road in search of animals that had died during the night with their valuable hides intact. He always hoped for a cow or a goat, but he counted it good fortune to find anything salvageable at all. Ashish often tagged along on these daily hunts. It pleased Virat to have him. The boy must learn, for one day he, too, would do this accursed work. The son of a *chamar* always grew up to be a *chamar*.

But very early that morning a runner had come from across the bridge, from the high caste side of the village, and—careful to keep his feet off the polluted path of the Untouchables—had called out, "Virat! Virat the *chamar*! Come and take away a dead cow!"

No one of high caste birth could touch a dead animal, of course. It would instantly pollute them. So, however much they might despise Virat, they could not do without his services.

"You must not come with me today," Virat had told his son. "Today you must stay with your mother."

But Ashish did not stay with his mother. As soon as Latha left on her morning trek to fill the water jars, the boy set out to follow his father. Virat was too far down the path for Ashish to actually see him, but that didn't matter. The child knew the way his father would go: he would take the small path to the main road where he would turn and follow it all the way to the river. So that's the way Ashish went.

When the boy got to the river, he caught sight of his father far ahead, on the other side of the bridge. Actually, Ashish could only see a faint shape, but he knew it to be his *appa* because the shape pushed a hand cart, and only his father did that. So Ashish had rushed across the bridge.

Beyond the clutch of mud huts, flattened dirt and dusty brush lined both sides of the pathway. With most of the trees cut down for their wood, the land lay barren—shades of brown and gray and sandy tan—broken only by a great patch of shimmering green up ahead. It was the scum-edged pond where Latha went each day to fetch water for the family. Only in the hot summer, when the pond dried into thick mud, did she risk going on to the river.

People of the washer caste lived around the pond. It was their job to clean the dirty clothes of anyone who could afford to own more than one garment. Already untouchable women had begun to gather at the side of the pond, dipping their jugs into the water as they chatted about their children. Farther along, dusty steps led from the washerfolk's houses down to the water. Stained *saris* and muddy *mundus* lay in piles on either side of the stairs. One washerwoman after another grabbed up a dirty garment and beat away the stains in scummy water. At a signal that only the washer folk knew, waiting children dashed into the water to grab the colorful cloth away from them and spread it out over the rocks to dry. Red, yellow, blue, green . . . like giant rainbow-colored flowers blossoming in the bleak land.

"Look at the funny man!" a child called as he pointed to Virat.

Other children turned to stare and giggle.

"Hush, hush!" the adults scolded. They kept their own eyes averted. They knew. A cup kept an Untouchable's contaminated breath off roads where high caste feet would tread. A broom was necessary to sweep away the pollution of untouchable footprints. A drum allowed the disgusting one to warn members of pure high castes that a polluted, worthless one headed their way.

That awful day had started out an especially fine day, blessedly too early in the year for the sweltering summer air that would soon blast the land and scorch the soul. The dead cow lay in a field directly across the river, in the section of the village reserved for Sudras—the workers. Even though Sudras were people of caste, not outcastes like in Virat's section of the village, they occupied the bottom rung of the caste ladder. Were a Brahmin to kill a Sudra, his penalty would be no greater than if he had killed a dog.

Virat worked efficiently. First he skinned the cow. He laid the hide aside to dry into fine leather which he would later fashion into sandals for the highest caste feet. Next Virat removed the best of the meat from the bones. He wrapped each piece in a section of cloth and laid them one by one in his cart to take back to his side of the river. Untouchables were meat-eaters. In fact, the promise of meat is what had persuaded the village elders to allow Virat and Latha to settle at the far edge of the village.

The rest of the cow, Virat left for the vultures. They also needed to eat.

With a smile of success, Virat had grabbed hold of the cart handles and tugged his way back across the rough slats of the bridge. That night, he would enjoy meat with his rice. Everyone in the settlement of mud huts would take pleasure in a meal of meat and rice. No doubt, Latha and the other women had already lit the cooking fires in anticipation.

Up ahead, a clutch of small boys chased after each other, clouds of sandy dirt billowing around their bare legs. Startled, Virat stopped to stare. For a moment, he thought he saw his Ashish running in the circle, laughing with the other children. But no. It was another skinny brown boy with black hair and scratched-up legs.

When the boys saw Virat staring at them, they stopped and stared back. Embarrassed, Virat moved on. The boys pulled together and drew away. Virat didn't turn around to see how long they continued to gape at him.

Past where the boys played, the land grew full and lush. Here the houses were larger, framed by verandas and sheltered by leafy neem trees. They were even made of wood, though the boards had weathered to a dull gray. Here and there Virat saw a mango tree, fragrant with blossoms. One house had a good-sized cart pulled up to one side and a plow next to that. At the end of the house stood an extra room big enough for a cow. Or maybe only a goat, though even a goat would be wonderful.

Nice, this part of the untouchable village. Nice in a drab sort of way.

✑❧

"Where is Ashish!" Latha had demanded as soon as Virat pulled his cart into their courtyard. "Where is your son?"

Virat stared at her, unable to comprehend the question.

Here at home. Here with his mother. Virat knew Ashish to be an obedient child, so he must be right here.

But Ashish was nowhere to be found. So Virat left his cart where it was—standing in the open, filled with the wrapped packets of fresh meat—and ran to search for his little boy.

"Have you seen Ashish?" he asked one person after another. "Have you seen my son?"

No, no, no, each person said.

But then three boys pointed down the road and told Virat, "He went that way. He went to the bridge."

That's when panic seized Virat. He had run to the bridge and on across without stopping, bellowing all the way, "Ashish! Ashish! Where are you, Ashish?"

✑❧

"You make a disgusting spectacle of yourself, *chamar!*"

Ranjun the potter sneered from behind the pretentiously bushy mustache in which he took such pride. On his head he balanced a huge load of newly fired earthenware pots, skill-fully bound together with twine. It made him look like a tree with globes of fruit growing out of his skull. Although he, too, was untouchable, his pots were used in the kitchens of the high caste houses—the most sacred place to be found in a house—so he considered himself better than the others on that side of the river.

"Do you really think a cup, a broom, and a drum will protect you from the wrath of the upper castes?" Ranjun laughed out loud. "Of course they will not! It is you who pollutes the ground! It is your shadow. Tell me, how will you walk through their land and keep your shadow off their road and away from their houses?"

Ranjun was a vicious man. When distressed or angry, he beat his wife with a stick, and his daughter too. Sometimes he did so even when he wasn't distressed or angry, just to make certain they knew their place.

Yet Virat answered Ranjun with respect. Not because he liked the man, but for Latha's sake. She considered Ranjun's wife Pooni her closest friend.

"I have business on the other side of the bridge," Virat said as he continued to walk.

Virat could feel Ranjun's eyes burning into his back. Business? Of course Ranjun knew what that business was. Everyone in the untouchable end of the village knew.

Only March, yet the day that had started out mild had grown increasingly hot. Little Ashish had crossed over the bridge into the Sudra's land. Why he would do such a thing, no one could imagine. Certainly he had never set foot in the high caste area of the village before. It could be that he became confused and lost his way. Or perhaps he simply determined to find his *appa*. But this much was certain: Ashish crossed over the bridge on a day that had turned unexpectedly hot.

One other thing was certain, too: At some point the little one had seen the village well and the community cup alongside it. Just a well like any other, except that it sat on the high caste side of the bridge. But the sun seared and the child grew thirsty, so he had stood on his tiptoes, reached for the cup, and he had taken a drink from it.

So normal a response. So innocent an action. But so dangerous for one of his caste.

⚘

"Your son desecrated their well," Ranjun called after Virat. "Of course they grabbed up sticks and beat him! Your boy should have learned the proper ways from you. This is your fault, Virat!"

Virat *had* taught his son. "Do not cross over into the high caste section of the village," he had warned, not one time but many. He had pointed to the rough-hewn bridge and explained to his son the great danger he would invite should he dare to so much as tread on the road next to it. Caste code, Virat said, and caste code *must* be observed.

And yet, Virat had not specifically forbidden Ashish to drink from that specific cup that stood beside that specific well on the other side of the bridge. That such a possibility might happen never occurred to him.

One time when Ashish walked with his father in the sweltering month of July, when nothing was left of the green-scum pond but mud, the child had complained of thirst. Spying the river, tiny Ashish had begged, "There, *Appa!* Please, we can drink there."

"Never dip your hands in that water!" Virat had scolded. "You must never drink from their water. Not ever!"

"Why?" Ashish had asked.

"Because we are unclean."

"Why?" the child had persisted.

"Because we displeased the gods. In our past lives, we committed terrible evil."

"I don't remember being bad," Ashish said.

"Neither do I, but it must be so, for *karma* made us what we are. If we drink the water or eat the food of the high castes—of the pure ones—we pass our pollution on to them. We make them dirty before the gods the same as we are dirty, and the gods will be angry with us all over again."

Virat had said nothing more.

"*Appa?*" Ashish had asked. "Why did the gods put so much water in the river if they didn't want thirsty people to drink it?"

Questions, questions, and more questions. It was enough to weary a father.

But Virat should have taken the time to answer his son's questions. Oh, why didn't he sit with his Ashish and explain? Before it was too late?

✍

When Virat had finally found his little son lying in a heap beside the well, he picked up the battered child and carried him home in his arms. He tried to awaken the boy, and when he could not, Latha tried. When Ashish still would not open his eyes, Virat ran in search of the herbalist. Latha built up the cooking fire and put rice on to boil, then frantically ran from market stall to market stall in search of appropriate offerings to accompany the rice sacrifice for the village god—sweet-meats, fruit, coconut, flowers.

Neither the herbalist nor vendors would wait for their pay. Virat had no money, so even as their son struggled for breath,

Latha pulled the glass and clay bangles from her wrists and handed them over.

As soon as little Ashish uttered a whimper, the healer forced him to drink first one herbal medicine and then another. Virat traded their earthenware storage pot for an amulet to slip over the child's head, and the healer chanted one *mantra* after another. But despite all their efforts, the little one seemed to linger between life and death.

The bruises that marred Ashish's small body darkened from red to purple to black, and his little face puffed up with welts. His breath came in short, agonizing gasps.

"If he cannot breathe, he will not live!" Latha moaned.

So Latha sold her two most prized possessions—beautiful painted pots, one for rice and one for curry, wedding gifts from her family. Virat unwound the *chaddar* he wore as a turban around his head and wrapped his son in the long cotton scarf. He picked the child up, and, with his wife beside him, carried the boy all the way to the medical hut in the next village. An Indian man met them at the door and took their money.

"Unwrap him," the man instructed.

Tenderly, Virat pulled his *chaddar* back to reveal his beaten son. The man looked at the limp child. He prodded him and put his ear to Ashish's chest to better hear the child gasp for breath.

"Take your son home," the man had said. "Most likely, he will die before morning."

Nothing more. Ashish was not even allowed inside the medical hut. "No, no! Unclean!" the man at the door said. He wrinkled his nose to emphasize his disgust. "Untouchable and unclean!"

Evenings, with his day's work behind him, it was Virat's habit to seek out a sliver of shade and settle down to rest. Ashish, surrounded by the other children of the mud hut settlement, would run past him and call out, "Look, *Appa!* Look at me!"

Virat adjusted the tin cup over his mouth and picked up his pace.

This evening he would not be watching the children. But what did it matter? If his own son could not run and play, why should he care to watch the others?

# 4

*D*rink the milk, my little one," Latha pleaded as she pressed a cup to Ashish's swollen lips. "Please? It will bring life to you. A few sips?"

But Ashish turned his head away.

Latha had traded her day's measure of rice to the milkmaid for that cup of milk. The rice mattered not in the least to her. How could she eat with her son lying in such a state?

"Eeeeeeeeeee . . . "

A piercing squeal, and from the very piglet she had promised Virat she would sacrifice to the village god. The longer Latha delayed the offering, the angrier the god would be. But how could she go up to the shrine and leave her little boy alone?

Any other family would simply call for a grandmother or an auntie to come and sit with an ill child, but Latha had no family in the village—none in all of Malabar, besides her husband and son. Everyone else lived far away beyond the hills in the village she and Virat had fled.

Latha leaned over her child and repeated the familiar refrain: "You are Ashish. You are a blessing. Always and forever, remember who you are."

When the little one failed to show the slightest response, she added in a desperate whisper: "Do not leave me, Ashish. Please, please, do not go!"

*

The door scraped open and Latha exclaimed, "Virat! You are back so soon?"

"No, no. It's only me," said her friend Pooni as she let herself in.

Of course, Pooni was always welcome in Latha's house. As soon as she crossed the threshold, she was as one of the family.

"Oh, Pooni, I'm glad you are here," Latha cried. "I promised Virat I would make a sacrifice for his journey and say prayers for our Ashish, but I dared not leave the boy alone in such a state. Can you stay with him so I can do my duty before the village god before it is too late?"

Pooni lowered her eyes. "Perhaps it is already too late. Surely the gods and goddesses are most displeased with you, Latha. "

Instinctively, Latha reached her hand up and covered the left side of her face—the ugly, accursed side—and bristled. "I do what I am supposed to do! Every year, I go to the sacred tree and lay out my sacrifices."

"Yet your *karma* continues to speak, does it not? Only one of the six babies born to you still lives. And even this one . . . well, look at him." Pooni pointed to the pitted scars on Ashish's swollen face.

"The goddess brought the pox to my child!" Latha snapped. "You said so yourself. You said I must not complain, and so I did not."

In truth, when Ashish fell ill with the dreaded disease, Latha had been too terrified to complain. Virat had run to fetch the healer who came with herbs and potions and prepared a bed of neem leaves for the tiny child who had only just begun to toddle. The healer made a drink of cheese, molasses, bananas, and milk to offer to the smallpox goddess, but he also gave some of it to little Ashish to drink.

"My son lived to be well and strong," Latha reminded her friend. "The same cannot be said for many others stricken with the pox, but my Blessing did live to be well and strong. He will grow up to wear his scars proudly. Everyone who sees him will know he was touched by the goddess of the pox."

Ashish tossed fitfully and cried out in his sleep. Pooni bent over him, but her words were to Latha.

"Life ends at the land of the gods. Everyone wants to go there, but only the good and pure succeed in their journey."

Latha clenched her lips.

Pooni turned to Latha and grasped hold of her hands. "If you made an error . . . " she implored. "If you sinned . . . Oh, Latha, I am so afraid for you!"

Pooni, a sharp and angular woman, moved with jerks and twitches. Not at all like Latha. In many ways, Latha was an attractive woman—graceful and rounded, with a fine sparkle to her face. Latha walked proudly and she spoke her mind, though in a pleasing way. No doubt her superior breeding had brought it all about. For she was of a higher *jati*—social strata—than Pooni. Much higher than Virat. An outcaste, yes. Untouchable, most certainly. But of a higher *jati* than anyone else in the settlement of mud huts, including Pooni's haughty husband Ranjun.

"Perhaps you have not heard," Pooni said in an ominous voice. "Ranjun told me this morning that Brahmin Keshavan pronounced a curse on your house."

Latha pulled her hands away from Pooni's grip. She clutched at the tattered edge of her faded blue and yellow *sari* and tucked it under so that the frayed edges wouldn't show. Even at a time like this, even with no one around but scrawny Pooni, Latha's instinct urged her to conceal her poverty.

"I must make my sacrifice," Latha said. "On my way back I will cut branches from the neem tree by the road, and we can take turns fanning Ashish. The cooling breeze will comfort him, and healing air will fly to him from the divine tree."

Pooni grasped Latha by the shoulder, but immediately let go. Latha's skin was smooth as *ghee*—boiled butter fine enough to enrich the table of a Brahmin. That's what Virat had told Latha the first time he touched her, when his hand brushed against her arm immediately after their wedding ceremony. Her good side still faced him, though, so he had not yet really seen her.

"Sow trouble and reap a harvest of disaster," Pooni intoned in that ominous way of hers.

Latha pulled away from her friend, but she said nothing.

"Your *jati* is higher than your husband's. You are of greater value than he is!" There. Pooni had said it. "That is not natural, Latha. It is going against the hair—like combing your tresses the wrong way."

"Virat is a good husband," Latha said, a scathing tone touching her voice. "He does not raise his hand to me. Never once has he done that."

Pooni flinched. But still she would not let the matter drop. "A cruel husband may not be pleasant, but it is natural. A husband who is lower than his wife is not natural. And it is not right."

Latha glared at the woman she called "friend." At the woman whose young daughter had already been pledged to marry Ashish as soon as the two reached puberty.

"Ranjun says you have an evil spirit," Pooni said, her voice barely above a whisper. "He says that is why your other children did not live. Ranjun says that is why this terrible thing happened to your Ashish."

Latha, her eyes flashing, demanded, "Who is your Ranjun to speak of evil or of good?"

"If Ashish dies, my husband will not allow you near me," Pooni said. "He says he will not permit your shadow to pass over our house ever again."

Latha's face hardened. "For the sake of my husband and son, I will go to the shrine under the spirit tree and make my sacrifice, for I am too lowborn to enter a proper temple. I ask you, if I am a Hindu, why can I not go into a Hindu temple to pray for my family? What is the great fault that traps me as too high for my husband and too low for the gods?"

"That is how it has been forever," Pooni said. "You cannot change it, Latha. And neither can I."

## 5

The sun rose high in the sky, heating the tin cup tied over Virat's mouth so hot that it scorched his lips. He longed to shift it to one side, but he dared not. Should a droplet of spittle escape his mouth and pollute the ground, it could cost him his life.

In rice paddies on either side of the road, Sudra workers—both men and women—bent over almost double as they planted seedlings in their fields. Back-breaking work under an unforgiving sun. Rivulets of sweat glistened across their bony bodies and soaked the thin cotton of their *saris* and *mundus*, and *chaddar* turbans. Their children hurried back and forth lugging buckets of water to pour over the seedlings.

When Virat was leaving to dispose of the dead cow, little Ashish had called out one last question: "*Appa*, why do the gods let animals die in lands where people must not touch them?"

"You ask too many questions," Virat had chided him. "Things are the way they are, and there's no more to be said about it. If you keep asking why, you will get yourself into trouble."

Now that Virat thought about it, his son had asked a rather good question.

"Who would take away your dead animals if it were not for me?" Virat demanded out loud, defiance ringing in his voice.

Beyond the rice paddies lay the land of the twice-born, the pure ones, the upper castes who were loved by the gods. Already the air smelled cleaner, and mango groves grew more lush and fragrant. Virat anchored his new drum under his arm and beat out a measured cadence. Through parched and blistered lips, he called: "Untouchable coming! Untouchable coming!"

As soon as he saw high caste villagers, Virat dipped low so that his broom would erase his unworthy footsteps from the dust on the road. Step, dip. Step, dip. Step, dip.

"What could such a one be thinking to walk openly on our road?" a stout man grumbled loudly to a younger man beside him. His companion made a face of disgust and spat noisily.

Virat bowed his head low and took care not to defile either of them with his shadow.

"Untouchable coming! Untouchable coming!" he called.

Fragrances of paradise floated on the breeze and intertwined themselves with spicy aromas. Surely it was true; the twice-born *were* favored by the gods.

Off to one side, sheltered under the spreading branches of a neem tree, squatted a square-shaped man, bedecked in red cloth and with a bright red turban wrapped around his head. A bushy gray moustache and beard obscured the man's face. He sat among half a dozen sacks, all of them standing upright and wide open.

The man glowered at Virat. "Stay clear of my spices!" he warned.

Virat slinked to the other side of the road.

A woman in a purple *sari* moved up to inspect the spice merchant's wares. "A measure of cardamom," she said.

The red-turbaned spice merchant dipped out a handful of cardamom seeds and wrapped them in a broad banana leaf.

"Cinnamon too," the woman said. "And cloves. Yes, and cumin, I believe. Hmmmm . . . and coriander as well."

"Very good," the spice merchant said to the woman. "You will grind masala today?" He dipped his hand into first one sack and then the other, wrapping each selection in a leaf.

Without realizing it, Virat paused to watch the transactions. When the spice merchant caught sight of him, he grabbed up a stone and heaved it. It caught Virat square in the chest and knocked him flat on his back.

"Be off with you!" the merchant hollered. "Don't you be polluting my market and my wares!"

Virat bowed as low as the broom would permit.

"Clean up your pollution!" a man from up the road ordered.

Adjusting the cup over his mouth and dipping to sweep while also staying off the road, Virat scurried away as quickly as he could.

Another accusing voice called after him: "Is it not enough that you pollute our water? Must you also pollute our ground?"

Virat leapt off the path and fell to his knees, for it was Brahmin Keshavan who spoke to him from the shelter of a mango grove. Virat caught a glimpse of the Brahmin's bone-thin features, harsh and holy.

"You do not keep to your place, *chamar*. It is not a mystery why you have raised so wicked a child."

"Next to the gods"—that's how Brahmin Keshavan referred to himself. It must be so. His *mundu*, tied halfway up his chest, was of spotless white linen, woven with a rich *kara* all around the edge—a lavishly wide strip of green and yellow silk threads. Even the wealthiest men only wore such finery for important occasions. Over the Brahmin's left shoulder, across his smoothly oiled body and on down under his right arm, hung the sacred thread that marked him as a member of the Brahmin caste.

Brahmin Keshavan's eyes squinted into slits and his thin mouth puckered in disgust. Still, his eyes never left the intruder. Virat fell to his knees and crawled past the great Brahmin, taking care to mind his shadow.

"This road is not open to you," the Brahmin said.

The first lessons an Indian child learned were to show respect to Brahmins and to gods. Even so, Virat gathered his courage and dared to speak.

"Show mercy to my son, I beg of you. He is but a very little child."

"*Varnasrama-dharma*," Brahmin Keshavan replied in a cool voice. "The sacred law clearly shows that *dharma* is not the same for everyone. All people are not held to the same rules. The *dharma* of a child is not that of an old man, just as the *dharma* of high birth is not that of the lowly. Still, a general conduct must be followed by all."

"Ashish is an innocent," Virat pleaded.

"Innocence is not the same as purity," Brahmin Keshavan said. "Pray that your son will die in defense of a Brahmin or a cow so that he might possibly secure a place in heaven. To die for polluting our water merely shows how little he learns as he passes from one life to the next."

His veneration for the Brahmin quickly turning to stifled anger, Virat said, "I wish to speak to the landowner."

"In that case, continue along the road until you reach the last house. You will find Mammen Samuel Varghese preening on his veranda." An unmistakably vicious tone tinged

Brahmin Keshavan's smooth words. "And, *chamar*, do not touch your feet to our road!"

Virat hurried away, taking care to stay off the road, to sweep away his footprints, to hunch low and to bow humbly.

"Your son cannot escape the law of *karma* any more than I can escape the passage of time!" the Brahmin called after him.

Life and death, rebirth and another death, over and over and over again. The endless circle spun around in Virat's head until he could hardly walk straight. Do good and be reborn into a better life. Do wrong and come back as something worse. Coming into life the son of a *chamar* was bad enough, but what if Ashish was doomed to come back as an animal, or a snake, or even a plant? And all for the sin of a drink of water on a hot day.

Word traveled fast. By the time Virat caught sight of the landowner's lavish home, Mammen Samuel Varghese would be ready for him.

# 6

*B*abu!" Mammen Samuel Varghese bellowed. "Do not make me wait!"

Mammen Samuel's Sudra servant rushed out to the veranda, head bowed, a fine embroidered rug slung over his bare shoulder and humble apologies tumbling from his lips.

"Place it under the jasmine vines," Mammen Samuel ordered.

With deft diligence, Babu threw the rug down on the veranda and straightened every wrinkle out of it before quickly ducking back inside the house. He reemerged bearing his master's flat wooden desk supplied with an inkwell and quill pen. One more run inside, and Babu laid down a thick leather-bound book in which his master recorded every detail of his business accounts.

"Go!" Mammen Samuel said, waving his servant away.

After settling himself stiff and straight on the rug, Mammen Samuel set about thumbing through the pages of his accounting book. He paused here and there to check this figure or recalculate that accounting, after which he dipped his pen in the inkwell and printed some notation or other in his tight, cramped script.

By the name *Sekaran*, he printed: *Baby born. Raise charge for family grain allotment.*

By the name *Debarma* he printed: *Wife injured, cannot work. Cut her rice allotment.*

By the name of *Usha* he printed: *Husband died, burial required. Double family debt.*

One man after another passed by on the road. Each in turn touched his forehead in deference to the small, stout man, so daintily put together, his moustache and beard always neatly trimmed. Mammen Samuel seldom gave any of them notice. When he did happen to look up, he would shout to whomever passed, "You! Where are you going?" The passerby always bowed low and answered politely, only to have Mammen Samuel dismiss him in mid-sentence with a curt nod and a wave of his hand.

"Babu! Bring me tea!" Mammen Samuel called. It wasn't really that he desired more tea. Rather, he clung to a deep belief that if he failed to keep constant watch, Babu—along with all the other servants—would stop work and stand about gossiping. He suspected that on occasion they even stretched out to nap. Well, they would find Mammen Samuel Varghese much sharper and more cunning a master.

"Babu! Work harder!" he called out at regular intervals. "Move faster, you lazy boy! I am watching you."

When applied to servants and women, Mammen Samuel considered gossip a most irritating attribute. When it affected him positively, however, he deemed it as nothing less than the passing of necessary information, or the issuing of an important warning. Whether gossip or warning, long before Mammen Samuel saw Virat or heard the beat of his drum,

Babu brought him word of the pitiful Untouchable coming up the road to see him.

"The *chamar*, is it then? The one whose son dared to drink from the pure well?"

Before Babu could answer, Mammen Samuel said, "As soon as he arrives, serve me my midday meal. Hurry now, and tell Boban Joseph he is to join me."

ℐ

"He's coming!" Mammen Samuel's fourteen-year-old son announced. "I see the wretch walking beside the road."

"Hush," Mammen Samuel scolded Boban Joseph. "Keep your eyes away."

He signaled Babu to lay out a silver plate for the savory *idli* cakes, and polished copper bowls of *chutney*, and a silver pot of *sambar* vegetable stew.

Virat stopped at the edge of Mammen Samuel's raised veranda, so comfortably sheltered by waving coconut palms. He looked with amazement at the banana and mango trees, and breathed in the fragrance of wild jasmine. Carefully he swept away his footsteps and laid his drum aside. Without a word, he knelt down and bowed low with his face in the dirt.

Rice. *Idli* and spicy hot *chutney*. More rice, with *sambar*. Curds to cool the heat of the hot peppers. Mammen Samuel busied himself squishing the fine food together between his fingers. He paid not the least notice to the prostrate *chamar*.

"Eat, eat!" Mammen Samuel urged Boban Joseph. "You are now a man, and food is plentiful."

Squishing, squishing the food between his fingers, mashing it together into a mush. Then, in one swift circular motion, Mammen Samuel gathered it into a ball and brought it to his mouth in his dripping hand.

"Mmmmmm," Mammen Samuel murmured happily. "Eat, boy. Eat your fill. Then you shall have more!"

Virat raised himself and looked up in wonder at the food spread out on the veranda. Such a feast, and on an ordinary day! How could it be? For the people who lived in the mud huts in the untouchable section of the village, most meals were rice flavored with a sprinkling of curry and a handful of hot peppers. Meat when an animal died, but when everything stayed healthy, mostly rice.

As Mammen Samuel's speedy fingers prepared his next bite, Boban Joseph stuffed a dripping bite into his mouth. Then another bite for Mammen Samuel, his two gold teeth glinting in the sun each time he opened his mouth.

A peacock, eager to impress an indifferent pea hen, fluttered onto the edge of the veranda and proudly strutted about. Shrieking for attention, it spread out a most remarkable tail of iridescent blue and green. With a startled cry, Virat fell flat on his stomach. Too terrified to move, he stared at what looked to be countless eyes staring out at him from the peacock's tail.

Mammen Samuel laughed out loud. He nudged his son and pointed to the frightened man lying in the dirt. The two roared together.

"Have I taught you well, Boban Joseph?" Mammen Samuel asked in a loud voice. "Do you fully understand the role of those who are dependents in the village? Of servants and Untouchables?"

"Yes, Father," Boban Joseph said.

To Babu, who stood mutely at the side, Mammen Samuel ordered, "More food for your master! And more food for your master's son!"

How long Virat knelt in the beating sun, perspiring among the mustard flowers and the preening peafowl, he couldn't tell. The spicy fragrance of the air, and the rumbling hunger inside his stomach, made him dizzy and confused.

A poorly plucked sitar whined from inside the fine house.

"My sister needs much practice before that can rightly be called music," Boban Joseph said. He shook his head, as if to free his ears of the jarring notes.

Mammen Samuel ignored his son and motioned instead for Babu. The servant hurried over with a basin of water. First father, then son, washed the remains of their meal off their hands and dried their hands on the towel tied around Babu's waist.

Mammen Samuel stood stiffly upright, the instinctive posture of short men. Freshly bathed and shaved before his meal, he wore white trousers that hung loosely and a *kurta*—a long-tailed, collarless shirt. His hard, expressionless eyes fixed on the still prostrate *chamar*.

"Why do you come to me?" Mammen Samuel demanded.

"You are a landlord," Virat replied, taking care to keep his head low. "You are a great man of power and wealth. I come to ask you to lend me money to get English medicine for my son. Please. I come to beg you to save my child's life."

Because his master ordered it, Babu brought Virat a clay cup filled with water. The Sudra servant would not hand it to the Untouchable, of course. Instead, he set it on a rock and walked away. As Virat grabbed up the cup and gulped thirstily, Babu hissed, "If all were as it should be, you would be living in a garbage dump."

"You know what you are," Mammen Samuel called out to Virat.

"Please, my boy is so little," Virat begged. "He has not yet seen his sixth summer."

At Mammen Samuel's command, Babu returned to the rock where the empty clay cup stood. He picked up another rock and smashed the cup to pieces. Such cups were intended for Untouchables simply because they could so easily be destroyed after impure lips touched them—another way to protect the pure upper castes from untouchable pollution.

"You know what you are," Mammen Samuel said again. This time it sounded more like an accusation.

Of course Virat knew. How could he not know? Everyone knew about the four *varnas*—the castes . . . and the outcastes whose *dharma* caused them to be trampled beneath righteous feet. Everyone knew the basic social order that governed Hindu society as outlined by Manu the ancient lawgiver in the *Manusmriti*.

Everyone knew Untouchables fell outside the four *varnas* of *Brahmin*, *Kshatriya*, *Vaishya*, and *Sudra*. Everyone knew the outcastes to be impure, subhuman, lower than animals and rodents and insects.

"Look ahead of you," Mammen Samuel told Virat. "Look to your right and look to your left. All the land you see belongs to me. Abundant fields, groves of cashews, mangos and bananas, and pepper vines climbing the trees. All of it is mine. Your pagan Hindu stories claim that the Lord Vishnu, by way of an axe, made a gift of this land to Rama all the way to the Arabian Sea. I say the God of heaven, the only true God, made a gift of it to me."

Virat lay on the ground before the landlord, sobbing into the tin cup still tied halfway over his mouth. He reached his arms out to Mammen Samuel Varghese and banged his forehead on the ground. "My Ashish is a good son. He deserves to live! Please, lend me the money. Please!"

"Stand up on your feet," Mammen Samuel said with a shade of disgust. "Take the cup off your face and the broom from your back, *chamar*."

✍

"My son is good and kind." Even though Virat stood before the landlord, he kept his head bowed, and he never ceased pleading. "He works hard, helping his father and his mother. I try my best to teach him to do right. Why must such a child be untouchable?"

"Because that's what he was born to be," said Mammen Samuel.

"His name is Ashish. His name is blessing. The boy is my blessing."

For many minutes the landlord, his face impassive, gazed in silence at the pitiful Untouchable. From his head to his feet, dirt and clumps of mud covered Virat. He dared not lift his eyes.

"Your son has the same number of years as my son, Saji Stephen," Mammen Samuel finally said. "For the sake of my own son, I will help your son. Also, because I am a Christian man, descended from a long line of Christians, I will take your Ashish to the English Mission Medical Clinic in my own bullock cart and I will pay whatever amount the medical man requires."

Virat fell to his knees. Tears flooded his face. "I will pay you back, kind sir. And whatever more you ask of me, I will pay that too."

"Come to the edge of the veranda so we can talk properly," Mammen Samuel said. "You can work off the debt in my fields. You and your wife."

"Yes, yes. Anything!" Virat said.

Mammen Samuel clapped his hands and Boban Joseph stepped forward with a paper and an ink bottle.

"To seal our agreement," Mammen Samuel said to Virat.

Because Virat knew nothing about letters or words, and because he could think of naught but his broken son, he unquestioningly dipped his thumb into the ink Boban Joseph poured out on a rock and stamped it on the line at the bottom of the agreement.

As Virat stood and waited, Mammen Samuel Varghese opened his book and printed: *Virat the Chamar.* Next to that: *1 man, 1 woman, 1 child.* Now all three belonged to him.

# 7

*I*t may be that the boy is breathing more easily," Latha offered hopefully. "He ate a bit of mashed rice and a few bites of curds. Perhaps—"

"What's done is done," Virat said. "We cannot go back." He took the *chaddar* from his head and wrapped it around his son.

With Latha beside him, Virat carried the child up the path to the place where it joined the main road. There they waited in silence for the landlord's cart to come for them. Latha, shading her good eye against the rising sun, was the first to spy a cloud of dust far up the road.

"Look, Husband!" she said. "It must be the landlord's bullock cart."

As the cart lumbered closer, Virat gasped, "The landlord himself sits on the bench!" Yes, and beside him, his son Boban Joseph, driving the team of bullocks—white ones with short hair, fine bullocks that showed off Mammen Samuel Varghese's wealth. In his hand, Boban Joseph clutched a sturdy, yet supple, branch he could use as a switch.

When the bullocks ambled to a stop, Virat obediently handed the boy up to the waiting landlord. Mammen Samuel took the child in his own arms and laid him in a box in the back of the cart, made soft with fresh-cut grass. But when Virat tried to climb up into the cart after the child, Mammen Samuel shoved him away.

"Not you," he said. "Only the boy."

"No!" Latha wailed as she pushed past her husband. When Mammen Samuel barred her way, too, she jumped at him, her fists pounding. "I will not leave my son!"

In a flash, Boban Joseph snapped his switch. It caught Latha across the face, sliced across her bad eye and slashed all the way down to her chin. She stumbled backward and fell hard against her husband, knocking them both to the ground.

"You will *obey* me," Mammen Samuel pronounced in an icy cold voice.

Stunned into silence, Virat and Latha stared up at the stout, perfectly arranged man. Boban Joseph raised his switch for another blow, but his father grasped his arm.

Resuming his more reasonable tone, Mammen Samuel said, "The English healers will not look at the boy if they see him arrive in the company of Untouchables. But if I carry him in my own arms, they will treat him with the tenderest of care. So you see, it is for the boy's own good that I must turn you away."

"No!" Latha sobbed. She struggled to her feet, but her husband grabbed her arm and held her back.

"The landlord is a wise man, Wife," Virat said. "He knows the ways of the English. We do not."

With an impatient sigh, Boban Joseph lashed at the bullocks, and the cart lurched forward.

"Pack up your belongings and move to the laborers' quarters," Mammen Samuel ordered. "Both of you. Take the pathway behind my fields, not the road through the village."

Virat bowed low. "We have our own house in the untouchable settlement," he protested. "We will not need to—"

"From now on, you will make your home on my land."

"It is not so far for me to walk each day," Virat protested.

"I will only return your son to you when you are on my land," the landowner said. The icy tone had returned to his voice.

"Please, Mister Landowner—" Latha cried, but Mammen Samuel Varghese had stopped listening. The cart already rumbled on with Ashish in the back.

❦

"I do not understand why we must leave our house," Latha insisted to her husband. "You could work in the landlord's fields during the day and come back to our mud hut at night."

"We will work in the landlord's fields," Virat corrected. "Both of us."

Latha stared at her husband. "But Ashish. Who will care for him?"

"The laborer's settlement is large with many children," Virat reasoned. "Probably old grandmothers look after the young ones. Don't worry."

"But why must we move there? The fields are not so far away from our mud hut."

"Because the landlord requires it," Virat said.

Two earthenware water jars and one clay bowl. Two earthenware cooking pots. A small sack of rice. Earthenware jars that held oil, dry vegetables, spices. Three woven reed sleeping mats. Virat's drying racks for the animal skins. One cotton towel. Between them, Virat and Latha could carry everything they owned.

Virat sneaked a look at his wife. In many ways she was a most attractive woman. Not in all ways, though. Her right eye shone a deep spicy brown, bright and expressive. But her left eye was cloudy and gray, and the skin around it scarred and twisted. Once she had told him she couldn't remember ever having two working eyes, but that's all she ever said and Virat didn't ask for more. Her eye belonged to her. Its story was hers to tell or to keep to herself.

"Remember when we first came to this village?" Latha asked. A tear glistened in her good eye.

"Pooni will watch over the house until we return," Virat said.

"Baby number five had just died and Ashish was not yet born," Latha reminisced softly. She spoke more to herself than to her husband. "I couldn't accept the *karma* of our village, so I begged you to leave your home and your family, and find us somewhere else to live."

"Pooni is a good friend to you," Virat said. "She will respect our house and care for it as her own."

"It was in the time of famine, remember? Your family shed no tears when we bade them farewell."

The wistful sadness in Latha's voice unsettled Virat. "Ashish will be with us tonight," he said.

"I should not have persuaded you to leave your home and your family. I am sorry, my husband."

Virat set the clay pots down on the ground, taking care to make a small indentation in the dirt for each one so they would stand upright. He laid the bowl down beside them. Even in so public a place, he dared to brush his rough fingers along the smoothness of his wife's arm. "In this village, I have achieved the most important things in life," he said softly.

"I made a place for us. I found friends for us. I fathered us a good son."

For the first time since her husband had carried Ashish to the road, Latha looked Virat full in the face. His skin was darker than hers by far, his face leathered by the sun. His chin and cheeks bristled with graying whiskers. Virat smiled his gap-toothed smile, cracking a blister the metal cup had burned on his lip. He picked up the pots and the bowl, and led his wife toward the path that would take them to Mammen Samuel Varghese's fields.

"*Chamar!* I am sorry to see you go!" Ranjun called out after them. Virat turned with a smile, his mouth ready to answer the unexpectedly kind words. But Ranjun had more to say. "I wish you were not leaving, *chamar*, because now we will have no one filthy enough to clean up the dead animals for us!"

*✒*

More than a hundred tiny thatched huts, huddled behind the fields of waving wheat, housed Mammen Samuel Varghese's laborers.

Latha frowned. "Not like our huts of mud in the village."

Virat said nothing.

"Which one is ours?" Latha asked as she gazed from one hut to the identical ones surrounding it.

"I don't know," said Virat. "One out on the far edge, I suppose."

Overhead, the sun burned hot. Latha sighed and set the earthenware containers on the ground. She swiped at her face with the edge of her *sari*. When Virat saw that she didn't intend to move, he leaned his drying racks against a rotting tree stump and piled his other burdens beside it. Because the land was devoid of trees to offer them shade, they sat on the hot ground and waited in the sun.

After the sun had moved so far across the sky that it cast an orange shadow over the settlement, Virat spied a lone figure striding toward them along a pathway between the fields. Virat and Latha stood up and waited uncertainly. The man's dark face was deeply furrowed, his bare back and sturdy legs burned almost black. A faded yellow *chaddar* wrapped around his head like a turban glowed golden in the setting sun.

"Come!" the man called out to them. "Follow me!"

The man was Anup, Mammen Samuel Varghese's overseer. He led Virat and Latha on a winding trail to the middle of the settlement. "This is your place," he said pointing to a hut no different than the ones surrounding it.

Virat hesitated. "I do not think so," he said with a polite bow. "I am but a *chamar*." He held up his drying rack as evidence. "I belong on the outskirts of your village."

"Not here," Anup said. "This is not like every other village. Here all *jatis* live mixed together." Anup gestured to the left. "A potter and his family live there." Then to the right. "Over there is a Sudra."

"They will live together with one such as me?" Virat asked incredulously. "With one who handles the dead?"

"All of us labor at the master's will," said Anup. "To him, we are all the same—laborers, all bonded to him. Nothing more and nothing less."

"Our son," Latha said. "Is he here waiting for us?"

Anup ran his hand over his stubbly black beard. "I know nothing of your son. I only know that you are to settle yourselves in your hut before nightfall. Tomorrow at dawn both of you will follow the other workers out to the field to begin work."

In a flat, open area, Anup pointed out a well with a community cup sitting beside it. "That's for all the laborers to use," he said. Off to the side and under a tree stood a mortar with two millstones. "Grind your grain here, either before you go to the fields in the morning or after you return in the evening. You will work in the fields from dawn to dusk. Not on Sunday, though. The master is a Christian, so we do not work on Sundays."

The hut consisted of one small room with a dirt floor, with nothing inside but a flat stone positioned in front of a small opening in the wall. A rim of mud and pebbles surrounded the stone. Latha smiled. A place for bathing, it was, and in the privacy of their hut too. More than she'd had in the mud hut. Nothing in there but the trunk of the date palm tree that supported the thatched roof.

"We must hurry, Husband," Latha said. "Everything must be in order when Ashish arrives."

Latha grabbed up the two jars and hurried to the well to fill them with water. These she set against the inside wall of the hut, on one side of the bathing stone. On the other side of the stone, she placed the clay bowl and cooking pots. Along the opposite wall, she laid out the sack of rice and her earthenware jars of oil, dried vegetables, and spices. Virat stacked their sleeping mats against the third wall. Because it was what she always did, Latha headed for the wooded area at the edge of the settlement to collect firewood.

"The landlord took my boy to the English healer," Virat said to Anup, who still stood outside the hut.

"Yes," said Anup.

"It is worth the debt I now owe to save the life of my son."

Anup said nothing.

"Even if we must work an entire year, it is worth it."

Still Anup said nothing.

"My son is but an innocent child."

"Of course he is not," said Anup. "If he were innocent, he would not have been born an Untouchable, and certainly not the son of a *chamar*. Everything has already been decided—for your son . . . for you . . . for me. Not one of us is innocent or we would not be here, slaving for the landlord."

The dusky hues of orange and pink that bathed the road washed over the long shadow stretched out behind Latha. Still, she would not leave her post. Surely, any moment now, a cloud of dust would arise in the distance and the landowner's bullock cart would appear bearing little Ashish to his mother's waiting arms. Perhaps the English healer's medicine would work so well that the boy would run to her, already well and healthy.

Virat laid his hand on his wife's shoulder. "We must eat," he said gently.

Latha shook herself as if from a dream. Yes, of course, they must. The day had been long, and tomorrow's work would begin at sunup. Silently, Latha laid wood in the fire pit in front of the hut, small kindling first and then a larger branch. The wife of the potter in the hut on her left busied herself doing the same, as did the wife of the Sudra on the other side. Except they both had children to help them. Latha put a handful of rice in one pot, poured in water, and set it over the fire. In the pottery bowl she measured out a fistful of flour, poured oil over it, and mixed the two together. With expert hands, she kneaded the dough. She sprinkled dried onions and peppers and a pinch of curry into the rice pot. The dough she formed into thin bread patties which she baked on rocks heated burning hot in the fire. *Chapatis*. Smoke rose from Latha's cooking fire and blended with the smoke from ninety-nine other cooking fires, all baking *chapatis* and boiling rice.

"Eat, Wife," Virat urged as he rolled rice up in a hot *chapati*.

But Latha could not. In front of a strange hut they must call home, surrounded by people whose names they did not know, facing a tomorrow they did not understand, she sat in silence and watched the sun sink behind the mountains. And still Ashish did not come.

⟡

Virat and Latha lay side by side on their sleeping mats on the ground in front of their hut listening to unfamiliar snores accompanied by the swish, swish of coconut palms in the breeze. Nighttime silence did not reign in the laborers' settlement.

"Soon our Blessing will be back with us," Virat whispered.

But Ashish did not come that night.

Before the stars faded in the sky, the settlement came to life again. Smoke rose from cooking fires, and soft voices floated through the air.

"We must be very evil people," Latha said.

Virat reached over and touched her butter-soft skin. "We can wipe out our sins with good. This day we will give rich gifts to the gods."

"We did that before. The best of the meat you brought back to the village always went to the village god."

"Not only the gods," Virat said. "We will also share generously with neighbors here."

"That, too, we did. You even shared with Ranjun. That cruel man never deserved anything from your hands, yet you shared with him."

For several minutes they lay together in silence. Then Virat said, "Our son is the goodness of our life. He is our Blessing. Our hope."

Latha said nothing.

🌿

Outside, in the breaking dawn, Anup waited impatiently for Virat and Latha.

"I will take you to the fields and show you where you are to work," he said. "Labor hard and mind your own business. Make this your home and forget what is past."

"We will not be here for long," Virat said. "Only until we earn enough to pay off our debt to the landlord. Then we will go back to our mud hut on the edge of the village."

"Pay off your debt?" Anup laughed a bitter laugh. "That's what my father said of his debt to the landlord's father. That was long ago before I was born. My father worked his entire life, and his debt was not paid off. I have worked my entire life, too, but his debt still is not paid off. Should the gods bless me with a son, he will also work for the landowner to pay my father's debt, but I don't believe he would ever be able to pay it off either."

Virat stared at Anup. He opened his mouth to explain that he was the village *chamar*, and that he had no family to carry on his work. To make it clear that high caste feet depended on sandals made by his hands and that Brahmin priests needed his hand-stretched drums for their sacred ceremonies. But he never got the chance. Anup had already started across the field.

# 8

*I* bring an outcaste child to you, beaten and abandoned for dead," Mammen Samuel Varghese announced to Abigail Davidson. The young missionary had opened the door of the English Mission Medical Clinic to see who bellowed outside. "Such an action was not required of me, mind you. I did it as a voluntary goodly deed from the kindness of my Christian heart."

Abigail stared at the short, squat man and shrugged apologetically. She couldn't understand a word of his language.

"Here, here! In my cart." Mammen Samuel raised his voice to an impatient yell, as if the young woman standing before him were quite deaf. "Come and see for yourself."

Abigail's bewildered gaze followed his gesture to the box behind the driver's bench. Stretching up on her tiptoes, she peered in. Ashish blinked out at her through blackened eyes.

"Oh!" Abigail gasped. "The poor, poor little one! Who did such a thing to him?"

Now it was Mammen Samuel's turn to shrug his shoulders and shake his head, for he could not understand her English language any more than she could understand his Malayalam tongue.

"Darshina!" Abigail called. "Darshina, come quickly! We need your help!"

❧

To Abigail, everything about South India seemed shrouded in mystery and myth, sprinkled with a heavy dose of wonderment. Barely more than a month had passed since she had arrived at the mission, exhausted and wide-eyed, riding on the back of an elephant. Yes, an elephant! The carriage in which she left the docks at Madras quickly became mired on the overgrown jungle path. In order to complete her journey, the guide to whom she had been entrusted quickly bundled her into a cage on the elephant's back. Barely more than a month ago, yet already she had been called upon to assist Dr. Edward Moore with a steady stream of Indian patients. They included snakebites (one man and two boys), many cases of malaria (two young children had died since she arrived at the clinic), and a badly burned woman.

Small and slender, with a round, smiling face generously sprinkled with freckles, Abigail knew better than to call herself a nurse. Certainly her two years' experience in a London hospital had not overly impressed Dr. Moore.

"Why headquarters could not have sent me someone with real experience and medical stamina, I do not know," the doctor sniffed when Abigail paled at the sight of the Indian woman's horrific burns. Never mind that before she arrived, the doctor had no help at all.

In Abigail's third week at the mission medical clinic, Darshina had appeared at the door, scrawny and half-starved. Dr. Moore prepared to send her away with a good meal and a night's rest when the girl amazed him by appealing in English, "Please, *Sahib* . . . *Memsahib* . . . please to be helping me?"

Abigail grabbed Dr. Moore's arm and exclaimed, "She speaks our language, Sir. She speaks English! God must have sent her to us!"

Dr. Moore, allowing that while there could indeed be some benefit to such a circumstance, extracted himself from Abigail's presumptuous grasp. "Yet, she is nothing more than an Indian," he pointed out. "And, no doubt, a Hindu as well."

Darshina stayed—with the proviso that she observe proper English decorum at all times and that she dress in a manner appropriate to an English mission medical clinic. To Dr. Moore, this meant she should speak only when spoken to and she should wear a white dress (though he finally conceded to allow a white *sari*, lightly starched).

"We shall maintain some semblance of professionalism, even in this heathen outpost," Dr. Moore had insisted.

❧

"This man, he being Mammen Samuel Varghese, *Sahib*," Darshina said to Dr. Moore. "He being a great landowner in the village. He saying the boy being an outcaste. He being beaten for breaking caste laws. He saying the boy brought here for you to be making him well again."

Dr. Moore, his dour expression unmoved, stared hard at Mammen Samuel. "I do not trust the man," he said. "Not in the least."

While the others talked and argued, Abigail lifted her white skirt and climbed up into the cart. Tenderly, she unwrapped the faded *chaddar* from around Ashish.

"Oh!" she gasped when she saw his battered body. "This poor child! Poor, poor little one!"

"Really, Miss Davidson!" Dr. Moore scolded. "Do you or do you not fancy yourself a medical assistant? If you wish to be taken seriously, even in this godforsaken country, you simply must learn to control your emotions."

⟐

Fractured ribs resulted in a seriously compressed chest, the doctor said. Pressure on the child's lungs—badly bruised, most likely—made it difficult for Ashish to take a proper breath. Immediately Dr. Moore set to work on the boy. When the little one finally gulped enough air to wail out a long cry of protest, the doctor heaved a sigh of relief. The pressure lessened; Abigail swabbed Ashish's wounds with alcohol and water. The doctor bandaged and wrapped his injuries. This just causes the boy to wiggle and wail all the more.

"Hold him still!" Dr. Moore ordered.

Abigail dipped a cloth in water and bathed the child's bruised face. "There, there," she cooed. "You will feel better soon, little one."

Dr. Moore flashed an impatient look.

Mammen Samuel, who had been delegated to the outside waiting area, pushed the curtain aside and roared an irritated demand.

"He would be knowing how much longer before you be finishing, *Sahib*," Darshina singsonged to the doctor.

Dr. Moore, his eyes flashing, glared at the man. "Tell him to stay out of my surgery. I will be finished when I am finished and not one moment before."

Darshina bowed and, in a gentle voice that in no way reflected the doctor's harsh tone, relayed the message.

Mammen Samuel's reply was clipped and curt.

"He be saying he must need return to his home before darkness be coming," Darshina said. "He be saying he must need
be going now."

"Tell him he is free to leave whenever he wishes," Dr. Moore
replied without looking up. "The boy shall remain here."

Abigail, her blue eyes flashing, snapped, "You tell that man
we will only release this little boy to his father and mother,
Darshina. Certainly not to him!"

Dr. Moore looked up at his young assistant, his eyes twin-
kling and his mouth turned up in the closest thing to a smile
that had crossed his face in a very long time. "Well, well," he
said. "It would seem that you have more emotions in need of
control than even I expected."

Darshina looked uncomfortable as she glanced from the
doctor to the impatient Indian man. Only when Mammen
Samuel Varghese barked an irritated command did she bow
reverentially and murmur a respectful reply.

Mammen Samuel slammed his hand down on the table and
glowered as he roared out a long string of angry words.

"He be saying the boy being his property because the boy's
parents being his property," Darshina said, her eyes fixed on
the floor. "He be saying he be going to his home now, and if
the boy be well or if he be sick, he be taking his property with
him."

Dr. Moore laid the bandages down, one by one, until they
stretched out in a neat row across the table. Abigail opened
her mouth, but the doctor shot her a warning glance, and she
closed it again without uttering a word. Dr. Moore stepped
toward Mammen Samuel Varghese. The doctor's height
allowed him to see over the short Indian man's head, yet
Mammen Samuel didn't flinch. He looked up and glared defiantly into the doctor's eyes.

Dr. Moore stared back, every bit as defiantly, with steely gray eyes. "Tell this man that the boy does not belong to him, but to Almighty God," Dr. Moore said through clenched teeth. "Tell him I will release the child to no one except his parents. Tell him that if the boy's parents do not come for him in due time, by which I mean a matter of days, I shall see that the child is sent to the mission orphan school in Madras. You tell him that, Darshina."

"*Sahib* . . . Doctor . . . Sir," Darshina stammered, "Please, you not be understanding the ways of India. This man being one of most great power."

"Tell him as I instructed you!" Dr. Moore insisted. His eyes held fast to Mammen Samuel.

"The authorities being with him, *Sahib*. He can be calling for them and—"

"Tell him as I instructed you!"

Darshina's face paled. Staring at the floor, she murmured the doctor's words.

Mammen Samuel's face flared with rage, and he spat a response. Without waiting for Darshina to translate, he stormed out of the clinic.

Calmly, without uttering a word, Dr. Moore turned his attention back to his patient. He mixed a concoction and handed it to Abigail. "See that the boy drinks this and keep close watch over him tonight. I will be in my quarters should you require my assistance."

After Dr. Moore left, Darshina ventured, "That boy, he not being accustomed to sleep on a cot, *Memsahib*. Shall I be putting down a sleeping mat for him?"

Abigail nodded her grateful agreement. And as Darshina spread out the mat, Abigail urged the whimpering child to drink the tonic. But even before he finished it, he was fast asleep.

"I be watching him this night," Darshina offered. "You please to be sleeping."

Abigail didn't answer. Instead, she asked, "What did that man say before he left?"

"The poor. He be saying the poor are with us always."

Abigail wrinkled her brow. "I see. And what else?"

"He be saying that sometimes the most kind thing, it be . . . it be—"

"It be *what?*" Abigail demanded.

"Sometimes the most kind thing, it be leaving one such as this child to lie in the corner and die."

✥

Generally speaking, Abigail refrained from taking tea with Dr. Moore.

All night, she had sat beside the child, keeping careful watch, comforting him and wiping his face with a damp cloth. Whenever he awoke, she urged him to sip water. When he cried out, she stroked him and hummed soft tunes and whispered words of comfort.

"He most definitely is cooler to the touch and seems to be sleeping peacefully," Dr. Moore announced when he looked the boy over in the morning. "I might yet make a nurse of you, Miss Davidson." The doctor instructed Darshina to lay out tea—for both him and his nurse.

Even though the doctor had never paid her a greater compliment, Abigail allowed his words to slip past without notice. "How can that man claim to own this boy?" she demanded. "No one can own another person's child! It isn't right."

Traces of that uncharacteristic smile again touched the corners of Dr. Moore's thin lips. "As neither of us is of the Indian persuasion, let us put the matter to Darshina, shall we?" To

Darshina he said, "Is it true that the pompous little man in the white skirt might indeed own this boy?"

Darshina bowed low. "Untouchables and women and Sudras—the Hindu scriptures be saying that the creator god made them as less valuable."

"What?" Abigail exclaimed. "You cannot really believe such rubbish!"

"That being the word of Manu the lawgiver. It be coming to us from ancient times."

"And the word of Manu the lawgiver," said Dr. Moore. "Does it stand true to this day?"

"Oh, yes, *Sahib*. Yes!"

"Created as less valued," Abigail said. "You are referring to the caste system, are you not?"

"According to the laws of Manu, Untouchables are less than human," Dr. Moore explained.

"How absolutely atrocious!" Abigail exclaimed. "You do not accept such a horrid belief, do you, Darshina?"

"Please, you to be coming from outside our country, *Memsahib*," Darshina said with pointed politeness. "Your ways being right for you, but they not being our ways."

"But . . . less than human? You would never dare defend such an atrocity of a belief!"

"Please, much about the Indian world cannot be to your understanding." Darshina's voice remained mild, but her eyes flashed with a frightening ferocity. "Even though you being English, you not knowing everything."

❧

Twenty-five years old, more or less. That's the age Darshina had told Dr. Moore she guessed herself to be. Five years older than Abigail. Married at the age of ten, Darshina—still without children—became a widow six years later. The day her husband died, she broke her glass bangles and wiped the vermilion marks from her forehead and from the part in her hair to show the world that she no longer had a husband.

Darshina had grown up in a Brahmin family, accustomed to the privileged life of the revered highest caste. But widowhood changed everything. She dared defy the decree her parents-in-law laid down that she honor her dead husband by committing *sati*—that is, by throwing herself into the fire of his funeral pyre and in the flames passing to the next life with him. Her parents-in-law were so furious that they banished her to a small cottage behind the family house where she was ordered to live out her days alone and in *purdah*. Utter isolation. Closed off from the world. A virtual prisoner for the remainder of her life.

But Darshina would not. With her huge dark eyes and her silky pale skin, she managed to catch the eye of the son of the Brahmin priest, a boy who had recently returned from Madras. She teased him and made him promises, and he bowed to her wishes and taught her English. Her father-in-law's bookkeeper caught her alone in the mango grove behind her cottage, practicing this strange language, but he did not betray her. Instead, he practiced English alongside her and talked of taking her away with him. But he never did.

Ten years after her confinement, Darshina ripped the gold bangles from her arms, pulled off her gold earrings and toe rings, and offered them all to the bookkeeper if he would smuggle her out of her prison. He took her gold and she rumbled away in the back of a cart, hidden under a mound of dirty *saris*. She planned to slip out of the cart and walk to Madras where she hoped to lose herself in the crush of the city. But the city was much farther away than she had realized, and the road that led to it, far more dangerous. Burning sun scorched her days, and terror plagued her nights. Hunger and thirst haunted her like a ravenous tiger. By the time Darshina had gotten as far as the mission medical clinic, she barely found the strength to stumble to the door.

"This night the child should rest more comfortably," Dr. Moore said to Abigail as he finished checking over Ashish. "However, you would do well to keep vigil over him once again."

Outside in the courtyard, Darshina pulled the soiled bedclothes out of the wash pan, squeezed the water out of them, and spread them across the ground to dry. She wiped her hands on her *sari*—something Dr. Moore had forbidden her to do, so she only did it when he wasn't around—and stepped back inside.

"What is it, then?" Dr. Moore asked.

"Please, the *varnas*—what you be saying as the castes— please, it is not a bad thing," Darshina said in her quiet voice. "Each caste is being good in its own way."

"How can you even say that?" Abigail snapped.

As Darshina spoke, she kept her eyes fixed on the floor. "Without workers, then no rice being harvested. No rice being harvested would mean all people be dying hungry. But without landowners, laborers have no rice paddies giving them work to do. And even if they be working, who can be telling them what to do or how to be doing it right? No one, you see."

Dr. Moore snorted. To Abigail he said, "Should ever you find yourself wondering whether we treat the natives properly and all that sort of rubbish, remember this particular defense offered up by one of their own."

"You please to be saying we should all be the same. But why should that be so?" Darshina persisted. "To you, we Indians not being the same as you English."

Ignoring Darshina, Dr. Moore continued to address Abigail. "You thought you would come here and tend to the sick, and that the grateful natives would beg you to tell them about the God that sent you. Well, now you know; they will not. They already have many, many gods of their own. Gods and manifestations of gods everywhere—in people, in trees, in animals, even in stones."

A blush of embarrassment washed over Abigail as she sneaked a peek at Darshina. But Darshina's face remained impassive.

"You cannot have missed their ridiculous temples as you passed through Madras," Dr. Moore continued. "Gods and demons staring down from those gaudy walls—thousands of them!—leering and fiendish and evil." The doctor snapped his bag shut. "An entire country of heathens. That's what India is."

"Mammen Samuel Varghese, he is being a Christian man," Darshina said. "He please to be descending from a long line of Christians. He please to be saying his line of ancestors traces all the way back to your Saint Thomas."

"Saint Thomas, the disciple of Jesus?" Abigail exclaimed. "That Saint Thomas brought Christianity to India?"

"Hogwash!" Dr. Moore said. "That is nothing but an unproven myth. Even if it were true, no one inherits Christianity. If that self-righteous landowner thinks he has any claim on the Christian faith because of some ancient ancestors . . . " The rest of the doctor's retort drifted off in disdainful mutterings.

Abigail knew she should hold her tongue. She saw how Dr. Moore turned his withering glare on Darshina. She watched as the Indian woman's courage faltered and Darshina dropped her gaze back to the floor. Abigail had no right to take issue with the director of the mission medical clinic, not on any subject. Of that, she was well aware. Even so, even knowing all this, Abigail could not stop herself.

"If Saint Thomas came to India and brought Christianity with him, would that not mean that Indians have been Christians longer than we English?"

"Hogwash!" Dr. Moore repeated more forcefully than before. "A disciple of Jesus Christ walking on Indian soil? A holy saint offering his life for . . . for such as *these*? No, Miss Davidson. No, I think not!"

# 9

No, Little Girl, no!" Sethu scolded. Her small daughter, in a struggle to scoop mush into the mouth of her tiny squirming sister, allowed the clay feeding bowl to tip at a precarious angle. The toddler grabbed at the bowl, and porridge slopped onto the ground. "Look at what you've done! You spilled the food! You and Baby will get nothing more to eat today!"

Virat glanced uneasily at Anup's family—each small child rushing about her chores, each cowering under a shower of reproach. Not at all like his own mornings with Latha and Ashish. His eyes kept coming back to the small girl with the bowl. She looked to be about the same age as his son.

"Your daughter—what is her name?" Virat asked.

Anup spat on the ground. "My daughter? I have *four* daughters! Four girls and not one son."

Morning had not fully broken, yet the eldest girl—a slight child of no more than ten years—hurried off for the vegetable garden beside the landowner's house. Master Landowner's cook would expect to find fresh vegetables waiting at his doorstep. It fell to the second girl to tend to the morning porridge that bubbled over the cooking fire. "Devi is the biggest one and Lidya is the one with the scars," Anup said to Virat. "These two—" Here he pointed to the small ones. "They have no names. We call them Little Girl and Baby."

With her small fingers, Little Girl scraped the last of the porridge out of the bowl and, after the slightest hesitation, put it into Baby's open mouth. Little Girl splashed water on her sister's face and on her own hands, and shooed Baby off to play in the dirt.

Gathering up baskets . . . shouting out instructions . . . scolding, worrying, crowding together . . . men, women, and children as young as Devi gathered in the courtyard in preparation of the day's work.

"Your woman," Anup said to Virat. "She will work alongside the laborers."

"But not today," Virat answered. "Today Latha must wait by the road for the landlord to bring our son to us."

"If Master Landlord wishes to see your wife, he will send for her. Until then, she will work the same as every other woman in the settlement."

"But someone must be ready to receive the child," Virat explained. "Someone must be ready to care for him. It is only because of our injured son that we came, and—"

Anup wiped his rough hand across his stubbly face and sighed loudly. "Can it be that you still do not understand? From now on, nothing is for you to decide. It is not for your woman to decide. You both belong to the landowner now, like his ox and his buffalo. Your lives are in his hands."

In the midlands of Malabar, shadowed by the great mountain peaks of the Western Ghats, where rolling hills and sloping valleys push their way to the sea, Mammen Samuel

Varghese's lands spread out rich and fertile. Fields, heavy with grain, awaited the spring wheat harvest. Once those fields were reaped and cleared, workers would open trenches that led from the river, allowing the fields to flood into paddies so they could prepare the land for the rice crop. With God's blessing, rice planting would be completed in time for the summer monsoon rains. To be a landowner in Malabar brought great fortune indeed. So lush was the land that it willingly yielded two crops each year—unless the heat and rain came at the wrong times, baking the wheat with drying heat or keeping it so wet it molded on the stalks.

Some laborers gathered up piles of scyths and set to work sharpening them at the whetting wheels, thus ensuring that the workers' cuts would be swift and clean. Others, with loads of fresh cut grass heaped high on their heads, moved toward the fields where the animals roamed in order to tend to them. The rest of the workers headed out to the harvesting sheds to ready them for the coming harvest. Latha went with that group. Virat intended to do the same, but at the last minute Anup beckoned to him and led him away.

Virat followed Anup out into the field, white and heavy with winter wheat. Anup stopped to pull off a handful of wheat heads and rubbed the grain briskly between his calloused fingers. He popped a couple of grains into his mouth and handed the rest to Virat. Virat followed Anup's lead.

"What do you think?" Anup asked.

Virat shrugged. "It cracks," he said as he bit down on the grain.

"Keep chewing." After a bit Anup asked again, "What do you think now?"

"Soft," said Virat. "Mushy."

Anup smiled. "First the crack, then the soft. That means the wheat is ready for harvest."

Anup pointed out past a row of waving coconut trees. "That field over there is a good one. So is the one on the other side of it. We will harvest those fields first."

"And this field where we stand?" Virat asked.

"Not so good. Many weeds here. Takes too much work to get too little grain. This field we will leave for last."

Without another word, Anup turned and headed back through the wheat field. Virat followed behind him. "If the landlord does not bring my son to me quickly," Virat stated, "I will take my wife and go for the boy myself. I will—"

Anup jumped at Virat. Before Virat could think, Anup grabbed him and threw him backward to the ground with such force that it knocked the breath out of Virat. Gasping, he did his best to kick and struggle, but Anup straddled him and held him to the ground in an iron grip.

"You would kill me for speaking against the landlord?" Virat cried.

"No," Anup said as he loosened his grip. He pointed toward the trampled wheat. There, its long body stretched high and its hood spread wide, a cobra swayed. Through yellow slits of eyes, it stared straight at Virat.

Virat sat up and ran his hand through his hair. "I didn't even see it!"

"Back away," Anup urged.

But Virat sat motionless, staring at the spotted hood of the snake. "Feet markings of the god Krishna," he breathed. "This snake—the Brahmin sent it. It is his curse on me."

Virat said nothing of the cobra to Latha. What purpose would it serve to trouble her further?

When Latha finally managed to leave the harvest sheds and head back to their hut, the sky already glowed with streaks of orange and pink. In the gathering dusk she lay wood in the cook pit and started a fire. In huts all around them, women were doing the same. Latha didn't say she had stolen every possible moment to stare down the road for a cloud of dust that might be the bullock cart, but Virat knew she had. She didn't say that again this day the landowner had not brought Ashish back to them, though Virat knew he had not. Latha put a handful of rice in the pot to boil along with dried onions and hot peppers. When the rice was soft, she added a generous pinch of curry. She spooned out a good helping of the spiced rice for her husband's meal. Only after he had finished would she eat hers. Custom required it.

That night Virat spread their sleeping mats outside next to the hut, and they lay side by side watching the stars.

"Anup and Sethu have four daughters," Latha said.

"Yes," said Virat. "I saw them today."

"Every day Devi, the oldest one, works in the landlord's garden. Lidya, the second one, cooks and gathers firewood."

"Yes."

"Lidya saw my scarred face," Latha said. "She asked me if boiling rice spilled on me. She has a scar on her face, too, and also one on her hand. Poor little child."

"I didn't notice."

"She also walks with a limp, that one. Once a cow trod on her small foot and crushed it."

Virat had not noticed that either. He had not really looked at Anup's older daughters. For several minutes, both he and Latha were silent.

"Do you think Ashish will have to work here?" Latha asked.

"I don't know. Not until his body has healed. Not until then."

For several minutes they lay in silence. Then, with an urgency that frightened Virat, Latha whispered, "We must not stay here, Husband."

"What?"

"We must get our son and go back to our mud hut on the far edge of the village."

Virat said nothing. How could he tell Latha that they could not go back? How could he explain that they now belonged to the landowner, like his ox and his buffalo? That their new master could keep them or sell them, work them or kill them? How could Virat possibly tell his wife that they were now the landowner's slaves?

# 10

As stars faded from the night sky, the laborers' settlement came awake. Latha grabbed up a handful of twigs and tossed them on the fire pit. Once she had a cooking fire burning, she threw rice into the earthenware pot—only half a handful, though, because the rice sack had grown much lighter than before.

"Quickly, Wife," Virat said. "Already workers gather in the courtyard."

Virat and Latha hurried to join the others, but then they hung back on the outer edges of the gathering. "Can you see what's happening?" Latha whispered.

"No," Virat said. But as he said it, he noticed a tree stump off to one side, so he jumped up on it and stretched himself tall until he could see over the heads in front of him.

"Anup covered up the opening to the well with some sort of thing," Virat whispered down to Latha. "Oh, now he is bowing down . . . bowing low, into the dirt. So low his forehead touches to the ground. I cannot see why . . . Oh, it is because of the landlord's son! The landlord's son who drove the bullock cart jumped up on the well and now he stands on it for all to see."

"Harvest!" Boban Joseph Varghese yelled out.

The people answered back with a ringing cheer.

"When the crop is in, every one of you will share in the celebration!" Boban Joseph promised. "My father has commanded that a feast be laid out for you in the harvested field. The greater the harvest, the greater the celebration!"

The workers roared their approval. To the chants of "Harvest! Harvest!" Boban Joseph jumped down and bowed his own head.

"Oh, now it is the Brahmin who comes!" Virat gasped to Latha. "It's the priest!"

Brahmin Keshavan Namboodri stepped forward. A garland of marigold blossoms hung around his neck. He folded his hands as if in prayer and lifted them high.

"He asks the gods to bless the harvest," Virat whispered.

Reciting *mantras* over and over in a loud voice, Brahmin Keshavan implored the gods to graciously grant a most bountiful harvest. If they would, he promised, they would be honored with many gifts and generous sacrifices.

As dawn broke, the workers filed out to the first field. But Virat and Latha were not with them.

Gasping at the sight of Boban Joseph outside her doorway, Latha shrank back into the hut. But Virat stepped outside and fell to his knees, prostrating himself, his forehead pressed to the dirt.

"Get up, get up!" Boban Joseph said. A touch of disgust tinged his young-man voice. "Father says you and your woman are not to go to the fields today. Father says both of you are to wash and oil yourselves and dress in clean clothes."

Virat lifted his head, but he did not get up. "The clothes we wear are the only ones we own," he said.

"Get up on your feet!" Boban Joseph ordered. "Wash yourselves, at the least. Wait here in your hut until someone sends for you."

"Yes, my master," Virat said. But still he did not get up.

Latha listened from inside the hut. "What does he want with us?" she begged of her husband after Boban Joseph had gone.

"I don't know," Virat said.

"It is about Ashish."

"Most likely it is." Virat's heart weighed heavy with dread, though he did not speak it to his wife.

Virat untied his *mundu* and slipped it off. He did his best to shake the dirt from the many yards of dingy cloth. Taking up one of the water jars, he carefully washed himself, including his hair and, last of all, his feet. When he finished, Latha unwrapped her *sari*, took the other water jar and did the same. With the last bit of remaining water, Latha did her best to rub away the worst of the soil and stains from their clothes. Then they put their clothes back on.

When Virat started to sit on the dirt floor to wait, Latha stopped him. "No, no!" she said. "We must not get dirty all over again."

So, awkward and uncomfortable, they stood and waited. And waited and waited and waited some more. With the last of the workers gone to the fields, no one remained in the settlement but the smallest children. Little One, though only in her fifth year, bore the sole responsibility for watching over Baby. Other toddlers appeared to be left to care for themselves. Latha watched as the little ones wandered about.

No old grandmothers' watchful eyes here. Among Landlord Varghese's laborers, old women worked in the fields right alongside the young ones.

When the sun had climbed halfway to its zenith, a servant from the landlord's house came bearing a neat stack of clean clothing, fresh from the washer men. He didn't enter the hut but called to Virat and Latha through the doorway: "Dress yourselves, then go to the road and wait."

"Look!" Latha gasped in wonder as she unfolded a bright green and yellow *sari*. "No stains. Oh, and the edges. See, Husband, they are not frayed!"

Also in the stack they found a fresh *mundu* of white cotton for Virat—one with no holes—and a bright yellow *chaddar* for his head.

"I am certain good news is coming our way," Latha said as she began to wrap the fresh *sari* around her waist—gathering it in the front before wrapping it around the rest of her body and up over her shoulder.

Virat said nothing. He had seen the cobra. He had seen the markings of the feet of the god Krishna on its head.

Virat and Latha were waiting, washed and wearing their new clothes, when the landlord's bullocks lumbered down the road pulling the cart. Mammen Samuel Varghese, on the front bench beside his son, motioned for the two to climb up in back. "I will take you to the clinic to collect your child," Mammen Samuel said. He didn't look at them when he spoke, but kept his eyes fixed straight ahead. "I will take you because I am a good Christian man descended from a long line of good Christian men. That is what you are to say to the doctor. Tell that to the English healer."

As the bullocks pulled the cart through the village, people stopped to pay tribute to the landowner. He ignored them all. The cart rumbled through the village, over the rough planks of the bridge, and on to the untouchable side of the river. Only after the lumbering bullocks had pulled the cart past him did Virat see Ranjun the potter on the untouchable side of the river. Whatever Ranjun might claim about his superior standing, at that moment, no one would mistake him for anything but an outcaste. He stood ankle deep in mud, his long *mundu* folded up and tucked into his waist in such a way that exposed his legs and knees for all to see. So disrespectful a display! Ranjun saw Virat, too. Most certainly he recognized the landowner as well. Virat could not miss the twitch in Ranjun's haughty moustache. With an imperceptible flick of his fingers, Ranjun's *mundu* fluttered down and covered his bare, mud-splattered legs.

Boban Joseph steered the cart away from the path through the mud-hut settlement where Virat and Latha's place stood empty and over to the wide road. The path led a much shorter route to the English Mission Medical Clinic, but since it required traveling on a polluted trail, no self-respecting person of high caste birth would consider using it.

For two long hours, the landlord bounced along in the cart, staring straight ahead. Not one word did he utter. Boban Joseph also sat in silence, except for the occasional command he called out to the bullocks.

Virat watched for another village. But instead they came to a compound with three small wooden buildings and one larger one, all neatly whitewashed. The large building had a cross fastened to the top. Boban Joseph steered the bullocks over to the shade of the single large mango tree that grew to one side of the largest building and called out for the team to halt.

"Doctor!" Mammen Samuel bellowed from his seat in the cart. "I have come back for the boy!"

But Dr. Moore didn't answer the call. Abigail Davidson did.

When Latha saw Abigail, her mouth dropped and her good eye opened wide. Such chalky white skin! And her hair . . . like the threads of Virat's new *chaddar*, it was! But Abigail's eyes really transfixed her. They shone with the hue of a spring morning. "A goddess!" Latha breathed. She eased out of the cart and lay flat on the ground before Abigail.

"Stand up, you fool!" Mammen Samuel hissed as he, too, climbed down from the cart. "This is but an Englishwoman."

Latha peeked up and saw that her husband stood beside her. Wide-eyed, yes, but he did not bow.

"Tell the doctor I have come to collect the boy." Mammen Samuel issued his order to Darshina in words clipped and tinged with rudeness. "I brought his father and mother with me. Tell the doctor that because I am an honorable Christian man and I desire peace, I have chosen to do as he requested."

Darshina repeated his words to Abigail, and Abigail called, "Dr. Moore! Dr. Moore! Do come at once!"

"What is all the commotion?" Dr. Moore insisted. When he saw Mammen Samuel Varghese, he said, "I see. Do step into the clinic."

Darshina translated, and with an irritated sigh, Mammen Samuel entered. Not Latha and Virat, though. They shrank back and did their best to make themselves invisible. But when Dr. Moore threw the door open wide, they could plainly see Ashish sitting just inside, spinning a bright red wooden top across the floor. He stopped his play, looked up, and stared.

"*Appa!*" the little boy cried. "*Amma!*"

Latha tried to run to Ashish, but Dr. Moore blocked the way.

"Come, come!" Mammen Samuel insisted. "I did as you instructed. Now we will take the boy and leave."

"Please, do sit down," Dr. Moore responded in a cool voice. He motioned Mammen Samuel to the best chair. "Let me come right to the point. It seems my assistant, Miss Davidson, has taken quite a liking to this child. It is her belief that he might well be better served in the English school for orphans in Madras, under the guidance of English caretakers, than growing up in some fearsome jungle. I must say, I am rather inclined to agree with her."

As Darshina repeated the doctor's words, Mammen Samuel's face flushed with fury. "You tell the doctor that if he is as honorable a Christian man as I am, he will keep his word and release the boy to me at once!"

Darshina looked helplessly from one powerful man to the other. Frustrated tears filled Latha's eyes, and little Ashish began to wail. Darshina repeated the landowner's angry words.

"Now, see here," Dr. Moore answered. "You may be an important chieftain or a clan head or whatever you fancy yourself in your village, but if you knew the first thing about being an honorable Christian man, you would welcome such an opportunity for the lad!"

Darshina did not have to worry about translating those words, however, for Abigail forced her way past the doctor and picked up Ashish. She hugged him tightly and kissed his soft cheek, then carried him to his mother.

"You have a wonderful son," she said, tears glistening in her blue eyes. "Take him home. I will pray to God that He will keep this little one in His care forever."

Stars shown in a black sky by the time Boban Joseph stopped the bullock cart on the road beside the path that led to the laborers' huts. He said nothing, and Mammen Samuel Varghese also stared ahead in stony silence, so Virat and Latha climbed out of the cart. Latha put Ashish on his father's back, and, with smiles on their faces, they walked to their new home.

"It is not wise to be outside the settlement in the dark," Anup called out as they passed by his hut. "Wild animals lurk beside the path. Not four days ago, a tiger got one of the master's goats."

"We brought our son back," Virat said.

Sethu hurried to the door to see. "Such a fine boy you have."

"Tomorrow, you stay with your son," Anup said to Latha. "One day to get him settled is not too much to ask."

Virat and Latha started to walk on, but Anup called them back. "Your food ration," he said as he handed them two sweet potatoes.

"What are these?" Virat said. "This is not food. This is feed for animals. We need rice."

Anup shook his head. "What Brahma has written, we must follow. The big man eats rice and butter every day. We work the fields and bring in a good harvest, but all we get is a potato. Brahma has written one kind of fate for us and another kind of fate for them. That is the way it is. No one can change it."

Virat took the potatoes, but under his breath he murmured, "That tiger eats better than we do!"

When Mammen Samuel Varghese reached his house, he immediately bellowed for Babu to bring him his wooden desk and leather-bound book of business accounts. He settled himself stiff and straight on the floor and thumbed through the accounting book until he found his latest entry: Virat. Mammen Samuel dipped his pen in the inkwell and—in his tight, cramped script—printed a new notation beside the name: *Injured son treated at English Mission Medical Clinic. Journeyed to deposit the boy; journeyed to bring him back. Fresh sari, mundu, chaddar for the journey.* He crossed out the amount of Virat's debt and doubled it. For several minutes Mammen Samuel sat and considered. Then he dipped his pen into the inkwell a second time, crossed out his changes, and doubled the debt again.

## 11

"You will go to the fields today," Anup said to Latha. Every trace of friendliness had vanished from his face. "The master commands it. Do not ask again."

"Only a few more days with my son," Latha pleaded. "Give me that and I will make no further request."

"You will go this morning and you will not ask again. Master's son will be watching for you. If you are not there, I do not want to tell you the punishments that will rain down on you and your family."

"But Ashish—"

"Little Girl will look in on him."

"Little Girl! But she is no older than he! What can she do?"

"This is how it is. Come quickly, now. The laborers are ready to leave." Anup turned his back and walked away.

❧

Brahmin Keshavan, dressed in his most impressively embroidered *mundu*, walked the road to Mammen Samuel

Varghese's home. The sacred thread of his caste, always over his left shoulder, glistened golden against the freshly oiled skin of his upper body. He did not pause at the entry steps to call out a greeting, but walked right up to Mammen Samuel's veranda. Mammen Samuel, bathed and oiled and smelling of sandalwood, sat crossed-legged on the most exquisite of his many fine carpets. Hand-carried all the way from Kashmir, he had chosen it for this day for the simple reason that its intricate patterns and vibrant colors proclaimed its lavish cost.

Mammen Samuel nodded to the Brahmin and said, "You honor me with your visit. Please sit beside me."

The landowner said these kind words, but he did not stand up to greet the revered Brahmin. Keshavan chose to ignore the slight. Brahmin Keshavan folded his long, thin legs and settled himself across from Mammen Samuel in the shade of the fragrant jasmine vine. He was older than his host, but not by a great deal. At forty-one and forty-nine, both men were considered advanced in years. Yet while the Brahmin's hair displayed a generous splash of gray, his skin remained smooth and light—the skin of youth—or perhaps simply of one who has never had to work in the sun or wind.

"Babu!" Mammen Samuel called to his Sudra servant. "Bring us tea. Quickly, now!"

Brahmin Keshavan pulled his own cup out from the pure white folds of his *mundu*. He need not say a word, for this gesture alone proclaimed: *You and yours are not pure enough for such a one as I.*

Mammen Samuel understood the insult. He smiled and nodded, but inside he seethed.

"May the gods smile on your harvest," Brahmin Keshavan said.

Mammen Samuel waited until Babu laid out the tea, then he answered, "The fields are rich and full, praise be to the one true God in heaven."

"You have a great crowd of workers," said the Brahmin. "They number in the many hundreds, do they not?"

Mammen Samuel shrugged. "Only enough to bring in the harvest and plant the rice paddies, and no more. The exact number, I do not know. I don't worry myself about such trivialities."

Both men knew that wasn't true. Mammen Samuel had every name of every bonded laborer carefully recorded in his leather-bound book, and each one was numbered—every man, every woman, and every child. He knew perfectly well that he had exactly five hundred forty-one slaves, and what was more, Brahmin Keshavan knew that Mammen Samuel knew it.

"My house is the first house in the Brahmin section of the village," Brahmin Keshavan stated.

Of course, Mammen Samuel knew exactly where the great Brahmin lived. Not that he had ever been invited inside his house. The few times in this life he'd had occasion to search out the Brahmin, he had been kept waiting outside for Keshavan to come out to him. But certainly Mammen Samuel knew where he lived.

"In my childhood days in this village, the Brahmin section had never been trodden by the polluted feet of a pariah," Keshavan continued. "Not a single Brahmin defiled his hands with labor of any sort. Untouchables did all the dirty work— but they did it far away from our street. Anything necessary to our comfort or welfare, Sudras carried in and out."

Mammen Samuel sipped his tea. He was not at all pleased with the direction of the conversation.

"Today, everything is different. Today our entire village is polluted. Potters and carpenters and scavengers and Sudras— all of them live together, and directly outside our village gates too. All of them work together in *your* fields. Unclean meat-eaters live just across the field from the Brahmin section of the village."

Mammen Samuel's jaw clenched.

"Why, not so many days ago a *chamar* walked the full length of our road on his way to your house. It happened to be the very same *chamar* whose son dared to defile our water. And now you have both that *chamar* and his son living right here, on your land. It is not right!"

Mammen Samuel lifted his tea cup to his lips and slurped with a vengeance.

"Stay inside the hut on your sleeping mat," Latha had told Ashish as she left for the fields. "Lie down and sleep all day. Sleep and get well."

But Ashish felt well already. He could take a deep breath and feel only a little pain. Most of all, he wished he could pull the tight bandages off his body. Ashish sat up stiffly and took out the red wooden top the pale English lady had slipped him when he left the clinic, and he tried to spin it the way she taught him. But it wouldn't spin on the dirt floor.

That's when he noticed the girl peeking through the doorway.

"Who are you?" Ashish demanded.

"Little Girl. I brought you milk to drink."

Little Girl came in and set a clay cup down beside him.

"My *amma* left me *chapatis* to eat," Ashish said. "Do you want one?"

*The Faith of Ashish*

"I have to look out for my little sister, Baby," Little Girl said. "She always finds trouble."

"Look what I have," Ashish bragged as he held out the red top. "If you come back to play with me, I'll show you how it works."

"I am not a man without power," Brahmin Keshavan stated. "Spiritual power, most certainly. That is obvious. But my family also has impressive political alliances upon which I can call at will."

"I, too, have an impressive family," Mammen Samuel said. He sat up tall and assumed his most arrogant tone. "In addition, I am endowed with the power that comes from intelligence, and also that which comes from hard work. My great herds of cows and water buffalo, and the many men I control with a single word, are ample proof of that."

Babu stepped in, bearing plates of sliced cucumbers and guavas, and a stalk of finger-sized deep red bananas. These he laid out between the two men. In the center of the presentation he set a golden bowl of cashew nuts.

"A village must have someone who can collect the prayers." Brahmin Keshavan's dark eye's flashed. His words were clipped and brittle.

Mammen Samuel reached for a guava and slurped it from its skin. "A village must also have someone who collects money." He reached for the golden bowl and scooped out a handful of cashew nuts. "Elsewise, who would support you while you pour out your endless flood of words?"

Brahmin Keshavan made a great show of sipping the last of his tea. Mammen Samuel offered to pour him more, but Keshavan waved him off.

"I am a tolerant and peaceable man," said the Brahmin. "The low castes are banned from public markets, yet I make it my habit to leave fruit out for them. Untouchables such as your *chamar* pollute anyone who dares to look upon them. I could have had that one of yours put to death for the abominations he has already poured out on this village, yet I willingly spoke to him, and in a most civil manner too."

Mammen Samuel tore a banana from the stalk. Expertly he ripped off the peel and popped the sweet fruit into his mouth. "Life cannot go on without the Untouchables," he said through his full mouth. "You know that as well as I."

"You mean to say, abiding the mixture of castes is a sacrifice we must make for our comfort and prosperity?" Brahmin Keshavan asked.

"Yes, yes. That is precisely what I say."

"In that case, the resulting prosperity must rightly be shared with me."

Mammen Samuel swallowed the banana. Dropping all pretense of a friendly visit, he shoved the fruit plates aside and glared at the Brahmin. "You dare to demand payment from me? You, who do nothing day and night but sit at your doorway and pass judgment on all who pass by? I most certainly shall not share my prosperity with you! No, not one rupee!"

"To collect a tithe is my right and my privilege," Brahmin Keshavan stated. "Did I not call out a blessing on your harvest?"

"Not one rupee!"

Sitting on his sleeping mat by himself had quickly become boring and tiresome to Ashish. He wished Little Girl would come back to play with him. He finally managed to get a bit of a spin from the top, but even that wasn't any fun when no one watched and admired his success. So he did exactly what his mother told him not to do; he went outside to explore this new settlement.

So many huts all crowded together, yet so few people! A couple of young girls struggled to tote a large bucket of water, but they paid Ashish no mind. Several other children scurried about searching for twigs and small branches which they threw into a pile. Gathering wood for cooking fires—Ashish knew that job quite well, although he didn't see many twigs or branches lying about.

Although Ashish often ran and played for hours on end, after only a short exploration of the settlement around his own hut, he felt weak and weary and ready for his sleeping mat. He looked at the hut beside him. Was that one his? No, it couldn't be this close. Maybe the next one? Or the next? To Ashish's dismay, every hut looked like his hut. He crept to the doorway of one after the other and peeked inside, but each time the pots lined up against the wall were not his mother's pots. And not one of those huts had a rack for drying animal skins propped up against the far wall.

Panic seized Ashish. He ran through the winding paths, searching frantically for something familiar. But weariness overtook him. He staggered and stumbled, then he tripped and fell flat. He wanted to scramble to his feet and hurry on, but he could not. What if he never found his *amma* and *appa*? His eyes filled with tears. He didn't know anyone in this settlement, and no one knew him. What would he do? A sob escaped his lips and tears ran down his cheeks.

Ashish struggled to his feet and swiped his dirty little hands across his tear-streaked face. That's when he spied the well. Exactly like that other awful well, it was. Even an earthenware cup on its side. Terror grabbed at him. Trembling, he threw his hands over his face and fell to the ground wailing.

"Ashish? What's the matter, Ashish?"

Slowly Ashish moved his fingers apart and peeked between them. Little Girl knelt in the dirt by his side and peeked back at him.

"I can't find my house," Ashish told her through his sobs. "And this awful well—"

"It isn't a bad well," Little Girl said. "That's where we get our water. Come with me. Baby and I will take you to your house."

Back in his own hut, Ashish fell exhausted onto the sleeping mat. Baby spied his red top and snatched it up to play. Little Girl sat beside Ashish. "Are you a bad boy?" she asked him.

"Yes," Ashish said. "I'm very bad. That's what the men said when they kicked me and hit me with sticks."

"I'm more bad than you," Little Girl said. "I'm so bad I had to be born a girl."

"I forget myself. You are, of course, a *meat-eater*." Brahmin Keshavan's carefully chosen words were the worst possible accusation, pronounced as though the words themselves were foul, disgusting things to be spat out.

"But not due to caste," Mammen Samuel quickly protested. "Christians are permitted to eat meat. Not carrion, of course. Not like a wild animal or an Untouchable or a savage. But fresh meat, yes."

Mammen Samuel Varghese took great pride in his claim of an ancestry line that traced all the way back to the ancient King Gundaphorus, famed for his quest to build the grandest of all cities. And Mammen Samuel never tired of telling the lesser-told tradition of the king's encounter with Thomas, one of the twelve disciples of Jesus Christ, shortly after Thomas arrived on the Malabar Coast aboard a trading vessel from the Red Sea. When Saint Thomas heard about King Gundaphorus' quest, he approached the great king and said, "Allow me to tell you of the greatest City of all—a City not made with hands." Under the tutelage of Saint Thomas, King Gundaphorus became an enthusiastic follower of Christ. And not only the king, but many members of his court as well, which Mammen Samuel Varghese insisted, included his ancestors. Saint Thomas himself had baptized the first Christians in Mammen Samuel's family. Or so the landlord said.

Mammen Samuel's eyes narrowed as he gazed at the pale-faced Brahmin who sat so smugly, his thin lips set tight. A Brahmin priest had killed the great Saint Thomas. Ran him through with a lance, he did. Could that ancient Brahmin have been an ancestor of this very Brahmin Keshavan Namboodri who sat so hautily on Landlord Varghese's fine carpet and drank his tea?

Mammen Samuel's nostrils flared and his eyes flashed. Though he did not raise his voice, his tone took on shadings of his ancient warrior caste past—Kshatriya ferocity.

"You Hindus speak of *karma*? Look around at the luxuries of my house." Mammen Samuel picked up the platter of fruit. "Look at the fine artistry in the silver of my vessels." He grabbed up the dish of cashew nuts. "See the rich gold of my bowls." He waved his arms about dramatically and exclaimed, "Look at the exquisite design of the rug on which you rest your body. Four thousand rupees I paid for this carpet! Surely a million of your gods have smiled on me. Can you deny it?"

Brahmin Keshavan could not. And although the expression on his face did not change, he simmered in fury at the injustice of it all.

"To accumulate gold bowls and silver platters and exquisite carpets is not the supreme goal of life," Keshavan said. "The supreme goal of life is to escape the never-ending cycle of death and rebirth as yet another human—or perhaps as an animal. The supreme goal is to finally become a part of the universal soul of Creator god Brahma himself. It is only achieved by living a life that is pure and good. As for me, I am but one step away from that supreme goal. For my life is indeed pure and good."

"Why, then, do you worry yourself about snatching away a share of my wealth?"

"To give is your destiny," Brahmin Keshavan said. "It is my destiny to receive from you and to bless you in return."

Mammen Samuel's lips tightened and his eyes flashed. "I can make my way quite well without your blessing," he hissed.

All afternoon, Ashish tossed in a restless sleep. When he awoke, Little Girl sat in the doorway of his house. Baby played in the dirt outside.

"Are you still sick?" Little Girl asked anxiously.

Ashish looked about him. For a few moments, he couldn't remember where he was.

"Are you still sick?" Little Girl asked again.

"I . . . I don't know," Ashish stammered.

"Your face looks strange. Do you hurt?"

"Not as much as I did before."

"The holy Brahmin came and blessed the harvest," Little Girl said. "Maybe he can come back and bless you too."

"I don't think so," said Ashish. "If he comes, I think he will hit me with a stick."

❧

Brahmin Keshavan sat straight and tall like a stone statue, his face rigid and angry. But he did not leave Mammen Samuel's veranda.

Mammen Samuel glowered and smoldered, yet he made no excuse to part ways either.

Finally Mammen Samuel said, "You are a Brahmin, a priest. You have your duties, and you have your privileges. I am a *Kshatriya*, a ruler-warrior. My duty is to bring order, to draw the incompatible together. Perhaps it is your place to limit contact between castes, to keep those who are unlike separate, and so to maintain the old ways. But the realm of a successful ruler is made up of unlike peoples, all rendered harmonious and productive together."

"And profitable for the ruler," Keshavan said.

"Profitable for the entire village," Mammen Samuel insisted. "The days of heroism and conquering enemies are past. Now it is the task of my kind to show our prowess by fighting against disharmony."

"Make yourself a king if you desire," Keshavan said with a dismissive wave of his hand. "What does a king matter to a Brahmin? We are *Bhudevas*, gods on earth. What is a mere king to a god?"

# 12

"I'm a *chamar*," Virat admitted to Anup. "I don't know how to harvest wheat."

"You'll learn," Anup told him.

By noon, Virat was walking across the wheat field in the middle of a long line of men, all of them swinging their scythes in rhythm, all taking care to slash the wheat stalks close to the ground. At first Virat stumbled along behind the others, hesitant and unsure of himself, too afraid to swing the scythe wide enough or low enough. But he watched the men on either side of him and learned quickly. Nor was Virat the only one new to the harvest. A fair sprinkling of other men had also come to the settlement since the fall crops came in. But Anup took care to intersperse the new ones among the experienced men, and by day's end, all worked together like veteran hands.

The women followed along behind the men to sort out the cut wheat stalks, bundle them together into stacks, and tie them securely. "Your job is only to gather the stalks into piles," Anup's wife Sethu told Latha. More experienced hands would come after her and form each pile into the right-sized bundle, then grab out a clump of stems and wrap it around, twisting the ends and tucking them in tightly so the bundle would hold together.

"When we finish with this entire field, we'll load the bundles onto our heads and carry them to the storehouse. The wheat will dry there until it's hard enough for threshing," Sethu said.

Before the sun reached its zenith, the muscles in Latha's arms burned like needles plucked from the fire. Her hands, unused to such harsh work, split to the quick so that each seedling she planted bore the stain of a drop of her blood. More than one worker staggered and fell under the blistering sun. Boys too young to swing scythes ran back and forth from the settlement well, laden down with jars of water which they passed along the lines of laborers. Only after the harvesters had had their fill did the women get a turn at the water.

When a water jug finally came Latha's way, she grabbed it and gulped greedily. As she turned to pass it on to Sethu, a rumbling tiger growl shook the field behind her.

All chattering stilled, every movement stopped. Even the swooping birds fell silent. But only for a moment. Latha leapt up and bounded back toward the settlement.

"No!" Sethu screamed at her. "Don't go *that* way!"

The terrifying growl still hung heavy in the air, but Latha could think of only one thing: her injured son, lying alone and helpless in the hut.

"Stop!" the women shrieked. "Come back!"

Ignoring the cries, Latha dashed through the unharvested field toward the path to the settlement. Directly in front of her, almost hidden in the uncut wheat, crouched the tiger. A gasp caught in Latha's throat and she froze in her tracks. Icy yellow eyes peered out at her through waving stalks of grain. The hairs on the back of her neck prickled out straight.

The tiger twitched and flicked its tail. Its muscles tensed.

*Step back slowly*, Latha told herself. But her feet would not obey.

On the breeze, musty tiger stench wafted across the field. The women's shrieks faded into ominous silence. But still Latha couldn't move. Her legs seemed to have turned to stone.

Joyoti's young son Kilas and little Anandraj hurried up the path from the settlement well, laughing loudly. Kilas lugged two large water jars and the small boy struggled with one. Before Latha could shout out a warning, the great animal swung around and thrashed its way through the wheat. With a powerful lunge, it flew at the boys.

"Tiger!" Latha finally managed to scream. "Tiger! Tiger!"

Kilas shrieked, "No, no! Anandraj!"

Like a streak, the tiger leapt up and bounded for the trees, dragging the small boy with him.

ℒ❧

"My Ashish will never go to the fields. I will make certain of that!" Latha announced to Sethu. The need for water had finally pushed the two mothers to venture out of their huts and to the well. "Never! My mind is made up."

Sethu sniffed. "Of course he will. He must work like everyone else. Anyone who does not work deserves to eat dirt."

"How can you talk that way?"

"My Anup and the men with him will find the tiger and kill it. Even if they don't, we will all be back in the fields tomorrow. Master Landowner will not stop the harvest simply because the tiger dragged off one boy, whose name no one even remembers."

Latha looked at her new friend in disbelief. "His name was Anandraj. His mother remembers," she said. "His brother remembers. And I will never forget."

"That boy's fate happened because of his *karma*, Latha. And it might be a good thing, too. Now his soul can move on to a different body, and he will have another chance in another life. Maybe his next life will be better than this one."

"I will not go to the fields tomorrow," Latha said. "I will stay at home and watch over my son."

The last of the purple and yellow bruises had faded from Ashish's face, and the wounds on his body were almost completely healed. He still wore the bandages, although they were so dirty and ragged Latha expected them to fall away at any time. Ashish seldom complained of pain and he had even started to run around the huts chasing after Little Girl. Even so, he was not the same Ashish as before the beating. He showed more fear now and shyness around everyone except his parents and Little Girl and Baby.

"Your boy is old enough to work," Anup told Latha. "The landlord will expect it. Everyone here must earn his keep."

"But Ashish is tiny and weakened," Latha pleaded. "The tiger would grab him first!"

"Forget the tiger. It has gone back to the jungle."

But Latha would have none of it. "Maybe it has and maybe it has not. But even if the tiger has gone, it will remember the taste of human flesh, and when it gets hungry, it will be back."

Anup was not unkind, but neither did he waver in his decision. "Ashish is part of the community now. He is required to work the same as everyone else is required to work. It is not your choice."

Virat suggested to Anup that Ashish might spend his days gathering firewood. Latha could use what she needed for her own cooking pit, and whatever was left, the child could trade for some of the fresh greens and cucumbers and chili peppers other families grew in their small garden plots.

"Work hard," Latha begged her son. "If you do not, you will be sent to the fields. Please, please, work very hard."

❧

Latha feared danger in the fields, but not she alone. Many women took to hiding in the settlement and refused to go out to work. No longer was the cadence of the harvest quick and sure. Now the workers hesitated, pausing frequently to look behind them. And when the sun started to sink below the hills, they glanced about anxiously and refused to work any longer. Boban Joseph rode his father's horse up and down the line bellowing, "Harvest! Harvest!" but no one listened to him. As one, the laborers abandoned their tools and hurried for the safety of their huts.

Boban Joseph, whose oversaw the harvest, carried the worrisome news to his father. "They fear the tiger more than they fear you," he said. "The harvest goes too slowly."

Late one afternoon, after the workers had deserted the harvest even earlier than usual, Latha—water jug on her head and Ashish tightly in her grip—stood with a crowd of women waiting for a turn at the well. Cheers suddenly erupted on the far side of the courtyard.

"*Amma*, look!" Ashish cried. "It's a baby elephant!"

And a magnificent elephant it was, too, beautifully painted with bright designs and decorated in red and gold. But most amazing of all, Master Mammen Samuel Varghese himself held the cord tied around the elephant's neck. He actually led it along! (Although a crowd of servants did follow closely behind him.)

"Can I touch the elephant?" Ashish begged his mother. "On its painted ear? Please, *Amma?*"

"No, no!" Latha said. "Hush now. Stay close beside me."

A small, wide-eyed boy sat straight and proud on a fancy blanket thrown over the elephant's back.

"I bring you my son, Saji Stephen!" Mammen Samuel announced to the gawking crowd.

The lively chatter dissolved into oooohhh's and ahhhhh's.

"Oh, such a heavenly child!" cried a woman at the millstone. She clasped her work-worn hands together in reverence and bowed low.

"Sa—ji! Sa—ji! Sa—ji!" the growing crowd chanted.

The procession stopped beside the well. A servant climbed up and lifted the boy down from the elephant's back and into the arms of Babu, who stood the boy on the rim of the well for all to see. A gasp of admiration arose as the crowd pressed in for a closer look. The boy could not have had more than seven years of life. Cleaner than any child the laborers had ever seen and smelling of sweet sandalwood oil, he was outfitted in elegant clothes that caused every mother to stare in disbelieving admiration—all pure white with what looked to be golden threads woven throughout.

When the gasps and exclamations began to die down, Babu lifted the boy onto his shoulders and paraded him through the crowd. Men and women alike bowed down and touched their foreheads to the ground as he passed by.

"You see!" Mammen Samuel called out. "All of us are safe from the tiger. The beast has crept back to its lair. If it were not so, would I dare to bring my precious little son out here among you? Would I expose my child to danger? Of course I would not. You know I would not!"

Ashish, transfixed, could not take his eyes off the child. A little boy, very much like himself. Oh, but nothing like him.

This boy wasn't bad or cursed. He looked to be almost like a small god!

When Babu approached with Saji Stephen on his shoulders, Ashish reached out his hand and held his red wooden top up to the boy. "For you," he said to Saji Stephen.

"Get away," Babu scowled, kicking at Ashish.

But Saji Stephen said, "No, no, Babu! I want it!"

Babu hesitated and glanced over to his master. When he saw that Mammen Samuel smiled, Babu reached down and took the top. He handed it up to Saji Stephen, who always got everything he wanted.

"Entirely safe!" Mammen Samuel called out. "Perfectly safe! I bring my own son to your settlement to show you."

The workers released a collective sigh.

"Tomorrow, the harvest will resume as before. Tomorrow, all of you will be in the field early and you will stay until dusk. And after the harvest is over, we will all celebrate its success together."

✿

"Little Girl!" Sethu scolded. "Baby will not stop her fussing and the noise exhausts me. Tend to her!"

Little Girl, near tears herself, swatted at her little sister. But all this did was set Baby to wailing. Fortunately, Devi returned from working in the landlord's garden just in time to see the difficulty. She tossed her armload of fresh spinach to her younger sister Lidya, who already busied herself at the cook fire, and rushed to pick up Baby. Balancing the little one on her own young-girl hip, she cooed and soothed the fussy child.

"Make yourself useful, Little Girl," Sethu ordered. "Take some of those greens over to share with Ashish's family. And take along an extra measure of rice too."

Little Girl scooped up a handful of spinach and the small bag of rice and ran off with glee.

The rest of the green leaves, Lidya tore into pieces and dropped into the earthenware pot over the fire where sweet potatoes and chilies already bubbled. She pulled two fistfuls of wheat flour from the flour sack and mixed in enough water to form it into a workable dough.

"The landlord's little boy rode into the courtyard on the back of an elephant today," Lidya told Devi.

"Saji Stephen? I don't like him."

"Hush that talk!" Sethu warned. "He is a beautiful boy."

"Everyone gives him whatever he wants," Devi said. "If they don't, he cries and yells until he gets his way."

"He is a clean, pure boy. The gods smile on him."

"If he is here, the tiger can't get us," Lidya said. "Can it, *Amma?*"

Sethu took the ball of dough from Lidya and patted it into thin cakes. "The landlord will protect us," she said in the voice that meant "say no more." One by one, she laid the cakes over the fire to toast.

❧

"Did the tiger *eat* the water boy?" Ashish asked his father. Latha hadn't wanted Virat to tell him about the tiger attack, but with it being on the tongue of everyone in the settlement, Virat insisted.

"Probably," Virat said.

"But why?"

"Because that's what hungry tigers do."

"Was the boy bad?" Ashish asked.

Virat grunted and gave no answer.

Questions and questions and more questions. That's how it had always been with Ashish. It used to be that his *appa* would take time to answer every one of his questions— patiently, calmly, with clear, easy words. And when he tired of answering, Virat would hug Ashish and tell him what a bright boy he was.

But Ashish's *appa* didn't answer his questions that way anymore. Now Virat's responses were vague, often impatient. Sometimes he didn't bother to reply at all.

Ashish wanted to ask his father if he were as bad as the boy who had been eaten by the tiger. He wanted to ask if he were as bad as Little Girl, cursed to be born both an Untouchable *and* a girl. But he knew his father would not be happy to answer those questions. Most likely, his father would pretend not to hear.

So Ashish lay down on the sleeping mat inside the hut, where the tiger couldn't reach him, and dreamed of the hungry tiger carrying the water boy away in his mouth, as though he were a goat or a chicken or a doll made of rags.

# 13

"A curse is what it is!" Mammen Samuel Varghese exclaimed. "He dares call himself a holy man, yet if he doesn't get his money, he conjures up an evil spirit and pronounces a curse on me!"

Parmar Ruth Varghese rushed into the room where her husband fumed and paced. "Whatever are you going on about?" she asked as she nervously smoothed the folds of her scarlet silk *sari*.

Though the wife of the great landowner seldom left her house or veranda, her sumptuous garments, each with a dazzling border of gold threads, bore witness to her husband's wealth. Even more, Parmar Ruth wore her wealth—gold bangles on her arms and ankles, gold rings on her toes and in her nose and ears. Her earrings were so large and heavy, in fact, that the pierced holes in her ears stretched large enough for her to put the tip of her finger through.

"That accursed Brahmin Keshavan Namboodri!" Mammen Samuel seethed at the sound of his name.

"What happened, Husband?" Parmar Ruth asked. "Did the Brahmin do you an injustice?"

Mammen Samuel opened his mouth to air further complaint, but he immediately thought better of it. "It is not a matter of concern for a woman. I shall take care of it myself."

He turned away shouting, "Babu! Call for my son! Call for Boban Joseph!"

✍

With Boban Joseph by his side, Mammen Samuel walked the short way down the road to the Brahmin settlement. Mammen Samuel's Kshatriya caste, though one level lower than the most revered caste of Brahmin, still carried the honor of pure and high-born. Both father and son could freely enter the Brahmin section of the village without threat of causing defilement.

"One day, you will have to deal with this haughty family of Brahmins," Mammen Samuel told his son. "Your grandfather struggled with them, and it cost him his life. I am wiser than he was. Learn from me to stand firm against them."

Even so, Mammen Samuel refused to allow Boban Joseph to accompany him all the way to Brahmin Keshavan's house. Halfway between the road and the first house, as they passed the huge mango tree that marked the entrance to the Brahmin section of the village, he told his son, "Wait here for me."

"Keshavan Namboodri!" Mammen Samuel stood outside the walled-in front entrance to the house and called. "Brahmin Keshavan, I must talk with you!"

"What do you want?" a woman's voice answered from behind the wall.

"I wish to speak with Brahmin Keshavan. It is a matter of great importance."

"He is not available to you at this early hour."

Mammen Samuel grimaced and rumbled an irritated grunt. Of course! The Brahmin's ridiculous ceremonies. Every day, Keshavan spent the entire morning, from dawn until the sun came close to its zenith, bathing and grooming himself and tending to his gods with prayers and *mantras*.

"Tell him Mammen Samuel Varghese waits to see him."

No one invited Mammen Samuel inside. Still, he was in no mood to leave, either, so he walked around the house to the veranda in back. The backdoor into the house had been left slightly ajar and Mammen Samuel could see Brahmin Keshavan inside. He sat perfectly still before an idol, his legs crossed, and stared straight ahead. Hands resting on knees, palms up, he punctuated his words with ritual gestures. The Brahmin did not see Mammen Samuel, though, so the landlord sighed impatiently and sat down to wait for him to finish his morning duties.

***

Boban Joseph made a face and kicked at a rock on the road. Stand and wait, stand and wait. Always, stand and wait. He kicked the rock again, and it rolled farther toward the Brahmin's house. Once more Boban Joseph kicked it, then again and again.

"Did you see the tiger?" asked a timid voice.

Boban Joseph looked over to see the Brahmin's scrawny son Rama watching him with shy eyes.

Boban Joseph hesitated, but only for a minute. "Yes. Yes, of course, I saw the tiger! Huge and vicious, with glowing yellow eyes . . . Evil eyes, and huge teeth, too!"

Rama shuddered. "How terrifying!"

"I wasn't afraid," Boban Joseph boasted. "Why should I be? I have a knife and I know how to use it."

As Rama's eyes grew wider and wider, Boban Joseph's chest puffed out with pride.

When two hours had passed and still no one called for him, Mammen Samuel rose to his feet and bellowed, "Keshavan Namboodri!" He made no attempt to hide his growing fury. "I have come to talk with you, Brahmin Keshavan. Not to your servant or some other person in your family, but to you!"

This time no one answered, not even a servant. Mammen Samuel had little choice but to continue to wait. He paced the length of the veranda, from the pungent pepper vines across to the fragrant jasmine blossoms, then back again. Back and forth he paced, back and forth, but still Brahmin Keshavan did not come.

Clattering tins echoed through from the kitchen, and the aroma of chutney with leeks, and curried potatoes, filled the air. Mammen Samuel, who relished eating meat, would never be tolerated in the Brahmin's house, let alone invited to share his table. But he knew, as everyone did, that every single thing in the Brahmin's kitchen was prepared in adherence with strictly observed Brahmin caste rules. Each food stayed in its place so that nothing touched the wrong thing. Only Brahmin hands were allowed to prepare food for Brahmin mouths. The food might be dropped into the dirt or nibbled by rats or covered with flies, but it must never be touched by lower caste hands. Nor did any left hand touch the food, only right hands. Left hands were unclean.

As Mammen Samuel considered how he might force his way into the house and confront Keshavan, the Brahmin at last stepped out onto the veranda. Without waiting for a greeting, Mammen Samuel stated through clenched teeth, "Keshavan

Namboodri, I have come to demand that you remove your curse from my harvest!"

Neither curiosity nor anger passed over the Brahmin's serenely passive face. "But it was I who blessed your harvest," he reminded the landlord.

"What you did was conjure up a man-eating tiger and set it to prey on my laborers!"

"Tigers are wild animals," the Brahmin said. "They roam where they will."

"You purposely disrupted my harvest, and now you insult me with great disrespect!" Mammen Samuel's face flushed scarlet with rage. "For over two hours, you have kept me waiting in the hot sun. No one offered me so much as a drop of water to refresh myself!"

"To bring in your harvest is your duty," the Brahmin said. "It is my duty to perform my daily sacrifices. I do not ask you to stop your harvest and talk to me at a time of my choosing, and I do not intend to stop my duties to talk to you whenever you decide to stand outside my door and yell my name."

"Your duties? You have no duties!"

"You are wrong. Every morning, I worship Brahma, the World-Spirit, by reciting the *Vedas*. I worship the ancestors by partaking of ritual water drinks. I worship the gods by pouring *ghee* on the sacred fire. I worship all living things by scattering grain on the threshold of my house for the benefit of animals, birds, and spirits. Only then do I worship men by showing hospitality to such a one as yourself."

"Hospitality!" Mammen Samuel sputtered. "After all the time you kept me waiting on your veranda, hot and without refreshment, you dare use the word *hospitality?*"

Brahmin Keshavan, his face placid, didn't bother to respond. Nor did he make any move to seat himself. He simply stood and gazed at Mammen Samuel with expressionless eyes and an unreadable face.

"What of the tiger?" Mammen Samuel demanded.

"What of it?"

"Is it an evil spirit?"

"The world is filled with spirits, both good and evil," the Brahmin said.

Mammen Samuel sputtered in exasperation.

"You are right about my spiritual powers," Brahmin Keshavan said. "Most certainly they are great enough to destroy any king or would-be king should he attempt to infringe on my rights as Brahmin priest. But I need not conjure up a tiger to do that."

"Pshaw!" Mammen Samuel spat. "You may present yourself to others as some sort of a god, but I know that you are nothing but a man! You are only a man like me."

"No, not like you," said Brahmin Keshavan. "You are a selfish, stingy man. You lavish money on yourself and your family, but you have not one rupee to charitably give to those around you."

"You mean, I have not one rupee to give to you! For my workers, it is I who allow them to live. I am like their father who makes it possible for them to eat. Even now, while preoccupied with the disruption of the harvest, I took care to distribute more rice to them. I am the one who permits them to survive. I am good to my laborers, and they love me for it."

Boban Joseph, his own tangle of hair wrapped up in a linen turban, pointed to Rama's freshly shaved head. "Is that for punishment or worship?"

"Not for punishment," Rama said. "I just attained the level of *Brahmacarin*, so I guess you would say it is for worship."

Boban Joseph considered for a moment. "Is it true that you never have to work?"

"Not like you do," Rama said. "Not in the fields. Not with my hands at all. But I do work. To attain *Brahmacarin* was very difficult. It required great discipline, harsh training, and much study."

"You are naught but a student!" Boban Joseph sneered. "That's not real work. What real work do you do?"

"I rise before dawn to honor my father as my *guru*. I spend much time reciting my devotions, and after that I attend to the gods in houses of people who are too old or too sick to do it themselves. The rest of the day I must study for my future spiritual work."

Boban Joseph scoffed. "Not one bit of that is real work!"

"To study the *Veda* is my *dharma*. And that is the highest work of all," Rama said a bit defensively. He quickly added, "After my initiation I will be twice-born. Then I shall wear the sacred thread of the Brahmins."

Again, Boban Joseph sneered. "I could be twice-born, too, if my family was Hindu. But I would rather work and be a rich man like my father."

"Even if you were Hindu, you couldn't be like me," Rama argued. "When I am twice-born and invested with my sacred thread, my third eye will be opened. I will see through my eye of wisdom. Then I will have the spiritual powers of my father."

Ah, yes. The power to pronounce curses and cast spells. To call up evil spirits. Boban Joseph stared at the scrawny boy, and a twinge of fear ran through him. But he mustered his bravado. "Your powers don't frighten me," he stated. "Your father's tiger doesn't frighten me!"

🖋

"My laborers respect me," Mammen Samuel said to Brahmin Keshavan. "They need a superior being to look up to, someone far above any ordinary person. They need someone they can depend on to deal with the forces that lie outside their control. For them, I am that person."

"Why, then, did you come to me?" asked Brahmin Keshavan. "Cast a spell of your own to rid your slaves of the tiger."

"I deal in the real world, not in the realm of superstition!"

"Then I ask once again: why did you come to me?"

Mammen Samuel didn't answer, so the Brahmin pressed harder. "If you feared the tiger to be an evil spirit, why did you dare carry your small son to within the reach of its deadly jaws?"

Mammen Samuel bristled. "I kept Saji Stephen safely in my care the entire time. Never was he in any danger."

"You are absolutely certain of that? Or is it that you would risk the life of your youngest son in order to ensure great profits from your harvest?"

Mammen Samuel's moustache twitched and his black eyes flashed, but fury so flooded him that his tongue could not form an appropriate reply. He turned his back on the Brahmin, ready to walk away. But then he paused. Without turning again to face Keshavan, he warned, "Work your spells, if you will. Call down a mountain of curses. What does it matter to me? I can gather others around me who will help me bring in my harvest. Savages from the hills and the beaches—I will bring them to my settlement. Of course, they and their families will live across the fields from your pure house!"

🖋

"I have decided to give more attention to my prayers," Mammen Samuel told his wife. "Prayer in the morning and evening, at the moment of night's darkness and the first light of day—that's what the Indian Hindu religion promotes. Pray at each union of day and night. It could be a good rule for a Christian too. I have decided that I shall follow that pattern."

Parmar Ruth looked at her husband most curiously, but she held her tongue.

It had been so long since Mammen Samuel had prayed that he wasn't sure he remembered how. He sat all alone in a room with his legs crossed, just as he had seen Brahmin Keshavan do. He had no idol, of course, but he stared straight ahead at a picture of Jesus that hung on the wall and intoned:

"Kill the tiger. Kill the tiger or move it far away from my fields." He paused to consider. "Prosper my harvest with much golden grain, and my thoughts with increasing wisdom." For good measure he added, "Bless everything I do and prosper me in all things. Bless me and prosper me more than you bless and prosper Brahmin Keshavan."

Satisfied with his prayer, Mammen Samuel smiled and said a hearty "Amen."

## 14

The savages! Yes! Such an inspired idea, and it had come to Mammen Samuel but a mere moment before the words leapt from his mouth. He immediately recognized the brilliance of his budding scheme.

It had been a particularly dry year. The previous summer's monsoons were disappointingly light, and since then not one drop of rain had fallen. Already a smattering of tribal people had drifted down from the mountains and up from the beaches in search of food—or money to buy food—and the hot weather had not even started. Many more were sure to follow. With Mammen Samuel's workers refusing to go to the fields before full daylight, and insisting they be allowed to return to the safety of the settlement before sunset, the harvest fell further and further behind. The tribal people's strong arms and backs could indeed be put to good use. But Mammen Samuel saw an even more appealing reason for elation: Brahmin Keshavan.

As much as the Brahmins despised Untouchables, they loathed tribal people even more. Not only did the tribals eat meat, including wild chickens and the pigs villagers kept to clean up the garbage, but they ate beef. Yes, they actually dared to eat cows!

Mammen Samuel chuckled as he imagined the Brahmin's raging: "Uncivilized! Filthy, polluting, stupid *savages!*" If it made Keshavan angry to see Untouchables mixed together on the other side of the field, now he would be beside himself!

Mammen Samuel sat back, folded his hands across his belly, and enjoyed his first hearty laugh in many days.

Generally, tribal folk took care to keep their distance from people of caste. Even now, when drought made them desperate, they pulled away from the offer to work in the fields of a rich, upper caste landowner. All except Hilmi, who had watched his fishing lakes dry up, his unused boat crack in the sun, and his family wither from hunger.

Latha and Sethu stood on the outside of the crowd gathered to watch as Anup led the fisherman and his family into the settlement. Fierce, they were. Small and wiry, their skin almost black. And Hilmi, the most fearsome of all, with teeth brown and cracked from chewing betel nut, and no turban to cover his wild hair. He wore his *mundu* tight and short, wrapped around him like a pair of shorts.

"Just look! His legs and knees exposed for all to see!" Latha exclaimed, clucking her tongue with disapproval.

Behind Hilmi walked two young boys, both older than Ashish, though not by many years. Hilmi's wife—Jeeja, a thin, nervous woman in a shabby, dirt-colored *sari*—followed after and two girls came along behind her. The girls looked to be older than Anup's two oldest daughters. Both wore metal collars around their necks, and their hair stuck out, dry and most untidy.

"I may be poor, but I do put oil on my hair," Sethu sniffed. "I do that."

A tiny girl—she looked to be the age of Baby—fussed as she struggled to keep up with the older girls. The oldest swooped the little one up onto her hip and carried her the rest of the way.

Anup didn't lead the family to a hut. Instead he indicated a clearing on the other side of the courtyard. Without a word, Hilmi and his sons set to work constructing a small dwelling of palm branches and leaves while the older girls wove a door from sticks. Jeeja busied herself laying down stones for a cook pit.

As interesting a diversion as the new family was, the workers couldn't spend too much time staring at them. Bigger concerns pressed on their minds.

"For the *puja*," a man stated as he propped a small idol up against the trunk of the single mango tree that grew alongside the courtyard.

Everyone had a house god. Several families who had more than one offered to lend the extra to the settlement for a village shrine. It would be a place for the settlement community to worship and pay homage and generate favor. Anup's daughter Devi and several other girls who worked in the landlord's garden brought fragrant flowers to sprinkle over the idols so they would feel like honored guests in their new home. An old woman brought a small pan of water so the gods could wash their feet.

"Coconut meat," a limping woman murmured as she laid out the first, precious offering.

All evening, as villagers prepared their meager meals, they brought pieces of baked *chapatis*, bits of rice, vegetables, and fruit to lay before the gods.

"Remember our kindness to you," they chanted. "Remember and preserve us from the tiger."

But when Latha laid out her handful of rice—which meant none would be left for her to eat that evening—she whispered, "Remember our family's sacrifice to you, and free us from this wretched place."

The next morning, the workers awakened to the unfamiliar sound of tinkling music. Someone was ringing bells for the *puja*, in honor of the new village gods at the break of a new day.

As Latha laid out her morning sacrifice, Sethu stepped up beside her with a split guava for the altar. Sethu nodded toward the hut of leaves and said out loud, "I will not work beside that ugly woman."

Sethu was not a tactful person. Often she said things that upset others and caused quarrels between them. Even so, Latha counted her as a good friend. Sethu, always willing to help, demonstrated her generosity in unexpected ways. Whenever her daughter Devi brought vegetables for her family from the master's garden, Sethu shared them with Latha. Only two days earlier, Devi had spent the day milking the landlord's cows. Her hands and arms ached so badly that she came home in tears. But she also brought a broken pot filled with fresh milk. Sethu set most of it to boil over her own cooking fire, but she sent Lidya to Latha with the last of the milk in the broken pot. "*Amma* says it's from a black cow!" Lidya had announced. "That means it's especially sweet and creamy."

"The woman cannot help being ugly," Latha pointed out to Sethu. "Look at my face. I, too, am ugly. I will work beside her."

Sethu shrugged. "Do as you wish."

Before the workers left for the field, Ashish began his search for firewood. Virat wanted to be certain Anup and the others saw his little boy hard at work. But because of the tiger, he gave the boy strict warnings: "Do not search in the woods. You must not even step the toe of your foot over the edge of the courtyard. Not even one time, Ashish. Promise me you won't."

"But then I can't find any wood," Ashish protested. "Someone else already gathered up all the twigs and little branches I can reach and burned them in their own cooking fires."

"I know it's hard for you," Virat said. "But it is your job. So many families depend on you now to bring them their firewood. But if you go out where the hungry tiger waits, there will be no Ashish left for anyone. Please, my son, work hard and do your best."

"And make certain everyone sees you working hard," Latha added.

After the laborers left for the fields, Little Girl called out, "Ashish! Come over here by the tree! Look at all the food!"

"That's not for us," Ashish said. "It's offerings for the gods."

"I think the gods are already full up," Little Girl answered. "Otherwise they would be eating right now."

Ashish looked at the ground around the altar: such a delicious spread of rice and cashew nuts and bananas and all sorts of good things. His stomach rumbled.

"Well," he said, "if you are sure the gods want us to eat it."

"Yes," Little Girl insisted. "But I don't think they want anyone else to know we did."

Even little children feared the gods, but not nearly as much as they feared the men and women of the village. Most of all, they feared Little Girl's mother, Sethu.

That evening, Latha worried over the diminishing weight of her rice sack. Instead of boiling a handful of rice for the evening meal, she took a handful of wheat flour from the earthenware jar, mixed it with water and kneaded it into dough. That night they would eat *chapatis* baked over the fire and dipped in spiced vegetable water. Not as good a meal as rice, admittedly, but enough to fill their stomachs. Latha boiled the last sweet potato from Anup, threw the remainder of the greens from Devi into the pot, and sprinkled in dried chilies and herbs. How she longed for curds—yogurt—to go alongside it. How she longed for a bulging sack of rice!

"The gods will bless us and bring us more food," Latha said as she handed a *chapati* to Ashish. "Because we have done what is right, the gods will reward us."

A lump of guilt rose up in Ashish's throat. "You can have my share, *Amma*," he said. "I'm not hungry tonight."

Latha, worried over Ashish's health, coaxed and pleaded with her son to eat. But he swiped at the tears in his eyes and steadfastly refused. Finally Virat said, "Leave the boy alone."

"I will not eat your food," Latha said to Ashish.

Virat took the boy's hand. "Come with me," he said. "We will take your *chapati* to the bull that lives in the field. It will be a special offering for the god Shiva from you. Would you like that?"

"Very much, *Appa*," Ashish said.

While Virat and Ashish were away, Latha gathered up the water jugs and carried them to the well. After she filled them and prepared to start back home, she noticed Sethu sitting alone beside the tamarind trees.

"Are you all right?" Latha asked.

Sethu nodded, though she certainly didn't look all right. "Come to my house and lie down," Latha said. "Virat and Ashish are away. You can rest for a bit."

"Did you hear what my husband Anup said when he saw that tribal savage with all his children trailing behind him?"

"No. What did he say?"

"First Hilmi said he regretted having so many children, and then Anup said, 'I shouldn't have so many children, either, but they happen. It is God's will.'"

Latha said nothing.

"I'm going to have another one," Sethu said.

Latha stared at her in surprise. "Is Anup angry with you?"

"He doesn't know. But I cannot wait any longer to tell him. Oh, Latha, we will have still another mouth to feed! Anup will be most displeased."

But before Latha could respond, Sethu brightened a bit. "But this one—I am certain this baby will be a boy. After four girls, the gods have to smile on me and give me a son."

"Yes," Latha said. "This one will be a fine, healthy baby boy."

"Anup blames me for all the daughters," Sethu said. "His family will fade away, he tells me, and it is my fault. The two of us will die working in the fields, he says, because we have no one to care for us in our old age. But now, finally, we will have a son who—"

"I like your daughters," Latha said. "They are kind and good workers too."

"They are a burden, is what. It will be very hard to get them all married. Where will we get the money to pay four dowries?

Devi is now in her tenth year. I wish we could find a husband for her very soon."

Everyone whispered about the tribal family, but Hilmi and Jeeja didn't seem to hear them or to care. They stayed to themselves. They worked hard in the fields, but seldom spoke to anyone. The two older girls and the boys also went to the fields each day, even though the youngest boy could not have been more than eight years old.

"The tiger will take him next," the villagers whispered to one another.

The tiniest tribal girl stayed alone in the palm-frond hut all day long by herself. Ashish told his mother he never saw her come out.

On the night of the full moon, a cloudless evening particularly bright and clear, the men sat together and talked while the women clustered together around the well. To everyone's surprise, Hilmi came outside and sat down—but alone and a bit away from the other men. Jeeja crept out, too, though she hung back from everyone, including her husband, and hunkered down beside a tree where she could watch the others in her dark, suspicious way.

"You are a fisherman, then?" Virat called over to Hilmi.

Hilmi wobbled his head in the singular way of South Indians that meant yes. "From the far away waterways," he said.

"Do you have wheat fields there?" another man asked.

Hilmi moved a bit closer to the men. "Rice paddies," he said. "People call our land *Kuttand.*"

"Land of the short people?" Virat asked. "Look at you. You are small but not so very short."

Hilmi laughed and moved still closer to the circle of men. "It is because the men in my area are always standing up to their knees in water. Either they are working in rice paddies or standing in the water casting out their fishing nets. People on land only see them above their knees, so they look short."

"Why are you here?" Anup asked.

"Too little rain," Hilmi said. The lakes have dried up and the fish lie dead on the muddy bottom. When the rains come back and the rivers flow once more, we will have fish again. Then I will gladly go home and throw out my nets."

"And sit under the mango trees when the moon is full and talk about us?" another man asked with a laugh.

"I will sit in the sand, in the shadow of a coconut tree as it waves in the cool wind, and watch the night birds," Hilmi said. "I will think of you not at all."

In the cluster of women, Sethu hissed to whomever would listen, "Why did the landlord have to bring those savages here? Even polluted untouchable land is further polluted by their presence."

Latha shot a quick glance at Jeeja. Her black eyes, hard and guarded, fixed on the circle of women.

"Maybe more workers have already been taken by the tiger," another woman suggested. "Just because we don't know doesn't mean it isn't so."

"The landlord should not have brought them here!" Sethu insisted. "They are savages. They do not belong with us."

That night, when Hilmi went out to prop up his sagging hut, one of his neighbors crept up from behind and, with his knife glinting in the moonlight, lunged at Hilmi.

"I thought he was a thief," the neighbor insisted as he limped away, battered from the encounter. Hilmi, untouched, never turned around to look back at the treacherous neighbor he had beaten off.

# 15

The next morning, the same as every other morning, Hilmi and his family gathered a bit away from the other workers as they prepared to go to the fields. No one mentioned the knife attack. But Hilmi's family held close together, and Jeeja's eyes, deep and dark in her sunken face, were more watchful and suspicious than ever.

Already Ashish had begun his search for firewood. "You must be sure the other laborers see what a hard worker you are," Virat told his son. "When we leave for the fields and when we come back in the evening, those are the times you must pay particular attention and work hard."

But not only Ashish scrounged for the hard-to-find pieces of wood. The sun rose higher and higher in the sky, yet his pile of sticks didn't grow. Desperate, Ashish decided to do what both his father and mother had strictly forbidden. He decided to climb over the piled-up rocks that separated the outer edges of the courtyard from the beginnings of the thick woods. As he stood on top of the rocks, Little Girl called out to him.

"Ashish! The master landowner's servant came looking for my *amma*. I must go to the wheat fields to get her, but I'm scared to go by myself. Will you come with me? Please?"

"I'm supposed to find firewood," Ashish said doubtfully. "My *appa* will be angry with me if I—"

"I know. But if you go with me, when we get back, I'll help you find wood." Little Girl's lower lip trembled. "*Please?*"

So Ashish carried his meager stack of wood to the hut, then followed Little Girl to her hut and waited while she closed her little sister inside. "Stay here, Baby!" Little Girl ordered. Baby banged on the door and started to cry. "If you go out the door or make noise, I will come back and hit you hard!" Little Girl threatened.

Ashish and Little Girl ran to the edge of the settlement and headed down the pathway that led to the fields.

"Lidya's supposed to go get *Amma* when the master wants her," Little Girl said. "But the servant couldn't find Lidya anywhere."

"Why does the master landowner want your *amma?*"

"Because a fancy lady is ready to have her baby. When fancy ladies have babies, they always call my *amma* to help."

Little Girl led Ashish past the grain storage sheds, then on toward the fields. "If we see the tiger, we must run back very, very fast," she said.

Ashish recognized the path. It was the same way his father had taken with him when they went to give his *chapati* to the bull. Fences fashioned from sharp thorn bushes surrounded the storage sheds and fields, and the path led between those thorny fences.

"I know what those prickles are for," Ashish said.

"What?"

"To keep the cows and the bull from eating up everything in the field. My *appa* told me so."

"Maybe they will keep the tiger from eating us too," Little Girl said.

Off to one side, a pool of water stood stagnant and muddy. Once the monsoon rains started, it would turn into a flowing stream. But before that time came, the sun would grow hotter and hotter, and the pool would dry completely into brick-hard clay. Ashish leapt off the path and squished his feet through the mud. Little Girl, laughing out loud, followed him.

"*Amma, Amma!*" Little Girl yelled when she saw her mother in the distance. "Come quickly! The master landlord's servant came for you!"

By the time the workers came in for the evening, Ashish stood proudly beside an impressive stack of firewood. He smiled through the praise and said nothing about Little Girl's help.

✒

When Devi came in from her work in the master's garden, a fresh cabbage tucked under her arm, she found Little Girl and Baby waiting alone beside the cold fire pit.

"Where is Lidya? Why is she not cooking our evening meal?" Devi asked.

"She had to go with *Amma* to help a fancy lady have a baby," Little Girl told her.

Devi sighed. They could be gone all night. Maybe tomorrow and tomorrow night too.

"But I got wood all ready for the fire," Little Girl said.

Devi didn't answer. Her father would be hungry, so she hurried to start the evening meal. Every evening, Anup returned to the hut long after everyone else, but he was the first to sit down and eat his meal. Sethu ate next, and the girls last. That's how it was in every family—unless the family had sons, in which case the sons ate second, after the father. But always the girls ate last.

Untouchable women think nothing of working throughout their pregnancies. It's expected of them. Many give birth in the fields, wrap the baby in a *chaddar*, and get right back to work. Not women of the highest castes, though. No, no, for them a great deal of fuss is made over an upcoming birth. Special foods prepared . . . painstaking ministrations provided . . . gifts and treats lavished on them . . . anything they might fancy, they get. And when the baby is ready to come, they send for a midwife. Mammen Samuel Varghese's large extended household preferred Sethu.

When Sethu's midwifery duties were finished the following day, she headed directly back to the fields to resume work there.

"So, you are midwife for the landowner's family," Latha said as she stacked a bundle of wheat stalks and held them for Sethu to tie. "Do they pay you for your services?"

"Not always. Not if the baby is a boy."

In answer to Latha's puzzled look, Sethu said, "Bringing a boy into the world is part of my job. But if the baby is a girl . . . and if they don't want a girl . . . I get rid of it for them. They pay me for that."

Latha stared at her friend. "You kill baby girls?"

"It's for the baby's own good."

"Sethu!"

"What kind of life is it to be a girl?" Sethu demanded. "What kind of life is it to be a woman?"

As he did every day at noon, Mammen Samuel Varghese took to his bed and rested through the hottest part of the day as his servant Babu waved a fan in an endless effort to stir up a cooling breeze over him. But in the late afternoon, when the sun ceased its relentless heat, Mammen Samuel called for his son Boban Joseph.

"Bring the horse and small cart," he ordered. "I want to inspect the progress of the wheat harvest."

But on its way to the harvested field, the cart passed alongside the farthest field where no harvesters had yet begun to work.

"Stop the cart!" Mammen Samuel ordered.

A barren patch stretched out to one side where a large, ragged swath had been chopped through the ripe field.

"What happened here?" Mammen Samuel roared in dismay.

"I don't know, Father," Boban Joseph said. "Maybe the tiger—"

Mammen Samuel hefted himself from the cart. He glared at the stubble left from the chopped-off stalks. Anger surged through him, and he ripped out a handful of the stubble. "Take me to Anup!" he ordered.

"But, Father, you haven't yet seen the harvested field."

"Now!" Mammen Samuel ordered.

Boban Joseph whipped the horse to a full trot and kept the poor animal trotting briskly all the way along the path between the thorn fences. They entered the settlement with the landowner bellowing, "Anup! An—up!"

Devi had just laid a bowl of rice and vegetables before her father, but Anup jumped up and ran to answer his master's call. Mammen Samuel held out the handful of chopped wheat stalks, clods of dirt still clinging to the roots. "These are from my fresh field! What is the meaning of this?"

Anup stared at the stalks. He fell to his knees before the landowner. "Thieves, Master. Thieves must have come in the night."

"Thieves! But what of the watchman?"

"No watchman stays through the night now, Master. For fear of the tiger."

"Tonight there *will* be a watchman!" Mammen Samuel ordered. "All night long. You see to it!"

"Yes, Master," Anup said. "I will have a man on the watchman's platform in the center of the field tonight."

"No, no," said Mammen Samuel. "I want the watchman to sleep on the ground and to move himself around to different parts of the fields during the night. I want the watchman's presence felt in every part of every field."

"It will be done, Master," Anup said.

For a long while after Mammen Samuel's cart had rolled back up the path between the thorn-bush fences, Anup stood alone. He unwound the *chaddar* turban from his head and mopped his face with it. With a sigh, he headed for Hilmi's hut.

Early the next morning, Ashish started his usual search for firewood. But already his most promising places had been picked clean. By midday, his stack consisted of nothing but a meager handful of twigs. Maybe Little Girl would help him. She always had good ideas for places to look. He went to her hut ready to call out for her when he heard cries coming from inside. Ashish knew that both Anup and Sethu had to be at work in the fields, and that Devi worked in the landlord's garden all day. He had just seen Lidya sweeping the main courtyard, so he knew she wasn't in the hut.

Ashish tiptoed to the door and pushed it open. Inside he saw the back of the master's big son, Boban Joseph. Devi, who was supposed to be working in the landlord's garden, huddled beside him. She pleaded with him to leave her alone. Boban Joseph shoved Devi, knocking her hard against the floor. She tried to push him away, but he made a fist and smashed it into her face.

"Devi?" Ashish whispered. "What are you doing?"

"Go away!" Boban Joseph ordered.

But Ashish suddenly felt as though his legs were made of solid wood. He told them to run away, but they wouldn't move. He had no choice but to stand and stare.

Boban Joseph kicked at Devi. He hit her again, then growled something that Ashish couldn't understand.

"Please, please, Ashish, go away!" Devi pleaded.

But Ashish could not. When the little boy didn't leave, Boban Joseph jumped up, shoved past him, and rushed out of the hut.

"Devi?" Ashish whispered.

"Go away!" Devi ordered.

That evening, when Latha went to get wood for the cook pit, she chided Ashish for the small pile he had collected. "You know what your *appa* told you," Latha said. "If you don't work hard enough, and collect enough wood, you will be sent to the fields." Usually when she said this, excuses and apologies tumbled out of Ashish's mouth, and promises to work harder tomorrow. But this time he bowed his head and said nothing.

"Well?" said Latha. "Have you no explanation? Were you so busy playing with Little Girl today that you could not do your work?"

Still the boy said nothing.

"You know what Sethu says. She says, 'A child who does not work can eat dirt.' Do you want to eat dirt?"

"The master landlord's big boy hurt Devi," Ashish whispered.

Latha set her water pot down. "What? How do you know this?"

"I saw him," Ashish said. At his mother's prodding, the boy told her everything that had happened.

❧

Latha found Sethu coming up the path behind the huts and rushed over to report Ashish's words. "It's a blessing that my Ashish came by when he did," Latha said. "Imagine what that horrible boy might have done to your Devi!"

Sethu's face grew hard. "It is no concern of yours. And tell your nosy son to stay out of our hut."

Latha stared at her friend. "You mean you *knew*?"

"It is not your concern." Sethu tried to push her way past, but Latha refused to let her go.

"Devi is hardly more than a child! How could you give that sweet girl over to so arrogant a fool who would hit her and kick her and . . . and . . . and use her?"

"It is easy for you to talk," Sethu said, her face hard and angry. "You have one son. But I have four girls. Why do you think Devi has so good a job in Master Landlord's garden? Why do you think we have papayas and plantains and spinach for our curries, while you scrape and beg for a handful of rice? Why do you think we have cauliflowers and cabbages, peas and radishes—enough to share with you, by the way? Why do you think we have an earthenware pot filled with lentils?"

"But . . . your own child!"

"She is just a girl," Sethu said flatly. "At least this way she is of some good to us."

✐

In the deep of the night, a terrifying shriek shook the settlement awake.

"What is it?" Ashish cried.

"Hush!" Virat said. He sat up on his sleeping mat and listened.

A low growl, then another shriek, this time long and horrible.

And then quiet.

# 16

All night, the settlement waited in uneasy stillness for dawn to break. Latha lay on her sleeping mat, her good eye wide open. Ashish nestled beside her, breathing long, deep sleeping breaths. But not Virat. He, like Latha, lay wide awake.

"We must get away from here," Latha whispered.

"You know we cannot," Virat answered. "Not yet, anyway. Until our debt is paid, the landlord owns all of us."

"Then we must work harder so we can give the landlord's money back to him. I can do extra jobs. Perhaps I could gather fodder for the cattle after I finish my work in the fields. And you could ask Anup for more jobs too. Watchman perhaps. And Ashish—even he can work more, sweeping or cleaning or doing other small jobs."

Virat said nothing.

Slowly the settlement came alive, though everyone felt far too edgy and nervous to move about freely outside. The night's long, horrible shriek still echoed in everyone's ears and chilled their blood. Even so, Jeeja and her daughters stepped out from their palm frond hut and lit their morning cooking fire as though it were any other morning. Latha watched them from her doorway—as did every other person whose doorway looked out at the palm leaf hut. Jeeja went for water and never looked behind her. One daughter baked chilies while another pounded grain and cooked it into mush over the fire.

And then the woven door opened again and Hilmi stepped out, alive and well. Not one bite had been taken out of him. The settlement of laborers caught its collective breath and let out a gasp of awed disbelief.

"Hilmi!" Anup exclaimed. "We heard the tiger roar! We thought it got you."

"No," Hilmi said. "I that got the tiger."

"What happened?"

All the men pressed around, eager to hear Hilmi's story. He had been sleeping in the far field, he said, when he heard a disturbance among some of the cattle in a field closer to the settlement.

"Those fields have already been harvested," Anup said. "So you knew it wasn't the thief."

"I knew it was the tiger," said Hilmi. "I could smell it. A most foul scent, it was. The smell of an injured animal, frightened and hungry."

"But what happened?" Anup demanded.

"I crept toward the poor beast." Hilmi crouched down to demonstrate the stealthy way he had sneaked forward. "I knew it would attack. What else could it do?" With movements fluid and agile, he showed how he had prepared himself for the inevitable. "I had to be ready." With a rapid pounce, then a twist and a scramble, he replayed his reactions to the tiger's attack. "My knife went right to the tiger's throat," Hilmi said. "The great beast did not suffer."

"You killed the tiger all by yourself?" Anup shook his head in disbelief. "Only with your hands and your knife?"

"I killed him the same way he would have killed me. My sharp knife was like a tiger's sharp teeth."

As Hilmi told the story, acting out each part, the women pushed in close behind the transfixed men. Children shoved their way near enough to see the tiger-killer's every move with their own eyes and hear his tale with their own ears.

No sooner had Hilmi finished the story than someone called out, "Tell it again!" So he did. But when that telling was done, another person immediately insisted, "Again! Tell it another time!" So Hilmi told the story yet again. And though, when he finished that telling, the people begged, "Again! Again!" he decided three times were enough. So Hilmi sat down and ate the mush and chilies his daughters had cooked for him.

Young Devi, humiliated and disgraced by the endless gossip that buzzed through the settlement, begged to stay away from the landlord's garden. "Can't Lidya go this one day? I would stay here and sweep the floor and prepare the meal," the girl pleaded. But Sethu said absolutely not, she must tend to her job. If she were wise, she would hold her head up high and look her accusers straight in the eye.

Devi pulled up the edge of her *sari* from off her shoulder and threw it over her head, low enough in front to shade her face. It couldn't hide the huge purple bruise on her cheek, though, nor her eyes, red and swollen from a night of weeping.

As Hilmi told his story for the third time, Devi hurried behind the push of workers and moved on toward the path that led to the landlord's garden. Unfortunately for her, a wizened old woman at the back of the crowd spotted her and called out through her few remaining teeth, "There she goes, that foolish girl, on her way to see the landowner's son again."

"Thinking herself good enough for the son of the master!" said another, clicking a scolding tongue.

"Her next life will most definitely be as a rat," said a third. "A female rat and nothing more."

Others turned to stare. And to whisper insults. And to cast sneers her way. Devi did the only thing she could do—she hung her head low and hurried past them all. She headed for the path that led back to the garden, and, inevitably, to Boban Joseph.

Hilmi was no different than he had been before. Still small and wiry, still dark and leathery, the exact same tribal man everyone had looked upon with such disdain. Still an outcaste of the outcastes. His wife Jeeja remained every bit as quiet and suspicious as before, and their children as silent and strange to the eye. The difference was that the workers no longer moved away when Hilmi passed by. And they no longer murmured insults about wild savages and where they did and did not belong.

Hilmi had killed the tiger.

At first, a few doubters among them whispered, "Why should we trust the word of a savage?" and "This could be but a ruse to keep from having to stand watch at night." But no more. That very morning Anup had taken four men out to dig a pit and bury the beast, and the men came back with amazing tales of their own.

Hilmi had indeed killed the tiger.

That evening, as the women started their cooking fires, Hilmi and his sons dug in the dirt until they had fashioned a long pit. This they lined with rocks and heaped with leaves and branches they brought back from deep in the woods.

When nothing more could fit into the pit, Hilmi lit it on fire. Leaving his boys to tend the blaze, Hilmi sat down with his legs crossed and assumed a position of meditation.

As the men of the settlement ate their rice and vegetables, Hilmi's boys tended the fire while their father meditated. When the settlement's men finished and their sons ate, Hilmi's boys stirred the dying fire with sticks and Hilmi chanted *mantras*. When the sons finished eating and the women dipped their hands into the food pot, Hilmi's boys hunkered down and kept watch over the fiery cinders while their father meditated some more.

When the settlement's girls—the last ones to eat—scraped together the leftover grains of rice and morsels of food from their family's pots, Hilmi's sons stirred the ashes in the fire pit into a bed of glowing embers, and Hilmi at last ended his mediation. Curious men and women gathered around to watch. The tribal fisherman paid them no mind. He stood up, looked to heaven, and stepped with his bare feet into the pit of red-hot embers. With unhurried steps, he walked across the glowing bed of charcoal.

"Why do you do it?" an old man asked after Hilmi reached the other side.

"It's my sacrifice of obedience," Hilmi answered. "Because the tiger lies dead and I do not."

⟋❧

"Is it not the master landlord's order that you post a watchman in the field without fail?" Virat insisted to Anup. "I could sleep on the platform every night. Or I could sleep on the ground, if I must."

"Why do you want to do that?"

"So I can pay back our debt more quickly," Virat said. "So I can take my family away from here."

"You think too much about the future, Virat," Anup said with a sigh. "You should be more like me. I do not think about the future at all. I want to keep my mind happy."

"Please, I beg you. I do not sit in judgment on your family, and I ask you not to sit in judgment on mine. My wife and I want to work hard and pay off our debt. But we need you to help us."

"Keep your mind happy," Anup pleaded. "Please, do not insist on thinking about the future."

"Don't take our sleeping mats outside tonight, Husband," Latha said as Virat pulled the mats from the corner. "Please, this night let us sleep inside the hut."

So Virat spread the mats out on the dirt floor next to Ashish, who already slept soundly, curled up in a corner. Latha lay down and Virat stretched out his weary body beside her.

"I talked to Anup," he said, because he knew the question Latha wanted to ask of him. "Maybe he will let me work as watchman in the fields or maybe he will not. But even if he does, I do not think we can pay our debt back quickly."

"Let's simply leave," Latha said. "Let's go back to our mud hut on the other side of the river. Pooni has kept it ready for us, I'm sure of it."

Virat reached over and ran his calloused fingers down Latha's arm. It shocked him to feel the scratched-up roughness of her skin. How the sun had baked it. No longer was it smooth as butter.

"You know we cannot," Virat said. "The landlord's servants would find us and drag us back. They would flog us bitterly—

even little Ashish, who could not bear it. The landlord would increase our debt so much that we could not hope to pay it off before the end of our days."

"We could go to the English clinic, then," Latha said. "The English lady loved Ashish. I could scrub their floors and cook their rice, and you could pick up the dead animals from their streets. The English healer wouldn't let the landowner take us back. He would protect us for Ashish's sake."

"No, no!" said Virat. "The English loved Ashish too much. They would take our son away from us and make him be English too. Already the pale woman said she wanted to keep him for her own. No, not the English!"

"What of Hilmi, then? When the rains come and he goes back to the coast, maybe we could go with him."

"I am not a fisherman. We don't know the tribal ways or customs. If we move to their village, they will look at us with the same suspicion and distrust that we look at Hilmi and Jeeja."

Latha said nothing. She longed to argue, but she knew that her husband only told the truth.

"Somewhere there is a village that needs a *chamar* to clean up its dead animals and dry their skins into leather and make sandals and drums for the upper castes," Latha said.

"Yes," said Virat. "But they are somewhere there and we are here."

For a long time, Virat and Latha lay next to each other in silence. Neither could sleep. Virat's mind stayed fixed on their plight, but Latha's mind drifted to the plight of the young girl in another hut.

"Poor little Devi. What can she do?" Latha asked, tears marring her voice. "To deny the landowner's son is to sin, because he is the son of her master. But not to deny him is also to sin. What can that child do?"

"We live in a time when nothing is right and all actions are sinful," Virat said. "What can any of us do?"

"The times. When will they change?"

Virat didn't answer. He had no answers.

"Please," Latha begged. "We must get away from here!"

Virat reached over to her with a reassuring touch. "You do not need to fear any of them."

"I do not fear them," Latha said. "I fear us. If we stay here, I fear what we will become."

## 17

$\mathcal{B}$andages, Miss Davidson!"

Had Dr. Moore looked up at her, he would have seen that Abigail already had the bandages in hand and ready for him. Yet another injury caused by the ancient plows local farmers used to prepare their rice paddies for planting. Abigail had assisted Dr. Moore in treating so many of these injuries at the clinic that she could easily have tended to this boy by herself.

"I will finish up with the patient," Dr. Moore stated. "You might as well start cleaning up."

Not that Abigail would ever get the chance to actually treat a patient. Dr. Moore was the doctor, of course. But she was the nurse, not simply a cleaning lady!

Like all the other injured men and boys, this one immediately got up off the cot, folded his hands together and bowed his head to murmur, "*Namaste.*" Thank you. He should stay and rest, at least for the remainder of the day. But, of course, he would not. Tomorrow morning he would be back at the plow, working all day behind a bullock or water buffalo.

136

"That boy could not be more than ten or eleven years old," Dr. Moore muttered as the child left the clinic. "A country of fools, that's what India is."

"Truly, Sir, it is not an altogether unpleasant country," Abigail said. She could be as positively positive as Dr. Edward Moore could be pessimistically pessimistic. But Abigail was also honest, so she allowed, "It is extremely hot. But all the same, it is not altogether unpleasant."

"Hot?" Dr. Moore said. He laughed out loud. "Hot for England, perhaps, but this is India. We are still in the midst of the comfortable season. Wait a few months and you will learn the true meaning of hot."

Abigail pushed back a stray lock of strawberry blonde hair and tucked it under her cap. "However uncomfortable it becomes, I shall not complain of the heat," she announced. "We are here to make a difference in people's lives, and I shan't complain about whatever inconveniences I am called to encounter along the way."

"You will soon repent of your resolve not to complain," Dr. Moore muttered, half under his breath.

Abigail paid him no mind. "I want to see the country. I want to understand the people. That's what you have done, is it not, Doctor?"

"I have seen the country, all right, but I have absolutely no understanding of the people."

"I want to ride again on an elephant. Have you done that? Oh, and I want to wash in the river."

Dr. Moore's eyebrows shot up. "I say, Miss Davidson! Have you completely forgotten yourself?"

"Oh, I don't mean wash like the natives do!" Abigail blushed a deep crimson. "Of course, I would keep my clothes on! It's only that I long to splash around in the cool water, you see, and—"

"And get deathly ill for your trouble? So that I shall have to care for you in addition to all my other responsibilities?"

Abigail knew perfectly well that so much talk would do her no good. She realized her chatter had already begun to irritate Dr. Moore. Yet she couldn't stop herself.

"I want to walk around and explore the countryside, you see."

The doctor laid down his armload of medical supplies. He adjusted his glasses that perpetually slipped down on his long, thin nose and, glaring hard at Abigail, demanded, "Why ever would you wish to do such a thing?"

"So I can meet the people. So I can see how the men work in the fields. So I can sit beside the women and observe them as they cook their meals. So I can watch the children at play."

Dr. Moore said nothing.

"I want to *know* the Indian people! If I don't know them, Sir, what right do I have to talk to them of important things? How can I tell them of the God who loves them so?"

"You are a foolish schoolgirl. Yes, that is precisely what you are—a foolish schoolgirl!"

He looked Abigail straight in the eye.

"You want to see how the men work in their fields, then? Well, I'll tell you. They work night and day in wretched conditions. You want to sit beside a woman as she cooks? Perhaps you have not noticed the protruding ribs on the bony bodies that come to us for help. Those women you want to watch have almost nothing to cook. They are not at home anyway, but are in the fields working alongside their husbands in the deep mud of the rice paddies. You want to watch the children at play, do you? Well, you shall have a right rotten time of it, Miss Davidson, for children here do not play. The fortunate ones work. The unfortunate ones lie down and die."

❧

*Lecture, lecture, lecture, Dr. Moore! Can you do nothing but lecture? Can you never once respect the opinions and thoughts of another?*

Exactly that, Abigail determined, she would say to the good doctor. Sometime . . . at the right moment. When that time came, she would let the doctor know that healing hands did not make up for a stone-hard heart.

Yes, yes! She must remember those very words. She would say, *Dr. Moore, your healing hands do not make up for your hard heart of stone.*

That afternoon, silence reigned in the clinic. Dr. Moore took his seat by the window, book in hand and spectacles perched on the end of his nose. Darshina left the clinic and went Abigail knew not where. Cook had left for home to be with her family until time to prepare the evening meal. At first Abigail paced restlessly from one window to the other. But when she saw the doctor nodding over his book, she hurried to her room and donned a straw hat. When she came back, Dr. Moore was fast asleep. Quietly, Abigail eased out the door.

❧

Abigail had no idea where she was, nor did she know where she might wish to go. She stepped carefully onto the dirt road, and for no particular reason, chose to turn to the right. Fields and fields and more fields. That's all she saw. She stopped to watch a mud-splattered Indian man guide a dilapidated wooden contraption—precariously tied to a scrawny bullock—through a field of slogging mud. A woman and a passel of small children hurried back and forth across the field with buckets, pouring water out over the mud, then hurrying back for more.

Wretched conditions! The woman hard at work alongside her husband in the deep mud of a rice paddy. Emaciated children, who should have been at play, running back and forth toting heavy buckets of water.

Abigail was indeed a foolish schoolgirl. A foolish, foolish schoolgirl.

When Abigail arrived back at the clinic, the doctor was again reading his book. He didn't look up when she came in. She closed the door behind her and tiptoed to her room, which was off to the side.

"Everyone who comes to India wants to change it," Dr. Moore called after her. "But with time, you learn better."

# 18

"No! No! No! No! No! No!" Saji Stephen screeched. "I want it! I want it to be my pet!"

"That animal has horrible claws, Saji Stephen," Parmar Ruth explained to her son. "And it isn't soft at all. Its shaggy hair is coarse and scratchy."

"I . . . want . . . it!" Saji Stephen yelled, stamping his little feet. "I want it and I will have it!"

"It" happened to be a toddy cat—a wild civet. The small creature—no more than seven pounds and not two feet long, unless one counted its equally long tail—had taken up an unwelcome residence in the trees surrounding Mammen Samuel Varghese's house. Small as it was, the toddy cat made enough of a racket to keep the entire household awake all night. It had actually made its home in the mango tree, but on occasion, such as the previous night, it raised an alarming ruckus fighting with its mate and clawing about on the roof. Babu had gone out to swat it away, and Saji Stephen followed. As soon as the boy saw the toddy cat's cute little face peeking out from among the mango leaves, its black markings making it look as though its eyes hid behind a mask, he determined he would have it as his pet.

"Talk to the boy," Parmar Ruth begged of her husband.

"He is your darling," Mammen Samuel replied. "You deal with him."

Mammen Samuel had more important concerns than the railings of a spoiled child. The rest of the household could comfort Saji Stephen. They always did. The cook plied him with figs stuffed with coconut. Parmar Ruth promised him a new toy . . . special treats . . . a tale of the gods. Babu tried to entice him with the promise of a ride on the elephant.

"Sunita Lois, play the sitar for your brother," Parmar Ruth instructed her daughter. "That always quiets his spirit."

Sunita Lois—older than Saji but younger than Boban Joseph—obediently lugged the unwieldy instrument from its place in the corner of the great room and sat on the floor, balancing the sitar between her left foot and right knee.

"Listen, Saji," she urged, "I'll play a special *raga* just for you." She plucked out a tune on the sitar's seven main strings and did her best to accompany it with the eleven sympathetic strings under the frets. But Sunita's hands were small and her interest in her lessons even smaller. So what came out was an incessantly ear-piercing twanged whine.

Even so, Saji Stephen stopped in mid-tantrum. "I want to ride the elephant," he said to Babu.

"Take the boy, Babu!" Mammen Samuel called in from the veranda. "Enough music, Daughter! Where is Boban Joseph?"

❦

Harvest was almost over. The two good fields stood bare and the laborers had already moved on to the close field. Much less yield was expected there. But for Anup, finishing the harvest meant the time had come to prepare the fields for rice planting. Once the stubble had been cleared away, river trenches could be opened and the fields flooded.

Already the carpenter and blacksmith, who lived side by side at the settlement, worked to ready the plowshares and other paddy-planting tools. First the blacksmith sharpened the flattened blades on the two plowshares after which he made certain both were solidly connected to the sharpened pieces of wood used to support them.

The carpenter busied himself checking the long pole that ran from the top of the plowshare to the wooden yoke. He must make certain that yoke would hold fast when laid over the necks of a pair of bullocks, secured with ropes and bars of wood cinched beneath the animals' necks. Also, he replaced the cracked wooden handles attached at the rear of the plow-share. So many workers had grasped those handles, jerking them to the right to steer the plow in one direction and then to the left to steer it the opposite way, that three were cracked and two of those hung loose. The fourth handle was completely gone.

Though rich and lavish, Mammen Samuel's house was not large. Besides a simple bed chamber for him and his wife and a small inside kitchen that opened to the outside kitchen, it contained but a single great room. All three children slept on mats on the veranda, except in the monsoon season when they spread their mats in the large room.

"Outsized luxury" is the way Mammen Samuel described the great room. Its major piece of furniture consisted of a not-so-comfortable couch with a pile of pillows stacked at each end. A perfectly white sheet covered it, and over the sheet, a deep green cover richly embroidered with elephants and river scenes and even a few Hindu gods. Across the room sat a second couch, this one small and brightly colored, firm and far more comfortable. A lotus-shaped bracket hung over the small couch, a painted picture of Jesus fitted inside. The copper bracket had been made to hold the portrait of a house deity, but since Mammen Samuel maintained a Christian household, it had been replaced with the Jesus picture.

Between the large couch and the small one stood a table and two straight-backed chairs. In the opposite corner, Sunita Lois's beautiful sitar rested—its round bowl on the floor and the beautiful neck of polished rosewood propped up against the wall. A drawing slab lay at the far side of the couch along with a pot of colors and brushes. These belonged to Parmar Ruth, though her daughter enjoyed painting too. A few books sat in a pile under the table, and a finely carved chess game— the white pieces from ivory and the black pieces from ebony— sat on top.

Four cages of pet birds hung from ivory tusks affixed into the wall. Mammen Samuel paid little attention to the small birds, though they chirped incessantly. But he did appreciate the great colored hornbill, too huge for its cage and always hungry for a mouse or lizard.

Normally, the family's women and children reserved the great room as their abode. The veranda was much more interesting and comfortable, and therefore the domain of the men. Not this particular day, however. For the veranda offered no privacy and Mammen Samuel wanted to talk to his son without the entire village pausing to listen.

"A fine harvest," Mammen Samuel began. "Even with the problems, an especially fine harvest. Thanks be to God for the bounty."

"Thanks be to God," Boban Joseph said.

"You supervised it well, my son." Boban Joseph did not miss the note of pride in his father's voice. "Now I will put you in charge of the rice planting. You must begin immediately, even though the wheat harvest is not yet complete. Tomorrow Anup should see that the two best fields are cleared of the wheat stubble. By early next week, I wish you to supervise the opening of the river trenches and begin swamping those fields before—"

"Wait!" Boban Joseph jumped up. "I am your son! Why must I work and work and work like one of your servants?"

"You are not a child. It's time you learn what it means to be a landowner."

"What about Saji Stephen?" Boban Joseph insisted. "He is also your son, but you assign him no work at all. He whines and cries, and the whole world is handed to him."

Mammen Samuel leaned back in his chair and folded his hands across his stomach. He stared hard into the face of his eldest son. "Sit down," Mammen Samuel said.

But Boban Joseph, still belligerent, refused. He folded his arms across his chest, planted his feet, and stared back at his father.

"Come, my son," Mammen Samuel urged. "Let us talk like men."

For a good while Boban Joseph hesitated, but finally he lowered his eyes and sat on the floor at his father's feet.

"Saji Stephen is a pet for our family," Mammen Samuel said. "That's what he is, and that's what he will always be. After I have gone to join my ancestors in heaven, Saji Stephen will inherit the one poor field near the laborers' settlement. But you, my son, will be the new master of everything else. The best rooms of this house will be yours, the ones that face east and south. That includes this great room and both the kitchens. Saji gets whatever is left. You will own all the good lands, and all the animals—the horses, the cows and bull, the goats and chickens, the bullocks and the water buffalo. All those will be yours. You will also inherit the laborers listed in my leather book. They will be your slaves to do with as you wish."

Boban Joseph stared at his father.

"You will care for your mother, of course—should she still be alive. And you will watch out for your brother. But you will be master, and they will obey you."

"Most of the laborers will be gone by then," Boban Joseph said. "Their debts will be repaid and they will have departed from our land."

"I have much to teach you, my son." Mammen Samuel reached for his leather accounting book. "The poor castes are all alike. They get paid for building a wagon, or for collecting a dead cow, or for bringing in a boatload of fish. They feel so rich that they quickly spend everything they earned. But then something unexpected happens and they have nothing left to pay the bills. So they must sell their few trinkets. If a second thing should happen—even something small—they have nothing left to sell. That's when they come to us begging for a loan."

Mammen Samuel opened his book and pointed to a row of names. "Whenever I make a loan, I require the family to move to the laborers' settlement until they work off enough to pay me back. What they do not realize is that I charge them fifty percent interest every month. I also charge them rent for their hut. Also, I add on a goodly sum for the food I distribute to them. Every *anna* and every *rupee* of that is added to their debt and more to reimburse me for my trouble."

"Don't they complain?" Boban Joseph asked.

"They don't know. They can't read the contract. But they sign it because I say they must before they can get the loan, and so it is law. These people are so desperate they will willingly affix their official thumbprint to anything I put before them."

"Are you saying it is impossible for them to ever pay off their debts?"

"That's right," his father said. "For a loan of thirty rupees . . . or twenty . . . or even ten, they sign away their lives. And the lives of their children and their grandchildren who are yet to be born. The arrangement is hard for them, but for us it is very good."

"But what if they fight us? Or run away?"

"Untouchables do not fight. To them, it is all *karma*. What they get is what they deserve. If they run away, we will send villagers and the authorities after them. They are low caste—or no caste—and they have no right to disrespect us." Mammen Samuel chuckled. "The Hindu religion is a very good thing for our purses."

Although Boban Joseph's face remained passive, inside him, his heart jumped for joy. When he ran from Devi's hut, he knew what he had done. He had brought ridicule down on his father's name. To get away with a sound scolding was the best he could hope for. More likely, he would face much harsher punishment. Yet here his father sat praising and rewarding him. Could it be possible that his father didn't know about Devi?

Mammen Samuel stopped talking. Once again, he folded his hands across his middle, but this time he fixed his eyes on his son and stared hard. Boban Joseph began to sweat.

"Anup's daughter is still a child, yet I did not complain about your behavior toward her," Mammen Samuel said. "I understand that she is but a toy for your indulgent pleasure. But you are not a child who needs a plaything. You are a man."

"Father, I don't know what you may have heard or what you think, but I—"

"I think you have acted as a fool. A very dangerous fool. Do you want to incite the entire settlement against you? Against all of us?"

"No, Father, I didn't do anything to that untouchable girl. I . . . I—"

"If you desire the girl, ply her with milk curd and *ghee*, enough for her and her family. Give her a bangle, if that would please you. But do not ever again step your foot into her father's hut."

"You don't understand, Father. All I wanted to do was—"

"Stop your blathering excuses and listen to me!" Mammen Samuel roared in a sudden rage. "I have worked hard to make the name of Varghese great in this village and in the surrounding villages as well. It is your responsibility to take that name up and make it greater still. You will not behave like a dog. You will not drag our respected name through the mud!"

"No work tomorrow!" Boban Joseph announced to the laborers as they lay down their tools on the final day of harvest. "Tomorrow belongs to you! And when the sun is at its highest point, my father will reward you for all your hard labor, exactly as he promised. You will enjoy gifts of fresh provisions and a magnificent harvest feast!"

The next day, as the first rays of morning sun shone over the mountains, the entire settlement came alive with eager anticipation. No one wanted to sleep away the day of celebration that belonged to them. No one wanted to miss a single moment of the magnificent feast—not even the preparations. At full light, Anup chose the most respected men in the settlement to dig a roasting pit. The women came after and filled the pit with wood and kindling. Anup lit the fire and tended it himself.

"Here they come!" Little Girl screamed. It was she who first saw four of Mammen Samuel Varghese's servants on the path. Two walked ahead and two behind, shouldering long poles between them on which hung young goats, fully dressed and ready to roast.

All day the wonderful fragrance of roasting meat wafted throughout the village. While the goat meat sizzled over the fire pit, Mammen Samuel's bullock cart arrived, bearing huge metal pots filled with rice. Smaller pots held curry and chutney, and a great deal of vegetable stew with red chili peppers floating in it. Bowls of curds . . . guavas and custard apples . . . stalks of red bananas.

Each man, woman, and child in the settlement got a banana leaf to pile high with the wonderful fare. And after the feast ended, each family received packages of rice, wheat, and spices.

The laborers were not alone in their joy. Whenever Mammen Samuel brought in a good harvest, the entire town rejoiced, for the powerful landlord took care to celebrate his good fortune with acts of generosity.

Prem Rao, the square-shaped, bushy-bearded spice dealer who wore a bright red turban, took sorrowful inventory of his sacks of spices. The day Virat had passed him on the road, sitting cross-legged and selling *marsala* spices to the village ladies, his spice sacks had stood upright. Not completely full, but still plenty plump. No longer. Now the sacks lay flat on the ground, all but empty. And because another vendor had started selling spices in the village, the women took one look at his depleted sacks, shook their heads, and turned away toward his rival.

So Prem Rao went to see Mammen Samuel. "My father sold spices in this village, and my grandfather before him. I must make my sacks once again plump with spices or I will have no spice market left. I cannot afford to fill all of them, yet if I don't, still more of my customers will pass me by and go to the new vendor."

"I did have a fine pepper harvest last winter," Mammen Samuel said in a most agreeable voice. "The pepper is especially strong and pungent, picked on the very day the first two berries showed red, almost ripe yet still hard."

Prem Rao licked his lips in eagerness.

"And my cardamom is already dried and carefully packed. The chilies, my workers continue to pick even while we talk."

"The three most popular spices," Prem Rao said.

"I can sell you a goodly amount of all three—on your good credit alone. Then you can use your money to buy the other spices you need."

Prem Rao's black eyes glistened with eager anticipation. He touched his forehead and bowed slightly. He belonged to the *Vaisya* caste, the merchant caste—third down from the highest. One caste below Mammen Samuel and two below the Brahmin. Still a respected caste, however, not servants like the Sudras.

"What must I do to earn your favor?" Prem Rao asked.

"A good man feeds his own family and gives help to others," Mammen Samuel said with exaggerated modesty. "For you, the interest charged will not be high."

At the end of the harvest, Mammen Samuel found opportunity to secure goodwill from as many people as possible— goodwill would continue on long after the tradespeople's storage bins, or spice sacks, were empty once again.

Mammen Samuel Varghese had learned to be a profitable landlord at the knee of his father, Nadir Lazarus. A cruel and haughty man, Nadir Lazarus Varghese, yet his business tactics made him extremely rich and greatly feared. But hated as well. Once, as he rode his horse alone on a dark pathway, a crowd of twenty-two armed men intent on breaking his iron grip on the village surrounded him. He escaped by turning the horse around and jumping it across one of the large ground wells he used to irrigate his fields.

Brahmin Keshavan's father, Brahmin Debarma, came to Nadir Lazarus and demanded a share of his harvest. "Go home, old man," Nadir Lazarus told him. "Do not bother me again. I will never give you one rupee." That night, Brahmin Debarma died in his sleep. Immediately, the Brahmin's family accused Nadir Lazarus of murder. Because everyone feared the Brahmins, authorities bound the great landlord in chains and locked him up in jail. The humiliation was more than the proud Nadir Lazarus could bear. The day he was released, he came home, took poison, and died in his bed.

No one in the village ever spoke the name Nadir Lazarus Varghese in Mammen Samuel's hearing. Mammen Samuel could not abide the humiliation. But in the privacy of his own house he said, "I am not like my father. The people love me. I am good to them."

As the sun sank low on the horizon, Mammen Samuel sat on his veranda where he could hear remnants of the echoed songs and laughter from the feasting laborers. He opened his leather-bound book of accounts, dipped his pen into the inkwell, and leafed though the pages one by one. Beside each laborer's debt, he added five rupees for each family member who sat at the feast. Fifteen rupees for Virat's family. The same amount as his original loan.

# 19

A very good harvest," Mammen Samuel Varghese said with a sigh as he settled himself on the veranda.

"Very good," Boban Joseph agreed.

"Oh, that wild man I brought in to help with the harvest . . . that fisherman . . . he killed the tiger. Did you know?"

"That is a very good thing," Boban Joseph said, but he kept his eyes averted from his father.

"The tiger had already been injured," Mammen Samuel said. His voice took on a harsh and brittle tone, no longer like a father talking casually with his son.

Boban Joseph's eyes darted from his father to the floor, then with desperation to the steps that led to the garden.

"Your friend—the one called Gokul who likes to run races on his horse—he suffered a serious injury in an accident, I understand. Two weeks ago, as I hear. You know about that, I assume?"

Boban Joseph swallowed hard. "Gokul can be foolish. And careless, too."

"So it would seem. The injury occurred while he was out on his horse, then? Participating in a race, you say?"

Boban Josepeh fidgeted uncomfortably. "I don't know," he mumbled. "Why are you so interested in Gokul?"

"Your other friend, then. Beeja Ram. The lazy boy who cannot be bothered to work or learn to read. I understand he wears a bandage on his arm and shoulder. He also suffered injuries in an accident?"

Boban Joseph, his face pale and distressed, stared at the floor.

"The same accident as Gokul, perhaps?"

Sullen resignation flooded over Boban Joseph and he slumped back against the wall.

"Two men came to see me today," Mammen Samuel said. "They were the no-good fathers of your no-good friends, Gokul and Beeja Ram. I paid a goodly sum to each man so they would take their sons home with them and say nothing of the details of their accidents to anyone."

"Yes, yes!" Boban Joseph blurted. "It is true that Gokul and Beeja Ram and I set out to kill us a tiger. We heard that one had entered the woods and we wanted to prove we were strong enough to kill it with nothing but our sickles and knives. But we couldn't do it."

"So you injured it and let it go free?"

"We had no choice!" Boban Joseph insisted. "That tiger almost killed us!"

"You left an injured tiger to prey on our village! You left an injured tiger to threaten my harvest!"

Boban Joseph jumped to his feet. "So what if the tiger got a water boy, Father? So what if it had gotten a couple of the women too? What difference do a few outcastes make to people like us?"

Mammen Samuel, eyes flashing and jaw clenched tight, glared in furious disbelief at his son. For a long time, he said nothing.

"You, Boban Joseph Varghese, are the son of kings and warriors," Mammen Samuel finally said, in a voice curiously calm. "Outcasts are not your enemies, my son. Your enemies are the Brahmins, because they envy you. That boy Rama, he is your enemy. He will smile to your face, but behind your back he will pronounce a curse on you and do his best to destroy you. The outcastes know their place, but the Brahmins are certain in their belief that they are better than everyone else."

"But it was because of Rama that I wanted to kill the tiger," Boban Joseph said. "I wanted to prove my strength to him."

"You proved your foolishness and your pride. Nothing more," Mammen Samuel said. "Right now, Rama is most likely deriding you for polluting him."

Boban Joseph slumped down and let his head sink into his hands.

"You must be stronger than the Brahmins, but not because you attack an innocent tiger. No, you must be stronger because you are smarter."

Mammen Samuel looked at his son and shook his head slowly. "Are you listening to me, Boban Joseph? You *must* be *smarter!*"

Morning and evening, darkening shadows of night and breaking light of day. Pray at the union of day and night. Mammen Samuel sat alone in the great room, his legs crossed, and stared straight ahead at the picture of Jesus on the wall. "Thanks be to God that I am not like all the others in this village." He paused. "Make my son Boban Joseph to be a good, obedient son, and a wise man. Make him to act in a way that does not damage our family's good name." For good measure he added, "Punish the Hindu son of Brahmin Keshavan for his

sins more severely than you punish my Christian son for his."
Mammen Samuel bowed low and said, "Amen."

The captive toddy cat shrieked and screamed in furious
frustration. It scratched and tore at the sides of its makeshift
cage with sharply pointed claws, screeching every time one
of its claws caught in the rough-hewn box. Another sleepless
night for everyone in Mammen Samuel Varghese's household.
But when anyone mentioned letting the animal go free, Saji
Stephen screamed and cried and stamped his feet. So the
toddy cat stayed. As always, Saji Stephen got his way.

# 20
## May

The hot season blasted in with a vengeance, scorching the earth so hard and black that the baked land cracked and fractured into odd-shaped scales. Under a blinding white sky, rice paddies floated in and out of focus. Heat melted everything into a shimmering blur.

Already, laborers had prepared the first field for rice planting. Anup commanded that trenches be opened to the second field to flood it. Workers followed to churn mounds of manure into the mud. At the completion of each section, teams came in to flatten the soggy ground, breaking up clods and leveling the land for planting. Virat, splattered with mud, drove one team of black water buffalo, yoked to a flat harrow. "Aim straight to the east," Anup told him. "Always aim straight to the east."

Latha filled her basket with rice seedlings that the women had grown in flat baskets covered with straw. She hunkered down in the muddy water of the first paddy and planted seedlings, one by one. Six inches apart. Row after row after row.

The sun beat down and burnt the women raw through their mud-caked *saris*.

"Where is the water boy?" Latha sighed.

"Water!" the woman next to her called out. The woman's hands had started to shake uncontrollably.

One by one, the other women joined in the cry. "Water! Bring us water!"

But the water boy didn't come. In desperation, the shaking woman next to Latha scooped up a handful of mucky water and gulped it down.

Before the sun reached full overhead, Jebar—a string-thin man with filmy eyes who drove another water buffalo-pulled harrow—toppled off the wooden bar and fell face down into the paddy. He lay crumpled in the mud like a dead man.

Virat ran over to him. "Jebar! Get up, Jebar!" When the man didn't move, Virat turned him over and splashed water on his face.

"You have to let us rest in the shade!" Virat exclaimed to Anup, who had hurried over to see what happened.

"Yes!" one after another exclaimed. "We cannot keep working in the sun like this! None of us can."

Anup, shading his own eyes from the glaring sun, sighed and ran his muddy hand across his face. "Work early and late, then. We will all take a break in the hottest part of the day."

Throughout the rest of the hot season, the settlement came alive as soon as the stars began to fade in the still-black sky. Latha roused herself from her sleeping mat outside the door and stumbled into the dark hut. She felt around for the bowl of cold boiled rice she saved back from the evening meal. Just a quick breakfast before she and Virat hurried off to the paddies. With first light, they would start work—harrowing, planting. Flattening the ground, planting. Later, weeding, weeding, weeding.

When the sun grew too hot to bear, when even the water buffalo teams began to slow, the workers splashed water over their arms and legs and headed back to their huts to eat and wait out the worst of the heat.

Latha, like every other woman in the settlement, started a cook fire with only a handful of small twigs. It made no sense to generate any more heat than absolutely necessary. She poured water into her earthenware pot and dropped in rice, chilies, and spinach seasoned with tamarind and salt. Since Master Landlord had replenished their supplies of rice and wheat, Latha allowed an extra handful of rice for her family. Enough to eat, some to save back to eat cold for the evening meal, and a bit more left over for the next morning.

After Virat had finished his meal, after Ashish had finished his, Latha skimmed her hand around the edges of the pot to scoop up the last bites of spicy rice. Outside, the men laughed and talked and told stories everyone had already heard again and again. Latha ran her hand around the pot one more time in hopes of finding a bit more rice. Satisfied that she had gotten every last grain, she poured water over the pot to clean it. She poured more water over her hands and even splashed a bit on her face before she stepped outside to relax with the other women.

"Come, Latha!" called a bent-over woman with gray hair who could plant rice faster than anyone else. "Come and hear the news!"

In every spot of shade, a cluster of women or men sat gossiping. Sethu hunkered next to the gray-haired woman, but she never looked up at Latha. That's how it had been ever since Latha tried to help Devi.

"Not today," Latha told the woman. "I'm too tired. Maybe I'll lie down for a bit."

A black crow flapped down from the tamarind tree, perched on the roof of Hilmi's palm frond hut, and set up a raucous noise.

"That means good luck for the fisherman," the woman with few teeth said.

The bird flapped down onto the ground, but never slowed its cawing racket.

"Or maybe good luck for someone else," another woman suggested. "Make a wish and lay down your lumps of rice."

"You too, Latha," urged the gray-haired lady. "Maybe the crow will snatch up your lump. Maybe your wish will come true!"

"I have no rice to spare," Latha said as she turned back to her hut. "And no wishes left in me."

❧

"*Amma*, see what I found!" Ashish, jumping up and down, could barely contain his excitement. "Come and see, *Amma*!"

Latha had barely settled herself on her sleeping mat. Too soon she would have to get back to work. But Ashish couldn't wait, so she sighed and followed him into the hut.

Latha expected to see a pile of dry twigs—most likely a small pile. Even that would be most welcome. Instead, she saw a huge pile of mangos, some rich and juicy orange, and some still green.

"I picked them!" Ashish squealed. "I climbed the tree and pulled them off, and threw them down to Little Girl. We can eat them all!"

Latha looked doubtfully at the pile. That mango tree, like all the trees in the settlement, was for everyone to use. "It wouldn't be fair," she said. "One or two, perhaps, but not all of them."

Ashish's smile melted and tears sprang to his dark eyes. "But I picked them special for us, *Amma*."

Latha didn't think about her crestfallen son. Nor did she consider the wonderful taste of the juicy ripe fruit, or the pungent green mango chutney she could make. She thought about Sethu. Probably this very minute Little Girl was telling her about the mangos. That meant that soon everyone in the settlement would know whatever Sethu chose to tell them, which most likely would not be kind.

"*Amma?*" Ashish ventured. "I could give the rest of the mangos to the other people. Maybe they will reward me for picking them."

"Yes, yes!" Latha said. Everyone would certainly be pleased. No one had the time or the energy to pick mangos, and here they were delivered to them. "What a good boy you are, Ashish!"

Ashish grabbed up an armload of the fruit and ran to the doorway, but Latha called after him, "First take mangos to Sethu. And don't accept anything in return!"

⌇

"A fortune-teller came to the village!" Devi exclaimed the next afternoon when she arrived home from the master's garden. "Master Landlord's wife sent for him. Master Landlord's daughter will marry soon, and his wife wants to find the best day to make a good marriage."

"I wish I could see a fortune-teller," Lidya said.

"He wouldn't tell you anything good," Devi told her sister. "I wouldn't even want to talk to him. I *know* he wouldn't tell me anything good!"

Sethu stopped kneading the *chapati* dough. She didn't say anything, but she listened intently to Devi's news.

"Bake the *chapatis* and feed your father," Sethu said to Lidya. She handed the girl the ball of dough, wiped her hands on her *sari*, and hurried outside.

Sethu went to Latha's hut and found her spreading out the glowing embers in her cooking pit. "This is for you," Sethu said. She handed Latha a freshly dug chili plant, dirt still clinging to its roots.

"Thank you," Latha said. She went to the side of her hut, poured out a puddle of water, then clawed out a muddy hole in which to plant the chili. She knew Sethu. This was her way of saying, "I'm sorry." Her way of saying, "Let us forget our dispute."

"My Devi brought news from the village," Sethu said, following behind Latha. She told Latha all about the fortune-teller.

"What has that to do with us?" Latha asked.

"I want that fortune-teller to tell me my fortune. I want him to tell me my baby will be a boy."

Latha said nothing.

"The master landowner owes me a double payment. I took care of twin girls for his sister. *Twin girls!* He owes me. When the others go back to the fields, I will go to the master's house and ask to see the fortune-teller."

An idea began to take form in Latha's mind.

Virat didn't sit outside and gossip with the other men for long. The sun burned too hot and his body was too weary. When Latha saw him coming, she said to Sethu, "Go home. Maybe I will find you before you go to see the fortune-teller."

Latha straightened the sleeping mat for her husband and brought him the water jug, freshly filled.

"Where is Ashish?" Virat asked.

"Carrying mangos to everyone in the settlement. I'm glad he is not here, Husband, because I want to tell you something."

Latha told him about the fortune-teller and about Sethu's plan to see him. "I want to go with her," she said.

"Why? You have no baby to ask him about."

"No, but I have a son. I have our Blessing. I want to ask the fortune-teller about him. I want to ask what will happen if we stay here and what will happen if we go."

"No!" Virat said. "You must not go. I forbid it."

"Why?"

"Because you will stir up trouble for us. Here is what I tell you: Do what you are supposed to do, and no more. Go to the fields and work, and leave Ashish alone to do his work."

Latha closed her mouth and said no more. But as soon as Virat shut his eyes, she crept away to see Sethu.

$\mathscr{L}$❧

"Foolishness and superstition," Mammen Samuel said to his wife. "I know the Brahmins and the low-castes demand fortune-tellers. But I say, leave the fortune-tellers to them. Let the fools follow their fallacies, if they will. But we will not."

Parmar Ruth smiled and bowed her head to her husband. When she first instructed Babu to arrange a time for her to take Sunita Lois to meet with the fortune-teller, she cautioned him to keep the meeting a secret from her husband. A young girl of but twelve years and soon to be married—was it not simple wisdom to look out for the girl's future in every way possible?

"And yet," Mammen Samuel allowed, "it is uncanny how often the foretellings of such a one do come true."

"Yes, Husband," Parmar Ruth said eagerly. "You are right about that. Foolish superstition for sure, yet uncanny nevertheless."

When the garden servant sent word to Mammen Samuel that the midwife Sethu had come with another worker to have her fortune told, Mammen Samuel's eyes glistened. "Tell her if she wishes to see the fortune-teller, then henceforth she must perform her duties as midwife—*all* her duties—without extra payment from me."

The fortune-teller was a slight man with a bent back and a mop of unruly black hair. With gnarled hands, he prepared a *jatak* for Sethu. A horoscope. Carefully he laid out the position of the twelve zodiac signs and printed them. He did the same for the positions of all the planets. After that he added the seven *chakras*. For a long time, he gazed at his notations and chanted *mantras* over them. He sought to determine the present effects of all the influences on Sethu. That done, he set about making calculations for the future. Finally the fortune-teller laid down his pen and gazed at Sethu.

"Well?" Sethu demanded.

"You ask about your baby," the fortune-teller said. "It will be a girl."

"No!" Sethu cried. "It cannot be!"

"It is so. The *jatak* does not lie."

Sethu, her face set like stone, stood up abruptly and prepared to leave.

"But it does not *have* to be so," the fortune-teller added.

"What do you mean?"

"The planets are like gods. To change the future, you must do *pujas* and chant *mantras* in order to pacify them. Also, I can sell you charms with the power to ward off the curse under which you are currently living."

Sethu sat back down. The fortune-teller eyed the carved bracelet on her arm, her last possession of any value. Sethu slipped it off and handed it to him. In return, the fortune-teller gave her two charms: a bag of dried herbs—"Wear it around your neck day and night"— and a bracelet woven of human hair—"This you are to wear on the wrist of your right hand, also day and night."

"Now my baby will be a boy?"

"It will be a boy," the fortune-teller assured her. "I have removed the curse of the girl child from you."

In her elation, Sethu pointed to Latha and exclaimed, "My friend here already has a son. She needs your help too."

"It it your own fortune you want read or your son's fortune?" the fortune-teller asked Latha.

Latha shot quick glances around her. She leaned in close and whispered, "I need to know one thing only. My son, Ashish. What will happen to him if we stay here?"

The fortune-teller didn't bother to prepare a *jatak* for Latha. He simply asked the date and place of her son's birth, and nothing more. "Why did you give him the name Ashish?" he asked. "Why didn't you name him for a god? Shiva, who could conquer evil demons, or Ganesh, who removes all obstacles, perhaps?"

Latha stared into the blank eyes of the fortune-teller and said nothing.

"Your son has a bad planet in his place of work and wealth," the fortune-teller said. "He cannot learn. He will not prosper in life."

Latha gasped.

"Your son is not a blessing," the fortune-teller said. "He is of no worth at all. Stay where you are and work, for if you leave you will all die. Your family is under a very strong curse and I can do nothing to lift it."

## 21

*I*n the soft stillness of the early morning, Mammen Samuel Varghese turned over on his bed and listened. Only bells tinkled in the distance, calling awakening families to their house altars to tend to the deities. Only the call of a bird from the mango tree outside the east window. Nothing more. Mammen Samuel stretched his arms wide and his legs long and listened hard. It took him several minutes to realize what was missing. The toddy cat! No clawing or scratching or screaming this morning. No unpleasant sound at all. For the first time in more than a week, quiet reigned.

Then an entirely different shriek—the scream of a furious little boy.

"It's gone!" Saji Stephen yelled. "My pet is gone! Look, his cage is empty!"

Mammen Samuel sighed and hefted himself from his bed. It would be a long, hot day.

"The cage door is wide open!" Saji Stephen wailed.

"Now, now, little one," Parmar Ruth cooed. "*Appa* will get you another pet. He will get you a better one."

"I don't want another pet!" Saji Stephen shrieked. "I want my toddy cat!"

"Shall I play a song for you on the sitar?" Sunita Lois asked. "I can make up words about the adventure of a runaway toddy cat. Would you like that?"

"No, no, no, no, no! I don't want anything except my pet back!"

Mammen Samuel sighed as he opened the door to face another day. Boban Joseph strolled past him, in from the veranda, his sleeping mat under his arm. The boy spoke no words of comfort to his brother. In fact, when Saji Stephen shrieked and stamped his feet, traces of a smirk crossed Boban Joseph's lips.

So. Mammen Samuel sat back down and folded his hands across his middle.

In time, Saji Stephen's screams quieted into incessant whines, but he still refused to be comforted. Finally, at the far edge of what he could bear, Mammen Samuel picked up his young son and set him on his knee. "The toddy cat never truly was your pet," he said. "You wanted that, but the toddy cat is a wild animal, just like the tiger was wild. The toddy cat would have bitten off your finger. It is the will of God that it has gone back to live in the wild."

"No, *Appa*, I—"

"Listen to me. You have cried and fussed long enough. Now I am going to give you a new pet. A real plaything."

For the first time that morning, Saji Stephen stopped wailing. "What is it, *Appa*? What will you give me?"

"A little boy to play with. A little boy all your own."

Saji Stephen's eyes opened wide and a smile crossed his tear-streaked face.

"The little boy in the settlement who gave the wooden top to you," Mammen Samuel said. "I will bring him here to play with you. But only if you promise me you will say no more about the toddy cat."

"Can you bring the boy right now?"

"Soon," Mammen Samuel promised. "Very soon."

❧

"Perhaps you do have the makings of a landlord after all," Mammen Samuel told Boban Joseph.

"You are not angry with me, Father?"

"Angry! Quite the contrary. A successful master does not strive to make everyone under his care happy. He strives to do what is beneficial for the majority. And he does it in a manner that will stir up the least criticism while bringing the greatest advantage to himself."

"I could not bear to hear that animal crashing about one more night! I opened the cage door and let the toddy cat escape. And I did it for *me*."

"You learned an important lesson, my son," Mammen Samuel said. "Most often, what is good for you is good for everyone."

❧

Devi hurried into the settlement calling, "Ashish! Ashish! You are to come to the master landlord's house with me now!"

Before she could see him, the boy ran and hid in a hole under Hilmi's palm frond hut. He thought Devi would grow tired and go away, but she did not.

"Ashish! Ashish, where are you? Ashish, you must come with me!"

Little Girl, who knew all Ashish's hiding places, headed for the hole and peeked in. "Why are you hiding from my sister?" she asked.

"Because I don't want to go with her!"

But Devi had followed Little Girl. She grabbed hold of Ashish's arm and pulled him out of his hiding place. "I don't want to drag you all the way to the master landlord's house. Please, come along like a good boy."

"My *amma* and my *appa* will be angry with me."

"It doesn't matter what they say," Devi told the boy. "The master landlord says you are to go his house now. He is the one you must obey."

Although he cried and protested the entire way, Devi half led, half dragged Ashish to the garden where Babu waited for him with a bucket of water and clean clothes.

"Here he is! My own little boy!" Saji Stephen squealed when he saw Devi and Ashish coming up the road.

Ashish was much shorter and thinner than Saji Stephen, and almost two years younger, all of which pleased Saji Stephen greatly. Even if this boy had a mind to fight back, Saji Stephen could be sure to win every time.

When Latha came back to her hut for the afternoon break, Ashish wasn't waiting for her as usual. The ground burned like a rock in the fire, so Latha couldn't bear to stand in one place very long. Even so she threw a couple of twigs into the fire pit and lit it hot enough to stir up a quick pot of porridge, flavored with chilies from her own chili plant. Still Ashish did not come.

"I cannot find Ashish," Latha said when Virat got back from the paddy.

"He's probably somewhere with Little Girl," Virat said.

Yes, of course! Latha scooped out porridge for Virat, then she ran to Sethu's hut to get her son.

But Little Girl told her sadly, "Ashish is gone."

"What do you mean, he is gone?"

"Gone to the master landlord's house. Devi came to get him and she took him away with her."

Latha stared at the child as though she couldn't understand her words. Then she ran from the hut, yelling for Virat.

"I disobeyed you, Husband." Latha's trembling words tumbled from her mouth. "You told me not to go to the fortune-teller, but I went anyway. I asked him Ashish's future if we stayed here or if we ran away."

Virat's face went pale. "Come, we will talk inside."

Inside the hut Latha waited and waited for Virat to speak, but for the longest time he said nothing.

"If you were Ranjun and I was Pooni, you would beat me until I couldn't stand up," Latha said softly.

"Do you not understand what you have done, Wife? That fortune-teller was in the landlord's employ. Did you not consider that he would repeat to Master Landlord every word you said?"

The idea had never occurred to Latha. Her eyes filled with tears. "Is that why the master landlord took Ashish away?"

Virat shrugged his shoulders. What did he know? What could he understand about anything?

Latha covered her face and wept. "The fortune-teller said Ashish is not a blessing. He told me our child is of no worth at all. The fortune-teller said it made no difference whether we stayed here and worked or left to die, because our family is under a terrible curse that cannot be lifted."

Virat reached out and touched Latha's weather-scorched arm. "Now I must confess something to you. Before the harvest, when Anup took me out to test the ripeness of the wheat heads, he suddenly jumped on me and pushed me to the ground. I thought I had done something to make him angry with me, that he might even kill me. But he saw what I did not see—a great cobra swaying high with its hood spread wide. All across that snake's hood were the footprints of Krishna. And I knew what Anup did not know. Evil spirits sent that snake. As a sign of the curse from Brahmin Keshavan. The Brahmin put the curse on us, and he can lift it off."

"But he won't. Oh, Virat, what if he won't?"

"Then we must get away from here," Virat said. "We must get far away!"

The landlord's usually quiet house buzzed with the excited talk of an upcoming wedding. Years before, an appropriate groom had been chosen for Sunita Lois, and now that she approached her twelfth year, the marriage would finally take place. The girl had not yet seen her husband-to-be, of course. That wouldn't happen until her wedding day. But Boban Joseph whispered to her, "Your new husband is in his twenty-fifth year . . . maybe. Or twenty-sixth. He lives in the next village. He is from a Christian family, and very wealthy." Sunita Lois asked if he might be handsome, too, but Boban Joseph just wrinkled up his nose and made a face.

"That fallow field beyond the garden," Parmar Ruth said to her husband. "It should be cleaned up and leveled for the wedding tents. And make certain it is packed hard."

"I'll send to the settlement for a couple of workers," Mammen Samuel said.

"Good ones," Parmar Ruth insisted. "And from as high a caste as possible so as not to unduly upset the Brahmins."

From a higher caste? No, no. Mammen Samuel would choose two men from the lowest caste. The savage tribal and the *chamar*, thoroughly polluted through and through. They would do perfectly. Since the field beyond the garden lay in plain sight of the road, Brahmin Keshavan could not help but see them there.

At sunset, when he sat cross-legged and said his evening prayers, Mammen Samuel would ask God to make certain the Brahmin saw the unclean laborers at work next to the garden. Better yet, he would ask God to bring them into direct contact with the Brahmin. He would also make it a point to thank God for bestowing on him only one daughter.

✍❧

As Virat made his way home from the rice paddy, he saw Devi coming down the path from the landlord's house with Ashish. The boy looked most unhappy. Virat met them and took his son by the hand.

"I don't want to play with Saji Stephen any more, *Appa*," Ashish said. "I want to stay here and gather firewood."

"I don't want to plow the muddy fields, but I do it," Virat told his son.

Ashish looked at his mud-caked father and laughed.

"*Amma* doesn't want to sit in the paddy water and plant rice seedlings, but she does that every day. All of us must do what the master landlord tells us to do, Ashish. For us, it is the law. It's our moral responsibility. It is our *dharma*."

"I don't like it!" Ashish said.

*Neither do I*, Virat thought. *Neither do I.*

When Devi arrived home, she repeated to her father the landlord's message about needing two workers to prepare the field for his daughter's wedding. Immediately, Anup set about considering which men he could best do without. But Devi said, "The savage tribal man and the *chamar* who is thoroughly polluted through and through. Those are the ones the landlord wants."

✑

Parmar Ruth looked out at the two men at work in the field—a scrawny man with a very dark face and teeth to match, and a mud-streaked collector-of-dead-animals with too many teeth for his mouth. "Why must you purposely irritate the Brahmin?" she asked her husband.

But Mammen Samuel paid his wife no mind. He knew Brahmin Keshavan watched from the road. And he knew it would not be long before the Brahmin found some pretext to come to his house.

Within the hour, Brahmin Keshavan, smelling of incense and his morning bath, approached the field. As always, the *mundu* tied high around his waist was crisp, white, and spotless. And, of course, his ever-present sacred thread glistened gold against the rich tan of his oiled body.

"You would build yourself an even larger house?" Brahmin Keshavan asked, doing his best to look nonchalant and somewhat pleasant.

"On the contrary," Mammen Samuel said. "I am making preparations for my daughter's wedding."

"Ah, yes. And I have come to recite blessings over the place of the wedding. This is the field where the guests will gather, then?"

Field, he said. Not pavilion, but *field!* A term that denoted a place unimportant and plain. Anger simmered in Mammen Samuel's breast.

"You need not disturb your Hindu gods for the sake of my family," Mammen Samuel said. He made no effort to hide the sharp edge to his words. Then, because he would not let such an insult from the Brahmin go by unchallenged, he added, "Your gods are blood-thirsty beings. Nothing but powerful demons, capable of all sorts of evil."

"Which is precisely why you should fear them," said Brahmin Keshavan.

Normally, in the afternoon hours, Mammen Samuel would have been lying on his bed while Babu did his best to fan away the oppressive heat. Brahmin Keshavan would also have been resting out the hottest hours of the day. But a chance for one to gain the upper hand over the other persuaded both men to stand outside in the blistering sun. As their debate turned to argument, Mammen Samuel edged closer and closer to the workers in the field. Afternoon was an unfortunate time for the Brahmin to be out, for the lowering sun caused the workers' polluting shadows to stretch out long across the field.

Each time his hoe thunked against the baked ground, Virat sneaked a glance at the Brahmin, busily engaged in an argument with the master.

Mammen Samuel motioned toward Virat and Hilmi. "Without my kindly help, these two wretches would be lying on the road, starving to death."

"It looks to my eyes as if you are the one receiving the help," Brahmin Keshavan retorted.

"A wise man knows how to use what benefits his neighbor to also benefit himself. It is my virtue to lend a helping hand and my *dharma* will be helped in return."

"Then extend a helping hand to me, as the law requires of you. A share of your prosperity is rightfully mine."

Virat watched for an opportunity to plead with the Brahmin to lift the curse from his family. But what if the Brahmin should grow so disgusted with the landlord that he walked away before Virat got the chance? Virat must not allow that to happen.

"Surely you will allow me to bless the field," Brahmin Keshavan stated. "Surely you will wish me to bless the preparations for your daughter's wedding."

"And how many rupees will that cost me?" Mammen Samuel demanded.

⁂

Virat edged forward. He glanced up at the sun to make certain it would not cast his shadow over the Brahmin.

"Keep your distance from me, *chamar*," Brahmin Keshavan warned.

Virat fell to his knees and bowed low before the Brahmin. "Please, I beg of you, remove the curse from my family."

"Stay away from me!"

Mammen Samuel noted the shrill touch of panic that ringed the Brahmin's voice and he could hardly contain his mirth.

Virat crawled forward. When the Brahmin tried to step back, Virat grabbed hold of his feet. "You pronounced a curse on me. Only you can remove it."

"Do not touch me!" Brahmin Keshavan cried. He tried to pull his feet away from Virat's grasp, but desperation had overtaken Virat, and he could no longer help himself. He clung all the more tightly.

"My son is a blessing. It is not right that he must live under your curse."

Brahmin Keshavan tried to run, but with Virat grasping at his feet, he stumbled and fell. He called out to Mammen Samuel for help, but Virat grabbed at him, begging, imploring, demanding.

"You touched it!" Brahmin Keshavan screamed. He clutched at his golden thread. "You filthy animal! You disgusting rubbish! Get away from me. For this assault, I double the curse. I pronounce it four times over!"

Virat shrank back, trembling. "No . . . please," he stammered. "Please, have mercy on me. On my family. Please!"

Brahmin Keshavan shook with fury. "For this great sin against me, you, *chamar*, will die!"

## 22

Abigail mopped her face and groaned. "How can human beings live in this heat?" she asked no one in particular. Dr. Moore adjusted his spectacles and kept his eyes on his book. Abigail sighed loudly and lifted the shade that covered the window. "Not one person dares to venture outside. The road is deserted."

"It will stay that way, too, at least until late afternoon," Dr. Moore said without looking up. "This really is a wretched country."

The hot blast of June parched everything barren and brown. The countryside looked as though it had been scorched by fire. Vultures hung in midair, shrieking harsh, thirsty squawks.

"I wonder if Ashish is faring well," Abigail said.

"No, he most assuredly is not," Dr. Moore answered. "Not in this heat. Not in this country."

"Poor little lad."

Dr. Moore's face assumed its well-worn look of annoyed resignation.

"Maybe he remembers something I said to him, though," Abigail persisted hopefully. "The prayers I prayed over him while he slept, perhaps, or maybe the songs I sang to calm him in the night."

With an irritated sigh, Edward Moore closed his book with a thump and dropped it on the table. "This is not the fairy tale land of your imaginings, Miss Davidson. This is real life in India. If that child still lives, he has forgotten you."

"I just thought . . . since his master is a Christian—"

"*Fancies* himself a Christian. I am well acquainted with his kind—Christian when it suits his purposes, Hindu when that brings him more advantage."

"Still, if he—"

"You will be fortunate to find even one of these heathens willing to heed the words of your prayers or songs. And if you think you can break down the centuries-old barriers of prejudice and suspicion that keep them oppressed and enslaved, you will be sorely disappointed. You cannot. This is India, Miss Davidson, not England. You would do well to remember the difference."

Feeling thoroughly chastened, Abigail sat stiff and still with her back to the doctor. Dr. Moore picked up his book and resumed reading. When he paid her no further mind, she slipped out to her own small room. Actually, she now shared the room with Darshina. Abigail had the bed and Darshina slept on a cot pushed up against the wardrobe. Dr. Moore's accommodations were on the other side of the great room. Abigail pictured them as luxurious, though she had never actually been afforded so much as a peek on the other side of his locked door.

Darshina had already stretched out on her cot to wait out the heat of the day. She didn't bother to open her eyes when Abigail spread out her mosquito net and threw herself down on her bed.

"Do you think Ashish is all right?" Abigail asked.

"Most certainly not," Darshina said. "He is being a slave boy."

"Blessing," Abigail said softly. "He is a blessing."

"Unclean. That boy being unclean. Nothing be changing that. My kind, we that are being 'pure' and 'blessed-by-the-gods,' we not allowing changes for his kind of people."

For a long while, Abigail lay on her bed lost in thought. *"This is India, Miss Davidson, not England. You would do well to remember that."* That's what Dr. Moore had told her. But how could she remember when she could not understand? And how could she understand when she knew absolutely nothing of India? The pitiful creatures that dragged into the clinic—more often than not they were already on their way to the grave. Yet they made up the sum total of her knowledge of this country.

"Tell me about India," Abigail said.

"Please, I am not to be understanding your question," Darshina answered.

"I want to know India."

"Then please to be coming with me to the next village," Darshina said. "Everywhere you be hearing peoples talking about the troupe of *jogis* coming there. Please to be seeing India with your own eyes."

"What are *jogis*?"

"Wandering singers. They be going from one village to the next village and to be staying for a fortnight in each place. Every evening, when the sun is to be falling low, they be singing and dancing the old tales of India."

"I don't know," Abigail said hesitantly. "I don't think Dr. Moore would approve. Especially if there is dancing. And I'm certain he wouldn't want me to mix with so many Indians."

Darshina shrugged. "When this day is to be growing cool, I will be going. Do what you wish—come with me or stay here and be watching the doctor reading his book."

*I could sneak away,* Abigail thought. *If I sneaked back in before dawn, Dr. Moore would never even know. I could tell him I must search for Ashish in order to check on his well-being, and then, I could claim illness and tell the doctor I must take to my bed and not be disturbed for any reason until . . .*

Abigail turned over onto her side searching for a more comfortable position. But comfort simply wasn't possible on the thin bed mat that passed for an Indian mattress. She sat up and reached outside the mosquito net for her bedside water glass. After a long drink, she poured the rest of the water onto her handkerchief and wiped her face and neck. With a loud sigh, Abigail flopped back down.

*I could simply tell Dr. Moore that I plan to go to the village. Well, why shouldn't I? I am an independent woman, here in India of my own free will!*

"Darshina," Abigail said. "I shall accompany you to the village."

❧

"I need *good* clay!" Ranjun the potter shouted at his youngest son. "Where did you find this terrible dirt? It is filled with pebbles!" He threw a handful of the clay and hit the child full in the face.

"In the rice field, *Appa*, where you told me to go," the terrified boy replied. "I will go back and get more."

"No! Your brother needs it now. He has sand all ready to mix with it."

The smaller child grabbed up a full pot of the soil and lugged it over to his older brother.

"Worthless, that's what you are!" Ranjun yelled after him.

All day, Ranjun had stomped around in an especially foul mood. Pooni warned the children to take care around him—the boys, certainly, for they had to work with their father. But even more she warned her little daughter, Mayawati. Ranjun shouted and bellowed at the boys. He threw clay and broken pots at them and slapped them, but he didn't beat them the way he beat his daughter . . . and his wife.

Ranjun strutted between the mud huts like a proud rooster among the hens. He was an outcaste like everyone else in that section of the village, but in his mind, he stood far superior to his wretched neighbors. Ranjun owned a potter's wheel, which he had made himself with the help of a carpenter. He had his own firing oven too. A simple enough affair—just a tunnel with a bulge in the middle. But with the wheel and the oven and the growing skill of his older son and the hard work of the small one, Ranjun could now make as many as five hundred pots each month. The imperfect ones that his son fashioned, Ranjun sold to the Untouchables. The fine ones went to the upper caste side of the river. The most perfect of all, Ranjun set aside for the Brahmins.

After Ranjun gulped down the last of his water, he pounded the water jug on the floor. "Where is the girl?" he bellowed. "I am in need of more water. Send the girl out here to me!"

"Run to Latha's house and hide yourself. Stay hidden until I call for you," Pooni said to Mayawati. "Hurry now. Go!"

Pooni waited until little Mayawati had time to hide before she carried a jug of fresh water out to her husband, along with a small bowl of cashew nuts. But when Ranjun looked up from his wheel and saw that his wife had come and not the child he demanded, his face twisted and his eyes darkened with rage.

"Beating is to be inflicted upon a donkey, a drum, and a woman," Ranjun pronounced in a voice as hard as iron.

Pooni had heard that Hindu proverb repeated far too many times. She dropped the jug and the bowl of cashews and ran.

But Ranjun was ready. He grabbed her by the hair and jerked her to the ground. "I do not deserve to be stuck with a bony old woman like you," he growled. "You are nothing but dirt beneath my feet."

Pooni scrambled on her hands and knees, but Ranjun grabbed her arm and hit her hard in the mouth. "A Sudra who speaks evil about a high caste person should be cut off," he quoted. Pooni wished she could laugh in his face. She would, if she were not bleeding and her teeth had not been knocked loose. Ranjun wasn't even a Sudra, let alone a member of a high caste!

"A Sudra who dares assume a position of equality with a person of high caste should be flogged," Ranjun recited.

How Pooni longed to say, "But if a Sudra—who is much higher than you, Ranjun—overhears the recitation of *Vedas*, molten lead is to be poured into his ears. Should a Sudra—who is much higher than you, Ranjun—repeat the *Veda*, his tongue should be cut out. Should a Sudra—who is much higher than you, Ranjun—remember a *Vedic* hymn, his body should be torn into pieces." She longed to say all that, but her mouth was too busy screaming.

"All the dancers, they are being people of low caste," Darshina told Abigail as they hurried along the road. "Only the low-caste please to be dancing in public."

Several bullock carts passed them by, but not one person offered the women a ride. So by the time they reached the next village—Abigail exhausted and drenched in sweat—the music had already started.

"It sounds mysterious," Abigail said. "A little bit frightening, too, I must admit."

Darshina laughed. "Are you not having flutes in England? And not having drums, too?"

"Yes, of course, but that other instrument. The one that makes a plucking sound. I've never heard that before."

"It to be going by the name of *lute*," Darshina said.

It took a minute for Abigail to realize that what she heard wasn't simply the playing of musical instruments. There were voices, as well. "The singers sound like another instrument," she said. "They sort of hum the same notes again and again. And they repeat identical words, too."

"The singers be calling to the gods. They be wishing to awaken them to be pleading for a blessing."

By the time Abigail and Darshina arrived at the village courtyard, the dancing was already underway. "Please to be watching the whole body," Darshina said as they pushed their way forward. "Indian dancing not being about arms and legs only. Every movement, even that of the little finger or the eyebrow to be having its own special meaning."

Abigail stared, transfixed with the hand gestures. "So beautiful!" she said. Darshina understood them all, and whispered their meanings. "It's like a secret language," Abigail exclaimed.

When the women dancers sat down, a man stood up alone before the crowd. He was unusually tall and slender but not scrawny. As the drums beat slowly and a haunting melody came from the flutes, the man moved alone in absolute glory. His motions were at once confoundingly complex and breathtakingly simple. Slowly he lifted first one leg and then the other. He planted each foot in turn, heel first. The man's almost bare body twisted as his arms and hands wove together, each with the other, forming complex shapes. His head moved forward and backward, side to side. It reminded Abigail of a chicken when it walked. The dancer's eyes, flooded with expression, looked at no one. He danced for himself.

"Please, he be interpreting," Darshina whispered. "Now he be telling of the dreadful heat of India's sun."

"Yes, yes!" said Abigail. Just watching him, sweat dripped from her face.

"Now to be telling of the cold of the rising moon," Darshina said.

Abigail's back tightened and a wracking shiver ran through her.

As Abigail watched, the dancer's eyes took on a gaze of indifference. Rhythmically they opened and closed, opened and closed. Ah, yes. Eyes of the cobra. And such eyes! They filled Abigail with a chilling dread.

❧

"Please to be knowing India now?" Darshina asked Abigail as they walked home by the moonlight.

"No," Abigail said. "But now I have some idea of how much I have to learn."

With a long day behind them and nothing special to look forward to, the road back to the mission medical clinic seemed much longer than when they had walked it in the late afternoon. "I wish someone would slow down and let us climb up on the back of their wagon," Abigail said.

"It is being better to walk," Darshina assured her. So they walked, mostly in silence. In her weariness, Abigail had little energy left for talk.

Suddenly, Darshina stopped. "Please! What is the sound I be hearing?"

"I didn't hear anything," Abigail said.

They took a few more steps and Darshina stopped again. The two women stood still for a moment, then Abigail heard the sound too. A whimper, perhaps. Or maybe only a breeze blowing through the cluster of trees ahead.

"Someone is in there," Abigail said, pointing to the trees.

"Come along, come along! Pease to be hurrying past," Darshina insisted.

But Abigail grabbed her arm. "What if someone is hurt? What if it's a child who needs us?"

"No! It's being foolishness to be stopping here. Someone could be wanting to hurt us. No persons be around to give us help."

Darshina spoke the truth, of course. Yet even as Abigail acknowledged it, she hurried toward the whimper. She paused at the edge of the trees and stared into the black grove. "Is anyone here?" she called.

Silence, except for the soft sound of Darshina's feet creeping up behind her.

"Does someone need help?" Abigail asked.

More silence. But as they turned to go, a broken voice wept, *"Eikku kudikkan entendilum tarumo?"*

"*Ate!*" Darshina exclaimed. "Yes, we can give you water!"

Abigail pushed through the brushy overgrowth. In a shallow nest of leaves lay Pooni, battered and sobbing.

⁂

Abigail strained to understand Pooni's talk, but to her ear it sounded like nothing more than melodic babble. "What is she saying?" Abigail asked Darshina.

"She wants for you to be understanding she be untouchable and unclean. She cannot believe you to be tending to women like her."

"Tell her she is my favorite patient all day," Abigail said.

Darshina laughed. "And should I also be telling her she is being your only patient today?"

❧

Because Pooni was a woman, and because her injuries did not require Dr. Moore's surgical services, the doctor offered to stay out of the surgery. Abigail was perfectly able to dress Pooni's wounds by herself.

Pooni, her eyes wide and troubled, spoke again.

"She's to be saying her husband is being angry with her because she is being very wicked," Darshina said. "She's to be saying pollution is on her and she must not touch the white sheet you wear on your bed."

"Tell her we are followers of Jesus, the Son of the one and only true God," Abigail said. "Tell her Jesus desired to mingle with sinners and outcasts, and with all the people others considered polluted."

Pooni's eyes opened wide as Darshina translated the words.

"Tell her Jesus ate with such people. Tell her Jesus sat with them and shared their food."

Pooni gasped in astonishment.

"She's to be saying she cannot be understanding such things," Darshina said. "She's to be saying such actions would make Jesus unclean too."

"Tell her that Jesus taught the truth: There is only one true God, and all people are made in His image. It is not true that some people come from His head, some from His arms, some from His belly, and some from His feet. Tell her that no people anywhere come from underneath God's feet. All of us came from the breath of God. We are all made after His likeness. Tell her that is the truth."

⚘

Abigail stayed with Pooni all night. The next morning she gave her water and porridge, and tenderly washed her face and again tended to her wounds.

"Doctor to be saying it be for me to be tending her now," Darshina said. "Doctor be saying it be for you to be resting."

When Abigail came out of the surgery, she found Dr. Moore waiting for her.

"It's so unfair!" Abigail said. "People like her and like Ashish. It is so terribly unfair!"

"Tragedy has a way of visiting those who can bear it the least," Dr. Moore said.

"But these were more than tragedies. They weren't diseases or accidents. These were purposeful, horrible beatings!"

"It is the way of India," Dr. Moore said. "I warned you before, Miss Davidson, do not expect to change it."

In the sweltering heat of the day, Abigail fell across her bed. She suddenly felt so very tired. Maybe if she lay down for an hour or so. Only until the worst of the heat passed.

Exactly how long she slept, Abigail didn't know. Longer than she had intended, judging by the length of the shadows outside her window. She hurried back to the surgery to check on her patient, but Pooni was gone.

"She is being gone back to her home," Darshina said.

Abigail shook her head in disbelief. "But why?"

"Because she feels condemned to be lowly," Dr. Moore said. "Because she sees it as her inescapable fate."

But Darshina said, "She be going back because she has a daughter there."

# 23

*W*hen Master Landlord's large house came into view, Ashish gripped Devi's hand. Up ahead he saw Saji Stephen waiting, dressed completely in spotless white, his hands on his hips. Ashish dug his fingers into Devi's palm.

"Let me go," Devi said, firmly, but not unkindly.

Ashish trembled and loosened his grip. He held his breath and fought hard against the tears that sprang to his eyes.

Babu approached so quietly that Ashish never saw him coming. The servant grabbed the boy by the shoulder and, pushing him ahead at arm's length, steered him over to the corner where a bucket of cold water awaited him. Babu stripped off the boy's filthy clothes, all the while making faces and murmuring "ghastly!" and "disgusting!" He scrubbed the tender little body until Ashish wept and begged him to stop. Babu sighed and handed Ashish new clothes. New to Ashish, that is. They were actually Saji Stephen's old ones. With clipped words that barely hid his disdain, Babu instructed the boy to dress.

"Hurry up with him," Saji Stephen ordered crossly. "I want to play."

Babu nodded and handed the still-dripping boy over to him.

Saji Stephen held out the wooden top Ashish had given him. "Show me how to play this game," he said.

Again and again, Ashish spun the top on the hard ground. Every time, Saji Stephen would say, "Let *me* do it!" But every time he tried, the top bounced and fell over on its side. And every time that happened, Saji Stephen stamped his feet and screamed a little louder.

"You must not do anything to annoy him!" That's what Ashish's *appa* warned. His *amma* had told him the same thing, and Devi whispered it again as she let go of his hand. Ashish started to shake so badly that he could hardly hold the top straight. When he tried to spin it, he dropped it and it bounced on the ground.

"Ha!" Saji Stephen said. "You are worse than me! I can throw it better than you can! You are a stupid boy! Now I want to play something else."

From then on, whenever they played with the top, Ashish took great care to bounce it so it would tip over. And when Saji Stephen chased him, he made it a point to stumble and fall. And when they threw stones at broken pots, he would be certain to miss every time.

"I'm better than you!" Saji Stephen bragged.

Only a little child, but already Ashish had discovered the secret of being a good slave boy.

No one seemed to know who renewed the settlement's flagging interest in doing *puja* before the pieced-together god house. Someone laid a couple of palm leaves over the idols, and one by one, people fashioned a structure to shade them from the burning sun. Most offerings were handfuls of rice, but some people still managed to leave a piece of coconut, or a banana, or even an occasional chip of fragrant sandalwood to please the gods.

When Latha suggested perhaps they should make a special offering, Virat said, "Why should we waste good food that we can save as a treat for our son?"

"Hush, Husband!" Latha warned. "You mustn't say such things in the presence of the gods!"

Virat shook his head. "We offer and we offer, yet no blessings come to us."

"One blessing did," Latha said. "We still have Ashish."

The fields, sun-baked to a warm brown, stood stark against the distant gray-blue mountains. Any piece of earth not covered with water dried hard and split open in the heat. Even the paddies were in danger of drying out. Virat shaded his eyes and looked to the sky. Not a single cloud. No hope for rain. Maybe a light shower would fall, if they were fortunate. Perhaps just enough to moisten the thirsty land, should the gods smile on them. Then again, probably not.

Two men sat idle in what mud remained in the rice paddy. Virat said nothing to them. He simply directed his team of sluggish water buffaloes around them. What could he say? Everyone struggled at the edge of exhaustion. The workers simply could not continue such strenuous labor under the relentless sun.

"You do not offer sacrifices to the gods?" Anup asked Virat.

"Latha will bring rice to the altar."

"Rice? That's all? Virat, one does not offer to the gods what one has. One offers what one likes best."

Virat, his face set, made no answer.

"Look at the luxury of the other offerings. Buttermilk and fruits and garlands of flowers."

"And rice," Virat said, pointing to the many lumps laid out before the various gods and goddesses. "Perhaps the ones who left those offerings, like us, live their lives under a curse."

❧

Ashish, tied up like a bullock and hitched to a little wooden cart, stood still and waited for Saji Stephen to hit him with a branch and yell, "Go!" Ashish hated this game. He struggled so to pull the cart. It hurt when Saji Stephen hit him with the switch. "Faster, faster! Pull me faster!" Saji Stephen commanded.

Ashish stumbled and fell to his knees. "Stupid bullock!" Saji Stephen cried. And he rained blow after blow down on the child's head and shoulders.

"You must not do anything to annoy him!" That's what his *appa* and *amma* had told him. That's what Devi said. Ashish's lip began to quiver and he felt the hot rush of tears. But at that very moment he saw a strange sight out on the road.

"Look!" he called to Saji Stephen. "A man crawling like a baby!"

Saji Stephen jumped up and down and clapped his hands. "It's a beggar!"

"What's wrong with him?"

"I don't know. He's sick or something."

"He could go see the pale English lady," Ashish suggested. "She would make him better."

"Phoo! He's too sick for the English lady to fix him. Let's go see who he is."

Saji Stephen ran toward the road, and Ashish followed after him, carefully choosing his steps.

So many beggars came along the road that Parmar Ruth Varghese had left strict instructions that a separate bowl of rice should always be available for them. But Saji Stephen didn't pay any attention to the bowl of beggar rice. When the boys got close, Saji Stephen stopped and called out to Ashish, "Look how funny he walks. On his hands and feet with his knees sticking out. He looks like a spider crawling along."

"The pale English lady would pray for him," Ashish offered. "She would sing him to sleep at night."

"Maybe he has leprosy," Saji Stephen said. "My *appa* says lepers are not welcome here."

Saji Stephen grabbed up a rock and threw it at the beggar.

"What are you doing?" Ashish cried. "You'll hurt him!"

But already Saji Stephen had grabbed up two handfuls of rocks. One large stone hit the man on his back. He fell to the side and cried out. The next rock hit him in the back of the head.

"Stop it!" Ashish cried.

With a laugh, Saji Stephen turned his aim and threw a rock at Ashish. It missed, so he threw another. It also missed. But the third rock caught Ashish on the side of his forehead and knocked him cold.

The next thing Ashish knew, he was coughing and choking. Babu had thrown a bucket of water in his face. As soon as the boy's eyes opened, Babu pulled him to his feet and led him to the veranda to lie down.

Mammen Samuel paused in his work to watch as the little child staggered toward him. "What happened to the boy?" he asked.

"The beggar has leprosy," Saji Samuel said. "Ashish kept running after him and it made him mad. I told Ashish to stop, but he wouldn't, so the beggar with leprosy threw a rock at him and hit him in the head. It's the beggar's fault. It's Ashish's fault."

"Fool!" Mammen Samuel chided Ashish. "Babu, get him to the girl in the garden and tell her to take him home."

"But I want him!" Saji Stephen howled.

"He is a stupid, stupid boy. But you can have him back another day."

✦

"Fire!" Anup called.

The laborers stopped their work to stare. Beyond the village, clouds of smoke poured straight up into the air. It couldn't be the landlord's house on fire. No, the smoke billowed too far away for that. It wasn't actually coming from the village at all. Even so, the sight of that smoky haze, growing and swelling so rapidly, struck terror into everyone. In the hot summer months, fire was the great fear. Dry stalks of grain could spontaneously ignite, and before anyone could stop it, an entire year's crop could be lost—not to mention nearby houses and the people who lived in them.

By now, Landlord Varghese's wheat had hardened. His sheds packed tight with sheaves of dry stalks could be the next to catch fire and burn.

Anup jumped up on the watchman's platform and called out, "We have work to do! Virat and all the rest of you in that front line, come with me now. The rest of you, get back to work in the paddy! Everyone, early tomorrow morning, we will begin threshing the wheat."

Anup pointed out the threshing ground on the other side of the storage sheds. "Plaster the floor with mud," he said. "It will dry quickly and hard in this heat."

Early the next morning, before the sun arose, Virat followed Anup and the other men to the threshing ground. With brooms made of twigs lashed together, they swept the newly mud-plastered floor smooth and free of loose dirt. When the other workers arrived, the threshing floor lay ready for them to spread out the stalks of grain. With a rustling that sounded like a great wind, hoards of rats—too many to count—scurried out from their nests in the wheat sheaves and ran for the safety of the fields.

After the workers had spread all the wheat out across the floor, a stocky man with bulging muscles—followed by half a dozen older boys—led ten animals to the threshing floor. Bullocks, mostly, and water buffalo, but also two cows. Virat and Anup fastened each animal to the large stake at the center of the floor and led the animals around and around and around it.

With grunts and huffs, the animals trod and stamped their heavy hooves over and over the stalks scattered across the floor. Round and round they went, their hooves knocking the grain off the stalks. Men hunkered along the sides, gathering up the untrampled stalks that had been forced to the outside, and pushed them back in under the animals' crushing hooves. Others rushed in between the stamping hooves to clean up after the animals.

Round and round the animals trod, trampling and stamping and crushing and flattening. One entire day. Two days. Three more days. They kept it up until those heavy hooves had knocked off every last grain. When the stocky man and boys finally led the animals back to their field, men swooped in with forked sticks to throw off the straw. Women followed them to sweep up the grain and chaff that remained on the floor and pile it into large winnowing baskets.

"Over here!" Anup called to the women. He and several other men climbed up onto ruggedly constructed three-legged stools. The women handed their winnowing baskets up to the men.

"Wind gods!" Anup yelled. "Do not hide your breath from us!"

"We serve you!" another man shouted. "Now you must not play your games against us!"

"Send the wind to blow!" the men ordered. "You have no right to withhold your breath and—"

As a sudden gust blustered, the men turned their baskets upside down. The wind caught the light chaff and carried it away, but the heavy kernels of wheat fell back to the threshing floor.

With cheers and shouts, other men rushed in with twig brooms and swept the kernels into piles so that the women could shovel them into sacks.

"A fine harvest!" Anup announced. "An extra measure of rice tonight for every man and every woman!"

⁂

When Latha got back to her hut, sore and exhausted from the hard day's work, she found Ashish inside, lying on the sleeping mat. She first noticed his black eye and the cut on his temple, surrounded by a huge purple and red bruise.

"What happened to you, my son?" Latha exclaimed.

The boy shook his head and turned his face away.

Latha sat down beside him. Ashish scooted over and laid his head in his mother's lap. The two of them cried together.

# 24
## July

All through the long, hot summer, Saji Stephen sent for Ashish to come and play with him. Ashish wept and begged to stay at home. He grabbed for his mother's hands and clung to her *sari*. But Virat gently pulled him away.

"It is not for you to decide, my son," he said. "It is not for your *amma* to decide, or for me, either. When the landlord calls, you must go."

No longer was Ashish the happy child who had scrambled about hunting for firewood with Little Girl. No longer was he the laughing boy who had scurried up the mango tree in search of fruit. Now he trembled at the sound of a raised voice and stammered when he talked. If he wasn't called to go to the master's house, Ashish huddled in the hut and waited alone for his *amma* to return. When she did, he clung to her and followed her everywhere she went. And when she sat down, he laid his head in her lap and wept.

"We cannot stay here," Latha whispered to Virat.

"We cannot go," Virat replied in a voice old and exhausted.

The rice paddies had been thoroughly weeded and the laborers were busy thinning the crops when the first clouds appeared high in the early July sky.

Everyone saw them and heaved sighs of hope.

The broiling sun shimmered on the horizon. It would have baked the earth, had everything not already been seared to a crisp. Three times, Anup had the men open the water trenches from the river wider in order to keep the newly planted rice flooded. One morning the laborers had found a dead leopard lying in the field. The poor animal was bone thin, his coat dull and faded. Not enough water for it to survive. Not enough water for his prey to survive, either.

A few days after the first cloud sighting, clouds grew darker and more numerous. The workers stopped to watch them rolling up in banks from the direction of the sea. "Back to work!" Anup ordered. "Finish the thinning quickly!"

When they came back to the settlement for their afternoon break, Hilmi walked out of his palm leaf hut, his family following after him in a straight line.

"We will leave here today," he told Anup. "Please give us our pay."

Anup ran his calloused hand across his face. "You have already received your pay," he said. "The landlord says to tell you it went to pay for your family's food and shelter."

"Our shelter? We built our hut with our own hands."

"But you built it on land that belongs to the landlord," Anup said. "Master Landlord charges rent for his land."

Hilmi stared hard. His wild black eyes bored into Anup.

"You are a good worker," Anup said with a heavy sigh. "I thank you and your family for that. But the landlord has his own way of payment. I cannot change his mind and neither can you."

A look of disgust crossed the dark, untamed face. Without a word, Hilmi turned and walked away from the settlement. His family, their eyes straight ahead, followed along behind him.

And then the rains came. Great pouring torrents pounded down. The mountains roared with thunder and flashed with lightning. A cool breeze crossed the settlement as the thirsty ground drank in the water.

"The rains!" the workers rejoiced. "Finally the rains have come!"

Men stood outside in the soaking deluge and laughed out loud. Women danced and sang. Children chased each other and slid in the mud. Soon the ground would be green again. Soon the world would be revived.

✿❤

Latha gave Little Girl strict instructions to call her when Sethu's baby came. "You don't need to tell your *amma* I said so," she added, for she knew Sethu wouldn't want help. Sethu might be a midwife to the fancy ladies, but she considered herself fortunate if she could simply bear her baby in the comfort and privacy of her hut. Each of her other babies had been born in paddies among the rice plants.

As soon as Latha saw Little Girl running toward her, she knew that the baby boy had arrived. She hurried toward Sethu's hut and shouted for joy when she heard the muffled cry of a newborn.

"Oh, Sethu!" Latha exclaimed as she ducked through the door. "I can tell he is healthy from his cry. He sounds so—"

"Not *he*."

"What?"

"It is another girl. The fortune-teller told the truth in the first place. He took my carved bracelet and gave me worthless charms even though he knew. I have borne my husband yet another girl."

Latha peeked over at the tiny, scrunched face and said, "Oh, Sethu. But she is such a beautiful one."

"What have I done to deserve this curse?" Sethu screamed. "What have I done to earn such a punishment?"

"Your children may be girls," Latha said, "but they are very fine girls."

"Pshaw!" Sethu sneered. "Only Devi brings money to the family, and she will be the first one married and gone. Lidya is a good cook and keeps the floor swept, and that is helpful to me, but she is scarred and ugly. Who will marry such a one? Little Girl and Baby are nothing but two curses on us. If they both disappeared tomorrow, no one would cry for them."

"Sethu!" Latha exclaimed. "How can you say such a thing about those sweet little girls?"

"Get out!" Sethu roared to Latha. "Get out of my house!

For two days, torrential sheets of water poured from the sky. Latha lit a cooking fire close to the hut, but it wouldn't burn long before the rain washed it out. "I'm sorry, Husband," she said as she handed Virat a bowl of half-cooked rice. "I couldn't keep the fire hot enough to cook it soft."

Rain washed mud into the hut and rain pounded Latha's pepper plant into the ground. Finally, on the third day, the rain began to slow. Although the sky stayed dark and threatening, every woman took the opportunity to gather wood and cook a real meal for her family. Then she paused to breathe in the rain-freshened air.

Already the trees were festooned with tiny buds of new leaves. Birds reappeared in their branches, and insects that had been burned away once again buzzed around people's faces and flew into their cooking pots.

"It's so wet and muddy," Virat said to Anup. "A most difficult time to have a new baby."

"Another girl," Anup said flatly. "My daughters hang around my neck like cursed millstones."

Virat could think of nothing to say.

"My brother has three sons," Anup said. "He is a wealthy man. I have four daughters. Five now. And what am I? An impoverished slave. Five girls! You tell me, Virat, where am I to get the thousands of rupees I will need to marry these girls off? If I cannot get the dowry money, I will be stuck with them forever, eternally disgraced by the unmarried daughters that remain in my house."

Sethu stepped out of the hut. "The baby is gone," she said.

Virat and Anup stared at her uncomprehendingly. But Latha, who stood off to the side, gasped out loud. "What have you done?" she cried as she ran to Sethu.

"I took away the added curse," Sethu said with not the least sign of emotion. "Now we have the four girls again."

"Oh, Sethu!" Latha cried. "What did you do to the baby?"

"I put her in an earthen pot and covered the opening, and I buried the pot deep in the ground. By now, the baby has left this life and is free to begin a new one."

A scream tore from Latha, and she fell to her knees in the mud. She threw the end of her *sari* over her face as her scream faded into an agonized wail.

"The fortune-teller told the truth," Sethu said. "That baby was born under the wrong star. The moon was in a bad position. It could not survive."

"If you didn't want her, I would have taken her," Latha sobbed.

"No, it is best that she be made to suffer for her sins," Sethu answered. "To suffer is her *karma*. If I didn't do this, the baby would have died some other way. She was not meant to live. She could not escape her *karma*."

"It is true that the baby is now a freed spirit," Anup agreed. "She does have a new chance now."

"Come," Virat said as he took Latha's arm. "Come on home with me."

"Yes, that would be best," Anup said. "Go to your own hut. We shall never again speak of the baby."

# 25

*R*oaring wind snatched the fronds off Hilmi's palm hut and tossed them to all ends of the courtyard. It ripped off the woven door and flung it into the well. Only Jeeja's cook pit and the rock Hilmi claimed as his favorite seat remained unmoved.

Devi picked her way through the storm and peeked into Virat's hut. "Come, Ashish," she said softly. "The landlord sent for you."

Ashish crumpled onto the floor and sobbed. "No, no! Please don't make me go. Please, *Appa*, please!"

Virat looked helplessly from his son to Devi. Such a young child she was. In her soul, she must have wept the very same words.

"If you don't go, the landlord will come looking for you," Virat said. "He will be very angry and will punish you."

"I don't care," Ashish said. "Please, *Appa*, don't make me go."

"Come along, Ashish," Devi said. "Maybe the road will be flooded. Maybe a tree blew down to block our way. If that happened I can bring you back home and the landlord can say nothing."

Ashish wiped his hand across his eyes and nose. He took hold of Devi's hand and walked out with her into the rain.

Latha, who could not trust herself to speak in front of Ashish, threw the end of her *sari* over her head and wailed.

Virat wiped his hand over his face. A good man should obey his master, but a good man should also watch out for his family. He should be honest and true to his agreements, but he should also protect his son. He should yield to *karma*, but he should also do what is right. Right there lay the big question, of course. What was right? Why did the gods accept his sacrifices and still permit evil curses to slither into his path and rip his family apart?

"When I was a despised *chamar* and we lived on the edge of the mud hut settlement, we were nothing," Virat said. "But look at us now. We live next to the great landlord, and work in his fields, and we are less than nothing."

Latha mopped at her face and hiccuped. "It is our *karma*," she lamented.

"No, it is not our *karma!*" Virat insisted. "We have been driven to this by people, not by gods or spirits or even demons!"

Once again, Latha started to sob.

"You were right from the first," Virat said. "We must leave here. We must get away."

Latha wiped the corner of her *sari* across her face. It shocked Virat to see how weary and drawn she looked. How tired and worn. How old his Latha had grown.

"Hilmi left," Latha said. "His whole family walked away and no one tried to stop them."

"The landlord didn't own them. They didn't owe him money."

"Our debt must be quite small by now," Latha said. "You and I have worked such long hours. And what of Ashish? Every day he goes to play with that awful boy. That must count as hours of work."

Virat said nothing, but a shadow of despair passed over him. He had heard Anup's words. The landlord had his own way of figuring debts and payments, and no one could change his mind.

Even so, the debt was not Virat's greatest concern. His greatest concern lay with Ashish. Virat and Latha were nothing but untouchable laborers who could do little work in these months of pouring rain. Long before the rice harvest, the landlord could get other laborers to move into their hut and do their work. But Ashish—he would not be so easily replaced. If Ashish were gone, the landlord's boy would stamp his feet and yell, and the master would do everything in his enormous power to force Ashish back.

"The monsoon rains could help us," Latha said, as though she could read her husband's thoughts. "It won't be so easy for the landlord's men to come after us."

The surging storm smashed against their hut, sending pieces of the roof flying.

"It won't be easy for us, either," Virat said.

The sun sank low, but Devi didn't bring Ashish home. Even when night fell, she didn't bring him home. Virat spread the sleeping mat out in the hut and he and Latha lay down side by side. The two children would not be able to come through the pounding rain and fierce winds. Certainly not after dark. But where was Ashish this night? Sleeping in the barn with Devi, perhaps? Certainly the landlord would not allow him in their fine house.

"Maybe we could make it to the coast where Hilmi's tribe lives," Virat said. "What difference does it make if they treat us as outcastes? We are outcastes here. We will be outcastes wherever we go."

"If we went back to our mud hut in the village, maybe the landlord's men wouldn't follow us until the rains pass. That would give us time to find another village," Latha said. "Pooni will help us."

For a long time they lay side by side listening to the fury of the storm.

"We did it once before," Virat said. The crushing weariness had left his voice. "We left everything and everyone we knew and found a new home in a different village in a different place. It wasn't easy, but we did it. If we did it once, we can do it again."

"Back then, no one chased after us," Latha reminded him. "When we left there, we thought our troubles were behind us, but now here we are again. Could it be that slavery is our *karma*?"

"We will speak no more of *karma*! I would rather we all die on our legs than live on our knees."

## 26

*E*very morning, Ranjun paused at the door of his shop, bowed low and touched the dust of the threshold to his forehead. "To guard my luck," he told his sons. "To keep my contact with the gods clear and strong."

Ranjun refused to eat rice and vegetables unless Pooni poured a generous amount of *ghee* over them. The clarified butter carried a high price, and no one else in the family was allowed to taste it. But Ranjun considered it an important part of his diet. He was determined to make himself fat. "Poor people are thin," he insisted. "Rich people are fat. I want everyone to see my prosperity in the layers around my belly."

If everything pleased him, Ranjun sighed and grunted and went about his work. If it did not, he flew into a terrifying rage.

"Do not go near him," Pooni warned little Mayawati. "If he calls to you, run away and hide."

But Ranjun's orders terrified the child. "You come when I call you!" he yelled, and he punctuated his command with a smashing slap that knocked the little girl flat.

Mayawati did everything she could to make herself invisible. She sank into the walls, she disappeared into the shadows, she hid away in secret places that only her brothers knew.

When Pooni came back from the English Mission Medical Clinic, she went directly to the fire pit and started a fire. The water jug was already full, so she filled the cooking pot and put in two handfuls of rice. She bent over the garden and cut vegetables, which was hard to do without cringing, for she still ached badly from the beating.

Ranjun and the boys were at work in the pottery shed. Pooni could hear the rhythmic thump of Ranjun's foot on the potter's wheel and his periodic bark of an order to one boy or the other.

"Mayawati!" Pooni called softly. "Come to *Amma*. Don't be afraid. You can come to *Amma*!"

No answer.

The child had taken refuge in one of her hiding places, Pooni thought. She'd probably been hiding ever since she saw her father brutally attack her mother. Poor little girl—so frightened. Poor, poor little child!

As the rice cooked, Pooni stirred in curry and prepared chutney, just the way Ranjun liked it. She scooped out a large helping of the spiced rice onto a pottery plate for her husband. Then she took out the jar of *ghee* and poured the clear liquid over his dinner. Ranjun, of course, would eat first, seated comfortably on pillows spread across the veranda.

Pooni stayed inside while Ranjun ate, slurping his food and smacking his lips loudly. His hand churned round and round as he grabbed up the pieces of rice, dripping with sauce and butter, and stuffed them into his mouth. *He is a wicked man*, Pooni thought. *A cruel and wicked man*.

When Ranjun finished eating, he pulled himself up and spread out the sleeping mat so he could rest while the boys ate their meal. Pooni longed to ask Ravi and Jinil about their little sister's hiding place, but how could she with Ranjun listening to their every word? So she brought food for her sons, but she said nothing.

As soon as Ravi and Jinil finished eating, Ranjun ordered, "Get back to work, you lazy boys!"

Pooni divided up what was left of the food onto two banana leaves, one for her and one to save for Mayawati. Pooni ate her share, but still the girl did not come.

✍

When dusk fell, Ranjun closed up the pottery shed. He and the boys cleaned themselves up and settled on the veranda.

"Ravi," Pooni asked her oldest son, "have you seen your sister?"

Ravi shot a nervous glance at his brother, but said nothing.

Cold terror crept up Pooni's back. She looked at Ranjun and demanded, "Where is Mayawati?"

Ranjun stood up. Carefully he adjusted his *mundu*, pulling it high at the waist in the manner of the upper castes. "Did I not tell you, Wife?" he said in a calculated, casual tone. "I sold the girl."

Pooni's legs lost their strength and she fell to the ground.

"Good money she brought me, too."

"Who did you sell her to?" Pooni gasped.

"A businessman of the *Vaisya* caste. He is taking her to a brothel where he will make himself even a better trade, I have no doubt."

"A brothel!" Pooni cried. "Where is it? We must find her and bring her home before it is too late!"

"Oh, no. That's not possible. It is already too late."

"I will find my daughter!" Pooni screamed. "If I must walk all over India, I will find her and bring her home!"

"She is gone," Ranjun said. "Forget her."

Pooni's voice rose to a shriek. She curled up on the ground and pounded her forehead in the dirt.

Her hands shaking, Pooni carefully measured a large portion of *ghee* into a new earthenware pot. She pulled her *sari* up over her head and, with the *ghee* clutched in her hand, hurried to the place of the village god. The rain had stopped and the sun smiled through the clouds. Too bad. On this day, Pooni would have preferred the rain.

"For my daughter," Pooni murmured. She laid out her offering and poured the entire pot of expensive *ghee* over it. "For my Mayawati."

When Pooni returned to the house, Ranjun demanded, "Where were you? I called for water and you were not here to bring it to me."

But Pooni's ears didn't hear him. For all the difference it made to her, she was in the house alone. Pooni said not a word as she gathered up firewood.

"Prepare a platter of sweets for me," Ranjun ordered. "With plenty of sugar and honey and butter."

Pooni loaded firewood into her arms until she could carry no more.

"I had planned to wait until the girl grew older and more beautiful, and take her to the temple to consecrate her to the god Shiva," Ranjun said, a taunting tone to his voice. "If I allowed her to be a bride of Shiva, I could save myself the high cost of a marriage dowry. But is seemed she would stay young forever and I grew tired of waiting. Besides, the businessman paid me a goodly sum for her."

Pooni carried the wood to the fire pit.

"I must tell you, too, that I dealt so wisely with the *Vaisya* that he thought me to be of his own caste!"

Pooni laid the firewood in a large pile on the cooking pit, then she turned her back on Ranjun and went into the house.

✑

Ravi and his younger brother Jinil should not have left their father's pottery shed early that evening. Even though their father stormed about in so foul a temper. Even though they had finished all the work they could do. Even so, they should have stayed until their appointed hour. Or maybe they should have gone to the rice paddy beside the river and collected more clay and sand. Anything except go home early.

When they saw the fire blazing so high, Jinil said, "*Amma* must be cooking something special for us this night."

Ravi quickened his steps.

That's when they saw Pooni jump into the blaze. With the fire roaring up around her, she sat down peacefully and folded her hands.

Jinil screamed and clutched at his big brother. Ravi knew he must do something, but all he could manage was a terrified gasp as he watched in horror.

Pooni opened her eyes wide and looked straight at her sons before the flames consumed her.

"That foolish woman!" Ranjun bellowed from behind the boys. "That filthy insect of a wife! Just look what she has done! Now who will gather fodder for the cow?"

Because he did not know what else to do, Ranjun sent Ravi to the master's settlement to fetch Virat. "He is a *chamar*," Ranjun said. "He knows how to handle the dead."

Virat, his eyes stinging with tears, dug a hole and buried Pooni's bones along with the polluted ashes. But he said no prayers over her and he offered no sacrifices. Ranjun was nowhere to be found, but Ravi and Jinil stood off to the side and watched in silence.

"Your mother was a kind woman," Virat told the boys. "Perhaps she will come back as a gentle cow."

"Her life held no hope," Ravi said, his voice flat and bitter. "That's why she could not bear to live."

After Virat left, Ravi picked up a large piece of firewood that had not burned and carried it to the pottery shed. Piled against the wall were hundreds of pots, all fired and carefully stacked according to their value. All were ready for sale. Bellowing with rage, young Ravi swung his wood club and smashed the entire stack of pots destined for the Brahmins. As he swung again, Jinil grabbed up pots from the other end of the pile and threw them against the potter's wheel. Ravi turned his fury toward the oven and clubbed it flat. Jinil pounded his way through the remainder of the pots.

When Ravi finally dropped his firewood club, and Jinil wiped the blood from his slashed hands, not one piece of pottery remained intact. They had completely destroyed their father's oven. And his wheel lay upside down, split in two.

"We have no mother and no father," Ravi told his young brother. "We have no little sister. But we do have a craft. You know how to make fine clay, and I know how to fashion good pots. It's easier with a wheel, but I can do it without a wheel. I can fire them without an oven, too, the way we used to do it. We can be the new potters in the settlement."

"Where will we live?" Jinil snuffled through his tears.

"In the house of Virat the *chamar*," Ravi said.

"What if Virat comes back?"

"If he does, then we will talk about it."

For almost a week, Ranjun hid out at his brother's house in another village. When he finally came back to his house and saw the destruction in his shed, he roared in fury. "Ravi! Jinil! Where are you wicked boys? I will find you and beat the life out of you both!" He found them at Virat's house. Spread across the courtyard lay row upon row of newly fashioned pots, drying in the sun. Fury overtook him all over again. "I am your father and you owe me your respect and affection. You owe me your loyalty, too!" he yelled. "Family members do not compete with family!"

"Go away," Ravi said. "We do not know you. We are our own family now."

"If you compete with me, you will starve to death!"

Family quarrels were not a common occurrence in the settlement. Certainly not loud, angry ones that forced everyone else to be involved. When difficulties did develop, friends were the greatest help at finding a way through the dispute. But Ranjun had no friends. Though many men stood close enough to hear every word he said, not one man came to stand beside him and speak in his defense.

An old carpenter, his face aged into leather, stepped up first. "I'll take two of your best pots there," he said to Ravi.

"They aren't dry yet," Ravi said. "We still have to fire them."

"When they are finished, I'll take two."

"Four for my wife," said the youngest of the weavers, who had recently taken himself a bride. "Two of a larger size and two smaller ones. And how about a large cooking pot for the fire pit? Can you make me one like that?"

"At the new moon, my woman will want an entire new set of pots," the village barber called out.

"Stop!" Ranjun ordered. "Do not talk to my sons as though they were men. I am the potter for this village!"

"Not if the villagers refuse to buy from you," the barber said. "Then you can either starve or leave this village."

"And you stay far away from these boys, too," the weaver warned Ranjun. "We in the village will watch out for them."

"Can you do the work for us?" the carpenter asked Ravi and Jinil.

"Yes. Yes, of course," Ravi said. "We will start tomorrow."

When Virat told Latha that Pooni was no more, she covered her face and wept. "Where are the gods?" she implored. "Where are the ones who demand our sacrifices, our obedience, our worship?"

"They are nowhere," Virat said. "Even *chamars* deserve better than this."

"We can never go back to our mud hut in the settlement, can we?"

"No," Virat said. "Our place in the village is gone. But we will find another place, Wife, and we will be happy there."

# 27
## August

*W*edding preparations spilled out of the landlord's house and spread across the village, all the way to the workers' settlement. The timing could not have been better. With the rice paddies flooded and more rain pouring down each day, Anup needed only a few workers to maintain the fences and guard the fields against thieves. But Mammen Samuel Varghese required all kinds of crafts people, and he had them ready in his settlement.

A singer to entertain the wedding guests? A stout man by the name of Hadia Behara, who lived in the hut behind Virat's, happened to be a professional singer already known in the village. And since he owed so great a debt to Mammen Samuel, his services would cost the landowner nothing. Potters to provide an entirely new set of fine pots to cook the wedding feast? Mammen Samuel owned many excellent potters. Carpenters to construct the wedding pavilion? Ten were already at work on it, and they had their own tools too. Tailors to sew new wedding clothes for the entire family? A whole array of tailors lived in the settlement. All Mammen Samuel needed to do was choose the best among them and let his family's wishes be known.

"If we ever hope to escape, now is the time," Virat whispered to Latha. "With so much happening around us, it could be days before anyone notices we are missing."

"We can head toward the mountains," Latha said. "We can go to my father's village."

"Our plans must be carefully laid. And we must watch every word we speak. Say nothing to Ashish."

"We have so few belongings to get ready," Latha said.

"Then let us leave in the dark of this very night. By sun-up, we will be well on our way."

*❧*

The entire village buzzed with gossip about the wedding. "There will be food for everyone," a woman in an orange *sari* whispered excitedly to Prem Rao when she stopped to buy pepper and turmeric at his spice stand. When the woman left, three others came along in search of *marsala* spices, and Prem Rao passed the news along to them. "There will be food for everyone, and all castes will be invited to the feast!"

One of the three women hurried home and told her husband, the seller of salt, "There will be food for everyone, and all castes will be invited to the feast, and all of them will sit together and eat together!" The seller of salt saw his neighbor mending a plow, so he stopped to tell the news: "There will be food for everyone, and all castes will be invited to the feast, and all of them will sit together and eat together for an entire week!" And so it went.

It pained Parmar Ruth to see her gentle daughter preparing to leave her home and family at the age of twelve. She herself had not married Mammen Samuel Varghese until she was a fully developed young woman—perhaps all of fourteen years old. Parmar Ruth had been considered a beauty, and many families had vied for her as a bride for their young men. Her hopes were so high, and then on her wedding day, when she finally gazed upon the man her family had selected for her, she sobbed.

"Tears of joy," the guests whispered, but of course, they were not. No one would call Mammen Samuel Varghese a handsome man, and his voice was anything but gentle. Still, his family had wealth, and he treated Parmar Ruth kindly. And their children, as well. Perhaps that was the most a wife should expect from a husband.

Mammen Samuel, who prided himself on being an astute businessman, counted and recounted the mounting costs of his daughter's wedding. Why, for the dowry alone he had been forced to pay a king's ransom in rupees! Yet, what could he say? His uncle had done well to arrange so fine a marriage—a Christian bridegroom, a man of twenty-six years, rich and perfectly qualified in every way. And since the money had already been spent, Mammen Samuel took every opportunity to brag about the prestigious union he has secured.

As for Sunita Lois, no one knew how she felt. No one cared. In her chest of personal belongings she kept a rosewood dowry box her grandmother had given her when Sunita Lois was but a little girl. "Put special things inside that make you happy," her grandmother had said. "You will need them when you marry. It is not easy to be a wife."

Sunita Lois took out the oddly shaped rosewood box and ran her fingers across the polished wood, then over the cast brass fittings. She drew the key from her shelf in her mother's wardrobe cupboard and fit it into the brass lock. She had only a few things inside the box: A jasmine blossom, once beautiful and fragrant, but now brown and crumbling. A gold necklace and a tiny solid gold leopard, both gifts from her father. A little book of Indian poems. Oh, and a folded paper with the words of Psalm 23 printed on it. Sunita Lois stumbled through the psalm, pointing to each word as she spoke it:

> The Lord is my shepherd; I shall not want;
> He maketh me to lie down in green pastures:
> he leadeth me beside the still waters.
> He restoreth my soul;
> he leadeth me in the paths of righteousness, for his name's sake.
> Yea, though I walk through the valley of the shadow of death,
> I will fear no evil:
> for thou art with me; thy rod and thy staff they comfort me.
> Thou preparest a table before me in the presence of mine enemies;
> thou anointest my head with oil; my cup runneth over.
> Surely goodness and mercy shall follow me all the days of my life;
> and I will dwell in the house of the Lord forever.

Sunita Lois folded up the paper and put it back in the dowry box, closed the box, and locked it. She put it away and slipped the key back into the cupboard.

⚜

Ashish bounded into his hut. "I don't have to go back to play with Saji Stephen for a long time!" he announced.

Latha looked at Devi, who stood at the door.

"At least until after the wedding," Devi said. "Madame Landlord says two boys are one too many."

Latha sneaked a quick look at Virat, but he kept his eyes straight ahead, his face impassive. Latha could not manage it. She smiled in spite of herself.

But Parmar Ruth was wrong. Without the attention to which he had grown accustomed, Saji Stephen became increasingly whiney, sullen, and demanding. He stamped his feet and shrieked and cried at the slightest provocation. When he interrupted yet another consultation to demand, "I want a ride on my elephant! Now!" Parmar Ruth exclaimed in exasperation, "Two boys are *better* than one! Send the garden girl to fetch Ashish! Tell her he will stay here until the wedding is over. She is to sleep in the barn with him at night."

When Devi arrived at their hut, Virat quickly grabbed up his *chaddar* and threw it over the stacked supplies he and Latha had made ready for their escape. "Say nothing about our plans," Virat whispered to Ashish. "Nothing! Not even to Devi."

Ashish took Devi's hand and went with her quietly. But when he turned to look back, his cheeks were wet with tears.

Latha pulled the edge of her *sari* over her head and sobbed. "The curse is on us. We will never get away from here."

"Maybe this wasn't a good day to leave," Virat said. "Maybe it isn't a Tuesday night. Everyone knows travel must begin on a Tuesday night if it is to be successful."

But Latha would not be comforted. She wrung her hands and wept.

"Leave everything where it is," Virat said. "The time will come, and when it does, we will be ready."

❧

Saji Stephen stood at the edge of the garden, waiting. As soon as he saw Ashish and Devi coming up the road, he jumped up and down and called, "Hurry, Ashish! Run!"

Ashish pulled back on Devi's hand and dragged his feet in the mud.

"I have peanuts for us!" Saji called. "Hurry!"

"What are peanuts?" Ashish asked Devi.

"You'll find out," Devi said with a laugh. "Go on to Saji Stephen. I'll come back and get you tonight."

Saji Stephen piled a large handful of peanuts on the ground beside him. "Sit down," he told Ashish. "One . . . two . . . three . . . four . . . five. Five peanuts for you because my *amma* said you have lived for about five rice harvests." Saji Stephen grabbed the rest and pulled them over to himself. "All these are mine because I am your master."

Ashish tried to eat his five peanuts slowly, but they were too good. When they were gone, he didn't want to sit and watch Saji Stephen smacking his lips over his pile of nuts, so he went to examine the rows of sunflowers that grew along the side of the garden. Ashish loved those huge blooms that reached up so high over his head.

Usually, so high, but not now. Now the huge flowers drooped low on their stalks, and the vibrant yellow-gold had faded from their petals.

"What happened to them?" Ashish asked.

"You did that," Saji Stephen said. "You polluted them. You're so stinky and dirty that you make the flowers die."

Ashish looked down at his mud-splattered legs and grimy fingers.

"Everything about you is dirty," Saji Stephen said. "Your face and your hair and your teeth."

Ashamed, Ashish tried to wipe at the dirty splatters.

"I'll show you how to clean your teeth," Saji Stephen said. He ran over to the neem tree at the corner of the house and scratched around in the mud at its base.

"What are you doing?" Ashish asked.

"Looking for a twig from this tree. Just a small one . . . Here! This will do." Saji Stephen held up a muddy twig. "Chew on this and it will clean your teeth."

Ashish took the twig and stared at it. "My *amma* says I'm not supposed to eat mud."

"Wipe the mud off, stupid boy."

Ashish wiped the twig on his clothes, then put it in his mouth and chewed.

At the corner of the veranda, Babu waited with the usual bucket of water and a set of clean clothes. He grabbed Ashish, pulled off his clothes, and started scrubbing. "Don't you get dirty again!" he ordered. "And don't you make Master Saji Stephen dirty, either."

At midafternoon, when the rain returned, the boys were relegated to the big room. "You can play chess," Parmar Ruth suggested. "Or paint a picture."

But as soon as his mother left with Sunita Lois, Saji Stephen bragged, "We have a sitar. I know how to play it." He pointed to Sunita Lois's magnificent instrument propped up against the wall. "I will teach you to play it too."

"No, no! I shouldn't touch it," Ashish protested.

"You have to do what I say," Saji Stephen insisted. "I am your master. I say you have to learn to play my sister's sitar, so you must."

"No, please. I can't."

"First, sit down with your legs crossed," Saji Stephen said.

Reluctantly, Ashish sat.

"Put the round part by your feet and hold the long, thin part straight up."

Saji Stephen grabbed the rosewood neck and pulled the sitar away from the wall. But the instrument turned out to be much larger than he had realized and much heavier too. When he tried to move it, it crashed to the floor.

"What happened?" Parmar Ruth called as she rushed into the great room with Sunita Lois right behind her.

Ashish sat cross-legged in the middle of the floor, and the sitar lay upside-down beside him.

"You naughty, naughty boys!" Sunita Lois cried.

Saji Stephen's face took on a look of great distress. He pointed to Ashish and said, "He did it! He wanted to play it. I told him to leave it alone, but he wouldn't listen to me. He dropped it on the floor!"

Parmar Ruth turned on Ashish in exasperation. "You are nothing but trouble! Saji Stephen brings you into our house to play with him, and you do this! Go back to your hovel and don't ever come back!"

"No, *Amma*," Saji Stephen wailed. "He will be good. I want him to stay and play with me. I'll make him be good."

Parmar Ruth sighed. "You are a lucky boy to have someone as kind as Saji Stephen to look out for you," she said to Ashish. "I only hope you appreciate him and stop causing such trouble." She patted Saji Stephen on the head and hurried to resume her preparations. Behind her back, Saji Stephen smirked and stuck out his tongue.

*⨯❧*

"Your uncle chose well for us. Sunita Lois will have a good husband," Mammen Samuel said as he came up behind Boban Joseph.

The boy gave a start and blushed with embarrassment. He had been staring at Devi as she worked in the garden. All day he had tried to talk to her, but whenever he got close, she managed to pull away.

"The next wedding will be for you, my son. Already your uncle has been talking with the parents of a prize girl in the next village. Her landlord father is even wealthier than I. The girl is pure and lovely, and much younger than that common Untouchable over there." His eyes went to ten-year-old Devi. "Five years from now, your wedding will be the greatest event either of our villages has ever seen. You shall be paraded through the town on the back of a splendid elephant, not a scrawny beast like Saji Stephen's pet."

Boban Joseph's eyes glistened at the thought. It would be the most important day of his life. No more would he be bossed around and treated as a boy. Once he married, he would be respected as a man. He would be free to do whatever he wanted. But it would not happen for five more years, and five years was a very long time.

Mammen Samuel also smiled at the thought. What prestige such a marriage would bring to his family! And great security too. For when he had a well-married son, and his holdings were joined to those of a family with lands and cattle and riches far beyond his own, it would guarantee a comfortable old age for him and his wife. Of course, Boban Joseph would attend to them until their dying days. As eldest son, it was his sacred duty to do so.

*❧*

In the early morning light, Ashish turned over on his bed of straw and reached out for Devi. "What's happening?" he asked.

"Hurry and get up!" Devi said. "They're getting the elephant ready for the bridegroom's procession."

It was the day before the wedding—the day to placate the evil spirits so that they would not harm the bridegroom. As Devi led Ashish out of the barn, they passed by the elephant groomers, already at work cleaning and decorating Saji

Stephen's elephant. Two men painted intricate designs on its ears and legs. Others laid a brightly colored banner, studded with gold and jewels, over the animal's head. Fashioned to fit between its eyes, it reached halfway down its trunk.

"Is Saji Stephen going to ride the elephant?" Ashish asked.

"No," said Devi. "The bridegroom will ride it. All the way through town, and maybe even out to our huts in the settlement. And all along the way, he will throw out handfuls of coins."

"Money?"

"Yes. And anyone can pick it up. Maybe even your *amma* and *appa*. Maybe mine, too."

"And then the evil spirits will leave the bridegroom alone?"

"Yes. If he throws out enough money."

"He could throw some to us," Ashish said. "Oh, Devi, I wish he would throw some to us."

✿

On the day of the wedding, Devi again roused Ashish early. Already Babu busily scrubbed Saji Stephen with a bucket of water that smelled of sweet sandalwood. He had a new set of pure white clothes to wear. Next came Ashish's turn. Using Saji Samuel's leftover water, Babu scrubbed Ashish from the tips of his muddy toes to the top of his gritty head. Fresh clothes awaited him too—though not new ones and not white ones.

"Don't you get a speck of dust on yourself!" Babu ordered Ashish. "If you do, I will beat you with a stick and make you wash these clothes until they are spotless!" To Saji Stephen he said, "Play inside and don't get dirty. If you do, it will make your *amma* very sad. And the evil spirits will come in the middle of the night and get you!"

Boban Joseph, already washed and dressed in his new clothes, went out to invite the bridegroom to the wedding. This would be his most important job.

"Otherwise, the bridegroom wouldn't even come," Saji Stephen explained to Ashish.

The bridegroom arrived like a king, sitting in a fancy chair with a fringed roof and two doors, carried on long wooden poles painted with gold paint.

"That's a palanquin," Saji Stephen told Ashish. "It's only for kings and very important people like my family. You must never ride in one."

Villagers crowded around to watch and to listen to the music.

"This has to be the best procession ever," Saji Stephen said. "Because *Appa* says people will talk about it for years. Only until I get married, though, because my procession will be much better. Better even than Boban Joseph's!"

Ashish and Saji Stephen sat stiffly on the couch in the great room and waited. When they heard voices out on the veranda, they jumped up and ran to watch.

"Your sister!" Ashish breathed. Sunita Lois wore a yellow *sari*, far fancier than any clothing he had ever seen.

"Those are her friends and our relatives crowded around her," Saji Stephen said.

Mammen Samuel Varghese, dressed in a white silk *mundu* and shirt trimmed with gold embroidered threads, raised his hands to receive his daughter. He picked up a silver cup and held it high for several moments before he put it to his lips and drank deeply.

"What was in the cup?" Ashish asked.

"Curds and honey," Saji Stephen said. "It brings good luck."

Ashish didn't see the actual wedding ceremony. When Parmar Ruth came to get Saji Stephen and take him out to the pavilion erected alongside the veranda, she told Babu, "Close that untouchable boy in a back room where he can't cause any trouble."

Ashish stayed alone in the room for a long time. Finally he lay down on the floor and went to sleep.

"Come!"

Ashish rubbed his eyes and looked around. For a minute, he couldn't remember where he was.

"Quickly!" Boban Joseph shook him awake. "Come with me. You must sit with Saji Stephen and keep him quiet."

More people than Ashish had ever seen in his life sat in groups on the floor of the pavilion. Everyone looked to be there, from clusters of upper caste people down to groups of Untouchables. As promised, they all sat on the floor together, an acceptable arrangement so long as everyone took scrupulous care to dip their hands only in their own caste's bowls of food. Also, as long as they positioned themselves in such a way so as not to cause them to gaze into the face of someone of a different caste.

But Ashish's eyes were not on the people. He stared at the food. Never had he seen so much! Never had he seen such a variety. Rice patty cakes of *idli* and big pancakes called *dosa*. *Chutney* and *sambar*. Plenty of fish and curds. Pitchers of *ghee* to pour over everything. Each dish had been prepared by Brahmin cooks, of course. That way, every caste could eat it.

"Over here," Boban Joseph said. He led Ashish to Saji Stephen who sat alone with bowls of food spread out before him. "Don't you get into trouble!"

As soon as Boban Joseph left, Saji Stephen said, "I don't want rice and vegetables. I'll get us something better to eat."

Saji Stephen jumped up and dashed over to a table off to the side, hidden behind a curtain. Ashish took the opportunity to dip his right hand into the bowl and grab a bite of *idli* and *chutney*. He smacked his lips and grabbed another bite. By the time Saji Stephen came back, his hands piled full, Ashish had popped a fifth bite into his mouth .

"Mmmmm, *ras-gola*," Saji Stephen said.

He stuffed one of the soft, syrup-soaked cheeseballs into his mouth. "Taste one," he said as he grabbed another for himself.

The spongy sweet had to be the most delicious thing Ashish had ever tasted! It melted into sugary pleasure in his mouth.

But by the time Ashish finished eating his, Saji Stephen had already finished the other two. "I'll get some more," Saji Stephen said. He ducked behind the curtain and came back with his hands full again—and this time, dripping with sticky syrup.

"Your clothes!" Ashish cried in alarm. He pointed to the brown syrup that ran down the front of Saji Stephen's new shirt. "It will make your *amma* very sad, and the evil spirits will come in the middle of the night and get you!"

"Babu always says that, but it never happens," Saji Stephen said. He held the sweets out to Ashish. "Do you want some or shall I eat them all?"

Ashish put a second gooey sweet in his mouth, and Saji Stephen stuffed two more in his.

"What are you boys doing?" Parmar Ruth demanded. Her brow wrinkled and her eyes flashed in anger.

Saji Stephen started to cry. "Ashish grabbed these from behind the curtain," he mumbled as best he could through his full mouth. "I told him to stop taking them, but he wouldn't!"

"No," Ashish said. "No, I didn't." But he protested softly because of his strict orders not to annoy Saji Stephen.

"He put one in my mouth. I tried to stop him, and he spilled it all over my new clothes!" Saji Stephen accused.

Parmar Ruth didn't look convinced.

Suddenly, Saji Stephen wailed, "My stomach hurts! It's Ashish's fault. He made my stomach hurt!"

"You are a naughty boy!" Parmar Ruth scolded Ashish. "Go back to your home and don't ever come back again!"

Ashish jumped up and ran before Madame Landlord had time to change her mind.

## 28

*A*shish ran all the way to his family's hut, still dressed in his fresh clothes and with his stomach filled with good food.

"I can't go back to the landlord's house anymore!" Ashish bubbled. "Not ever again! Madam Landlord said so! I don't have to play with Saji Stephen, and I don't have to go back to that house!"

As Latha picked up her laughing son and hugged him tight, Virat grabbed hold of his *chaddar* and pulled it off their piled belongings.

"Where's Devi?" Latha asked Ashish.

"I don't know. I followed the path by myself."

"Everyone is at the wedding dinner," Virat said. "If we hurry, we can get away before they come back."

Virat wrapped up the filled water jars and earthenware containers of rice and meal, together with the collection of small pots, in the middle of his *chaddar*. He stacked the large cooking pots together, taking care to leave the one holding all the baked *chapatis* on top, and tied them with a piece of fabric ripped from Latha's *sari*.

Latha grabbed a small pot filled with water and mango leaves and set it down outside the door.

"No, no!" Virat warned. "The others will see that and know we are gone."

"But we dare not leave on a journey without looking back at a full pot," Latha said. "If we do not, fortune will not protect us."

"But we must not leave that pot by our door for all to see!"

Virat held his ground. So did Latha. In the end they agreed Ashish could stay behind at the hut, but only temporarily. Virat and Latha would walk away and pause to look back at the full pot, then turn and go on ahead. Ashish could throw the pot down and smash it, and run to catch up with them. That way, they would be safe but also protected by fortune.

Latha lifted the load tied up in the *chaddar* onto Virat's back. She pulled the ends of the strip of cloth forward, under his arms, then tugged them back up and around behind his neck where she tied the ends together. The other load, she lifted onto her own head.

"I can take the drying rack," Ashish said.

"We will leave it here for someone else to use," Virat told his son. "You and I can make another one when we need it."

They also left the spice and dried vegetable containers. Not the sleeping mats, though. Virat had rolled them up tightly, and he and Latha each carried one tucked beneath an arm.

Taking care to cross the threshold right foot first, taking care to breathe deeply as they passed from the house and to make certain the pot full of water and mango leaves was the last thing they saw, taking note that they crossed the threshold with the lucky number of two people together (Virat and Latha, since Ashish stayed behind), they turned their backs on Mammen Samuel Varghese's slave settlement.

"What day of the week is this?" Latha asked with a note of anxiety. "If it's Saturday, we should go to the west. The planet Saturn only looks eastward and so it cannot see us going to the west."

"It is not Saturday," Virat said. "Saturn doesn't care which direction we go."

*✿*

The wedding pavilion rang with the sound of musicians playing flutes and lyres and sitars and drums, with joyful songs and dancers performing ancient dances. Cheers and laughter punctuated the merry-making.

So much food spread out! Enough for everyone, regardless of one's caste or standing in the village. So many specially prepared dishes! And, of course, the favorites—fish and rice and curds and fruit. Oh, and so many sweets.

"The entire village is here," one person after another after another exclaimed in amazement. "Mammen Samuel Varghese is a great and generous man."

Brahmin Keshavan and his son Rama were there, of course. They sat at the front of the pavilion, in a place of honor. The Brahmin officiated over the Hindu portion of the wedding ceremony, in fact. The Christian Bishop sat next to him at the feast, dipping his hand into the same bowl, for he, too, came from a high Brahmin family.

A simple melody, sung by a single voice, echoed through the pavilion. Temple music, it was. Of course, Mammen Samuel didn't call it by that name. To him it was simply Indian music.

*✿*

The wedding feast lasted until late into the night. When the final dance ended and the singers had sung their last melody, Mammen Samuel stood before the crowd and called out, "Tomorrow I call a holiday for the entire village! No work for anyone!" Cheers rocked the pavilion.

Devi turned to look for Ashish. Where was he? She must get him to the barn for the night.

"He went home a long time ago and he isn't coming back," Babu said in answer to the girl's questions. "Saji Stephen is sick, and it's all the fault of that wretched child."

"He went to the settlement all by himself?"

"What difference does it make? He's gone. That's all I care."

But Ashish was Devi's responsibility. What if something happened to him? She ran all the way to Ashish's hut. "Is anyone here?" she called. "Ashish, are you here?"

No one answered. Virat and Latha must still be at the pavilion, she decided. Maybe they saw Ashish there and were sitting at the feast with him right now. Still . . .

Devi peeked inside their hut, squinting in the darkness. Something didn't seem right. She stepped inside and waited for her eyes to adjust to the dark. The pots. That's what she noticed first. They were all gone. The food containers were gone too. Oh, and the water jars. And the sleeping mats. Devi looked around in confusion. Maybe she had stepped into the wrong hut. But that couldn't be. The animal skin drying rack still stood propped up against the wall. Only a *chamar* has use for such a thing. Only Virat.

Something had happened to Ashish and his family. It had to be something bad. And most certainly she would be blamed for it.

Devi ran back down the road screaming, "*Appa! Appa! Appa!*"

❦

"Can it be possible that they left?" Anup said as he looked over the bare hut. He walked outside and kicked at a broken dish which lay upside down beside the door. Three mango leaves lay crushed under it. "Yes, Virat and Latha are gone. Most certainly they took their child and left."

"You must tell Master Landlord immediately!" said Sethu.

"Two hundred additional people are in the village, and they will continue to be in the village for many days. No one will miss one skinny *chamar*, his half-blind wife, and their little boy for a very long time."

"Virat is your responsibility," Sethu insisted. "This very night you must tell the master what has happened!"

"Tonight is his daughter's wedding night. He will not want to be bothered with news of one *chamar*. I will tell him tomorrow."

In the dark hours of the early morning, storm clouds blew over the village and dumped out the rain they had held back throughout the day of the wedding. For three hours, it poured down in torrents.

*Travel quickly, Virat,* Anup murmured in his mind as he listened to the beating rain. *Your footprints will be washed away. Oh, but you must hurry!*

# 29

Virat and Latha walked throughout the night.

"You are a brave boy," Latha said to little Ashish. Whenever his footsteps dragged, Virat urged, "Don't look at the mountains up ahead, my son. Look at the small steps at your feet." Sometimes, when the road grew too rough, Virat picked the child up and carried him.

The deluge of rain hit in the wee hours of the morning, but the family pressed on. They had no choice. Ashish whimpered, but he did his best to be brave and keep up.

"I don't like the rain!" Ashish cried.

"Rain is a blessing," his father told him. "When the landlord discovers we're gone, he will look for our footprints to see which way we went. But because of the rain, our footprints will be washed away."

"And we need not be afraid of wild animals," said Latha. "When they sniff the air, they will not smell us . . . only the rain."

"Our water jugs too," Virat added. "When they are empty, we can find plenty of fresh ponds to fill them up again. Sometimes blessings come to us in disguise."

"Like me?" Ashish asked.

"Oh, no, not like you," Virat told him. "You, my son, are a blessing that looks like a blessing."

At long last, the black path before them began to grow lighter as dawn approached. The rain stopped and the sky lit up a lovely golden pink.

"Sun!" Virat exclaimed. "Today it will shine just for us."

"The landlord's men will see our footprints," Ashish said.

"No, no," his father said. "We are too far away now."

Once the sun shone full in the sky, Virat found a rocky spot where they could sit and eat their breakfast. He untied his pack and Latha lifted off her headload. She pulled out three *chapatis*, all baked and loaded with vegetables and spices.

"Only one for each of us," she cautioned. "That way we will have enough to last us four days."

No road led toward the mountains—only a path beaten down by the feet of the few travelers who passed that way. Sometimes Virat couldn't even find a path.

"Where are we going?" Ashish asked.

"Over the hills," Latha said. "A very long way away from here."

Although the sun rose higher and higher in the sky, and the day grew warmer, their wet clothes continued to cling to them as they slogged forward in the thick mud. Ashish found it especially difficult, and he moved more and more slowly.

"Can't we rest?" he begged.

Virat glanced over to the side where a thick forest loomed. "Not here." He thought it best not to mention the possibility of hungry leopards and tigers. "You stay between *Amma* and me," he told Ashish.

After they walked a little longer, Ashish suggested, "Maybe we could give someone your money coins and they would let us sleep in their house. Maybe they would share their rice with us too."

"Whatever do you mean?" Virat asked. "We have no money coins."

"The ones the bridegroom threw out for the people when he rode through the village on the elephant. The coins he threw so the evil spirits would leave him alone. Devi said he might come to the settlement and you could pick up some of the coins."

"He never came to us," Latha said. "We never even saw the bridegroom riding on the elephant."

Ashish wrinkled his brow and frowned. "Then I hope the evil spirits do get him!" he said.

"No," Virat chided gently. "We will never wish such a thing on anyone, whether they have been kind to us or not."

As the day dragged on, the travelers grew more and more quiet. Talking took too much energy. Their clammy wet clothing made walking that much more uncomfortable.

"Look!" Latha said.

Up ahead stood a rough hut with a most inviting fire burning brightly in front of it. As they drew closer, they saw that a yogi holy man sat off to one side, his legs crossed, chanting his prayers.

"Come," the yogi called to them without opening his eyes. "Sit beside my fire and dry yourselves. Rest your feet and your souls."

Latha grasped Ashish's hand and held him back, but Virat walked over without hesitation. A large log lay close to the fire. Virat sat down on one end of it and called for Latha and Ashish to come and join him. Within minutes, the little boy fell fast asleep, his head on his mother's lap.

The yogi paid them little mind, though every now and then he paused in his prayers to recite a thought that might or might not be relevant. "When a man is not conscious of his relationship with the world, he lives in a prison with walls hostile to him," he intoned. "When he finds the eternal spirit in all things, he is freed, for he then discovers the full meaning of the world in which he was born."

Virat said nothing. He had no idea what to say.

Sitting before the fire, warm and dry, listening to the calm cadence of the yogi's prayers, Virat fought the almost overwhelming desire to spread out his sleeping mat and lose himself in a deep sleep. But he dared not. He must rouse Latha and Ashish and move on. Still, before they left, he longed to ask one question of the yogi. "Please, tell me, holy man," Virat said, "you are up here all alone, with no one chasing after you and no one tormenting you. Do you have peace?"

The yogi stopped his prayers, and for the first time, looked at Virat. "No," he said. "No, I do not yet have peace."

Virat thanked the yogi for his kindness and bade him farewell. But the holy man didn't answer. Already he had gone back to his prayers.

*❧*

From the beginning of the deluge, Anup lay awake in his hut listening to the rain pour down. He knew the moment it stopped. He saw the first cracks of morning light, but for another two hours he pretended to be asleep.

Sethu prodded him with her foot. "Why do you lie there, Husband? You should be on your way to the landlord's house!"

"This is the morning after his daughter's wedding," Anup said. "I will not disturb his household too early."

Of course, he could not use that excuse much longer. He knew that perfectly well.

"I will send Lidya over to sweep out Virat and Latha's hut," Sethu said.

"No!" Anup said. "I am the one who gives the orders, not you. I will say when it's time to sweep."

Anup understood perfectly the reason for Sethu's urgency. More superstition. If a room was swept immediately after a traveler departed, the belief was that his journey would fail and he would have to return to the house. But Anup had already made up his mind that he would not interfere. If it was Virat's *karma* to fail, he would fail on his own. If it was his *karma* to succeed, Anup would stay out of the way.

"Master Landlord will be angry at the delay," Sethu insisted. "And on whose back will the punishment land? Yours!"

"Then let it land on my back. Do not bother me about it again."

✒

Anup bowed low before Mammen Samuel Varghese, low enough to touch his forehead to the ground. "The *chamar* Virat left the settlement," Anup said. "Fortunately, he is not an important person. He has an ugly wife who is half blind and a most impertinent son. His is not an important family. You will not miss them."

"What?" Mammen Samuel roared. "I know that family. What do you mean they left the settlement? Where did they go? When?"

"During the wedding feast, Master. We were all so filled with joy over your generous celebration of the marriage of your beautiful daughter that no one missed the *chamar* until today."

"I will have the *chamar* dragged back and flogged! I will see that his entire family is soundly beaten!"

"Perhaps the *chamar* has an explanation, Master. By your gracious order, no one works today. Perhaps he will be back tomorrow."

"He *will* be back, if not tomorrow, then the day after," Mammen Samuel vowed. "Even if I must drag him back by a hook through his untouchable nose, he will be back!"

Long after Anup had left, Mammen Samuel paced back and forth across the veranda, mourning the injustice of his loss. "This would happen right after every crook in the village bled me dry with exorbitant wedding costs!" He vowed revenge. "First I will have them flogged, then I will multiply the *chamar's* debt ten times over. No, twenty times!" When he thought about the embarrassment he'd certainly suffer in the eyes of the village, rage seized him. "After all I did for those lazy village sluggards, after all the money I poured out of my coffers on their behalf, they will see that a foolish *chamar* has escaped from my settlement and they will gather together and mock me!"

The *chamar*—phew! His scarred, half-blind wife—blah! And the boy. "Nothing but trouble!" Mammen Samuel spat. "Trouble at the well. Trouble at the English Mission Medical Clinic. Trouble in my own house with my own son! And now this!"

Mammen Samuel paced the length of the veranda, and with each turn, his fury burned hotter.

"When I find that boy, I will break each one of his legs in two pieces and sell him as a crippled beggar!"

The path Virat followed led closer and closer to the forest. Suddenly, he grabbed Ashish by the arm and pointed up ahead. An enormous crowd of pale monkeys, each with a black face, sat on the path and perched in the bushes around it. Ashish gasped, and the monkeys all turned to stare at him. One cried a monkey cry, and the bushes came alive with a mad scramble of hundreds of monkeys all dashing for the trees.

"We disturbed their morning walk," Virat whispered. "They're angry with us."

"Will they hurt us?" Ashish asked, his voice quaking.

"No, no. They're harmless."

Virat took hold of Ashish's hand and the two walked down the path together. The monkeys stared down at them from the trees, watching as they passed, calling out monkey comments.

After a while Virat said to Latha, "Your father will not be pleased to see us."

Latha said nothing.

"Pooni said all our troubles came to us because you sinned by marrying me," Virat said. "She said I fall too far below you to have taken you for my wife."

"What did Pooni know about husbands and troubles?"

"Will your father say the same thing that Pooni said? Would I be an embarrassment to him, a carpenter, who lives in a house with two rooms, wood pillars, and doors finely carved with flowers, fish, and birds?"

"I once told you our son is a blessing despite my sin of marrying you," Latha said. "But then I said something else. Do you remember what it was?"

"Yes. You said, perhaps our son is a blessing *because* I married you."

For a long time, neither spoke.

"My people do not like slavery," Latha finally said. "Before my birth, they left their village after the Great Mutiny because they didn't want to be servants of the English."

"They don't like slavery for *them*, but what about for others?"

Again, Latha fell silent. For a long time she did not speak a word.

"You asked me what happened to my eye. I told you my mother and father never spoke of it, and that is true. But when I told you I couldn't remember what happened, that was not true."

Virat said nothing. He waited in silence for Latha to speak again.

"My father performed his craft as a carpenter very well, but he could not get work in a village that didn't know his family. I was very little then, a burden my family bore unhappily. My father talked of borrowing money from a moneylender so he could pay a blacksmith to make him tools acceptable for an Untouchable but that could be used to do more intricate work on wooden portals. But my uncle insisted he must not involve himself with such people as moneylenders. Instead, my father allowed my uncle to take me to a band of thieves and pay them to make a good beggar out of me. They used a hot knife on my face and blinded my eye."

Virat stopped and stared at Latha. "Your father allowed such a thing to be done to you? Why didn't you tell me?"

"Because I did not want you to think poorly of him. He only did what his *karma* forced him to do."

"We will not go to your father's village," Virat said. "I will not live with such a man. I will not have my son live with him."

"We have no choice!" Latha pleaded.

"We do," Virat said, "We always have a choice."

When Mammen Samuel ordered Anup to gather up men to pursue Virat, he took note of the way Anup kept his eyes averted from him. Anup might command the workers to search, but he would not command them with his heart. Better to depend on Sudras, even though it meant paying them. Mammen Samuel knew how to pass along such a cost. He would add it to the ledger account of the other slaves. They should by rights bear a good part of the fault, after all, for every one of them failed to notice the escape or to stop it. Anup's account would be charged double, for he was doubly responsible.

"I will lead the search myself," Boban Joseph told his father. "I'll find the runaways and bring them back with ropes around their necks."

"I want them alive and ready to work," Mammen Samuel said. "I want them to pay for their insolence for the rest of their lives."

"Let me take a horse," Boban Joseph said. "That way I can keep the search moving fast. I'll have the runaways back here in two days. Maybe less."

✑❧

Had they been going to Latha's family's village, Virat and Latha would have stayed on the path that led over the mountains. But now where could they go?

"Out to the coast to find Hilmi's village," Virat suggested. "No one would think to look for us there."

"We can look up and see the mountains and head toward them, but how can we know the way to the coast?" Latha asked. "And if we should get to the coast, how could we find Hilmi's village?"

As they worried what to do, clouds gathered overhead. Before they decided on a route, monsoon rains once again flattened the earth. Ashish, exhausted and soaking wet, sat down in the mud and wailed.

Latha wept, too. "What are we to do, Husband?"

A bullock cart rumbled along the narrow path, churning its way toward them through the mud. In the front, driving the bullocks with one hand, sat a fine, slender man with a pale face and sharp features. He held an umbrella over his head with his other hand. He had a *chaddar* over his shoulders, but peeking out from underneath Virat spied the glimmer of a gold thread.

"It's a Brahmin," Virat gasped. Quickly, he and Latha bowed down in the mud. Latha pushed Ashish down beside her.

"Please, stand up," the Brahmin called. "Do not kneel in the mud before me, a mere man."

But Virat and Latha were afraid to move. It could be some sort of a trick. Why would a Brahmin be out alone in a monsoon downpour?

"My house is up ahead," the Brahmin said. "Please come and dry off. Please rest yourselves."

"We are Untouchables," Virat explained, his face still to the ground. "I am but a *chamar*."

"You should not be out in this weather," the Brahmin said. "Please come. You are most welcome at my house."

Virat stood up and glanced around him hesitantly. But he followed the cart nonetheless. And Latha and Ashish followed Virat.

Around the bend stood a good-sized house. The Brahmin got out of the cart, walked up to the door, and opened it. "Do come in," the Brahmin invited most courteously.

The Brahmin's servant rushed forward to give Virat water to wash, and also a dry *mundu*. He did the same for Latha, giving her a dry *sari*. "I have no clothes for a child," he said to Ashish. "So you shall get the seat closest to the fire."

When they were clean and dressed, the Brahmin invited the three to eat. Yes, to eat in his house! Beside him! At first, Virat and Latha refused. But the Brahmin insisted so strongly, and they were so hungry. The delicious food, Virat decided, might well have been the best he ever tasted. When he finished eating, and the servant poured out water to wash his hands, Virat spoke the question that nagged at him: "Please, forgive me for my rudeness, but I must ask you: Why are you so kind to us?"

"I am a Brahmin, yes, but I am also a Christian," the man said. "I act with love to you because that is what the one true God would have me do."

Virat licked his lips and took a deep breath. He bowed low and said, "You have been much more than kind to us. Please, forgive me for my insolence in asking still more. Yet I have one more request."

"Look me full in the face, then you may state your request," the Brahmin said.

Virat looked up into the face of the Brahmin. "Brahmin Keshavan put a wicked curse on me. He sent a cobra to trap me in the wheat field, and many evil spirits to threaten and torment me. Please, could you free me from Brahmin Keshavan's curse?"

"There is only One who can free you," the Brahmin said. "It is not me and it is not Brahmin Keshavan. It is only Jesus Christ, the Son of the one true God."

Virat stared at him.

"In the Bible, which tells words and thoughts from the true God, in Colossians 3:16-18 and 4:1, it says: *Let no man therefore judge you in meat, or in drink, or in respect of a holy day, or of the new moon, or of the Sabbath days; which are a shadow of things to come; but the body of Christ Jesus. Let no man beguile you of your reward in a voluntary humility and worshipping angels, intruding into those things which he hath not seen, vainly puffed up by his fleshly mind. . . . Seek those things which are above, where Christ sitteth on the right hand of God."*

"Let no man beguile you?" Virat asked.

"Trick you," said the Brahmin. "Let no man trick you."

"You mean the curse is not real?"

"When a person's mind is so filled with terror, it can be all but impossible to see the truth."

Yet even as the Brahmin spoke such reassuring words, Virat looked nervously around him. "We must hurry on," he said.

"Yes. I fear your pursuers are on their way," the Brahmin said. "I heard gossips speak of those who would search for you." Virat gave a start. "But you have time to rest. They will not travel in the rain or the dark."

Virat slept that night, but uneasily. Stars still shone in the dark sky when he roused Latha and Ashish. They dressed in their own clothes, which the servant had washed for them, and crept out of the Brahmin's house.

As the sun rose over the hills, the perfume of wild herbs wafted on the breeze. Had they been at their real home, in their own mud hut with their neighbors nearby, it would have been the beginning of a most lovely day.

❧

The path grew rougher and narrower until no one could rightly call it a path at all. Virat, followed closely by Ashish and then Latha, slogged up one hill after another. Finally Ashish, bruised and weary, flopped down on the ground and wept. Despite his parents' prodding and cajoling, he refused to move.

"We cannot continue uphill," Virat said. "The road isn't passable. But we cannot head for the coast, either, because I cannot find the way." So Virat turned toward the east. He headed back toward the land he knew, on a trail that would lead them out of the mountainous area, toward rolling hills and flatter land.

They walked through field after field, over hills, then through more fields.

Not once did they pass another traveler. Not even one of the roaming holy men who walk the length and breadth of India, constantly moving from one shrine to another. Even they had settled down to wait out the monsoon rains.

"What's that?" Ashish cried. He pointed to a gristly sight on the path—streaks of blood touched with bits of pale fur.

"A monkey," Virat said.

"A tiger ate him?"

"Not a tiger, but some wild animal, and very recently, too, or the rains would have washed away these remains."

Ashish started to cry. "Will it eat me, too?"

"No, no!" Latha said. She clutched the boy's little hand. "Your *appa* would never let that happen, and neither would I."

The rain wasn't Virat's biggest worry, nor the slogging mud. Even hungry animals that might be prowling along the path were not the worst of it. Virat's biggest worry was the bright sun that had replaced the heavy clouds. With no rain falling, the master's searchers would come after them at full pace. The searchers would find it much easier to follow their footprints too. If the landlord's men were close enough for the Brahmin to hear gossip about them, Virat knew it was only a matter of time. Around some bend, over the crest of a hill, through one field or another, they would run into the landlord's men.

Who would be leading them? Would it be Anup? That would be good. Anup wouldn't allow the men to kill them outright . . . though maybe it would be easier if he did. Otherwise Virat and Latha would surely face a horrible punishment. And as for Ashish? Oh, poor little Ashish!

"We must hide the boy," Virat whispered to Latha. "If we escape, we can come back for him. If we do not, at least he will have a chance."

"No!" Latha cried. "I will not leave my son alone out here!"

Virat sank to his knees and bowed his head to the ground. "I do not know what else to do! If any gods are watching me, please, what would you have me do? Please tell me, what can I do?"

# 30

"Are you angry with me, *Appa?*" Ashish asked.

"No, my son. How could I be angry with you?"

"I won't eat any more *chapatis*. You can have them all."

"If we had any more *chapatis*, we would want you to eat them," Latha told her son. "But they are all gone. So we will all be hungry together."

"Maybe the monkeys will share their food with us," Ashish suggested. When no one answered, he whispered, "Am I still Ashish? Am I still a blessing?"

"Always," said Latha.

"Forever," said Virat.

❧

"It is not at all proper for a young woman such as yourself to gallop all over the Indian countryside, wild and unescorted, yet you insist upon doing exactly that," Dr. Moore complained to Abigail. "Can you not see that such behavior lends an unprofessional air to the mission medical clinic? Might I suggest, perhaps even an *immoral* impression?"

Abigail gasped out loud. Of course the doctor's comments insulted her greatly. Yet if she had learned anything in her six months at the English Mission Medical Clinic, she had learned to keep her indignation in check. So she took a deep breath and carefully measured her next words.

"I must say, Sir, that I can think of little that is more professional—or even more moral—than to go out into the highways and byways, to reach my hand out to the very people we have come to serve, and compel them to come in. Is that not what Jesus taught?"

Dr. Moore heaved an exasperated sigh. "Miss Davidson, please consider the circumstances. A young woman such as yourself—a young *white* woman—roaming about, alone and unescorted! Really, it is most unseemly."

"Come along with me, then," Abigail pleaded. "Oh, do come and see the things I see. Explore the countryside with me and meet the Indian people—I mean, those who are still quite healthy."

"See here!" Dr. Moore exclaimed. "I am a doctor, not a tourist. Nor am I a social activist, or some sort of a . . . a . . . *politician!*"

"I don't mean come along for the sake of England, Sir. I mean for the kingdom of God."

Dr. Moore's face hardened, and his mouth clamped tight.

*Oh, dear, once again, I have said too much,* Abigail thought. Even so, she didn't stop.

"If you will not accompany me, Sir," Abigail added, though in a much milder tone of voice, "I shall go anyway."

How Abigail Davidson had changed since she first arrived in India. To some degree Dr. Moore himself had helped to bring about that transformation. Though he would never admit it, his words were much tougher than the man who spoke them. The physician talked in lofty terms about the best interest of the clinic, about what could be most advantageous for his own professional future, about what might one day lead to the establishment of an actual church on the mission site.

Yet when a terrified woman came to him, battered and oppressed, his face softened, and he treated her with utmost dignity. When a man others called "untouchable" crawled into his presence, bowing and scraping before him, the doctor's face seethed with frustration. He reached out and lifted the man to his feet before readily tending to his malady, however unpleasant the condition might be. Whenever someone found a helpless child abandoned at his door, Dr. Moore made certain the little one received loving care until he was able to find a home for him . . . or for her.

Without a doubt, Abigail had changed because she had come to know the hidden part of her employer. But that wasn't the entire reason. She also changed because of her association with Darshina.

"But I shan't be alone, Sir," Abigail added. "Darshina will come with me. She told me about a field of herbs over toward the hills. We shall gather them, and when we get back, she will teach me to make them into healing agents."

Dr. Moore let out another exasperated sigh.

"You said yourself that some of those ancient folk cures do more to treat native ills than any of our modern medicines. Is that not so?"

"Do as you will," the doctor said, dismissing Abigail with a wave of his hand. "If you get caught in a rainstorm, or step on a viper, I will be here to tend to you alongside my other patients. Of course, I shall have no one to assist me."

"I shall watch both the sky and the ground with utmost diligence." Abigail headed for the door. "And I shall bring back the most fragrant herbs and brew the most wondrous cures for your surgery."

Virat looked at Ashish, trudging along behind him. The little boy—his forehead creased in concentration, his small jaw clenched tight—stretched his legs out as far as he could and tried to walk in his *appa's* footprints. But he could not. Poor boy. Poor, poor little one. So small a child doing his best to bear the burdens of a grown man.

Anup would say, "Life is hard." He would say, "Many children die young." He would say, "Whatever happens, it is the will of the gods. Pray that the next life will be better." Virat was glad Anup was not with them.

Virat slowed his pace. He rested his hand on his son's head and said, "You are a good boy, Ashish."

Ashish tried his best to keep up with his parents. He really tried. Though he stumbled and faltered, he kept on trying. But when he tripped on the rough ground and fell flat, it was the end of what he could endure. He didn't even attempt to get back up.

"I am weary," Virat said lightly. "I believe it is time for a rest."

Latha looked anxiously at the path behind them. They had left a clear trampled trail through the high grass.

Once again, clouds gathered ominously overhead. Virat pulled a couple of fallen branches together and quickly fashioned a make-shift shelter. As they climbed inside, the rain began to pour down. Virat hugged Ashish to him, and within minutes, the boy fell soundly to sleep.

"Where are we going, Husband?" Latha asked. "It seems that you are leading us toward our old village."

"No, we cannot go back there," Virat said. "But maybe to the other village beyond it. Or to still another beyond that one."

❧

"The air always smells so good after a hard rain," Abigail called down to Darshina from her perch atop the carriage horse. "That is also true in London, of course, although London air is never quite so fragrant as this."

The doctor had only one horse. But even if he had one hundred, Darshina wouldn't have climbed up on a horse's back. She much preferred to walk. And without Abigail slowing her down, she could cover a lot of ground quickly.

Darshina carried Abigail's basket on her arm, taking care not to spill out any of her collected treasures: Leaves of basil, to draw the poison from insect bites; bitter menthe to reduce fevers; wild onions, to boil into a soothing balm; amaranth, to calm the stomach. ("And to be mending a broken heart, should such a break ever be coming to you," Darshina told Abigail with a teasing smile.)

❧

Virat had torn the shelter apart and dragged the fallen limbs away. Latha had filled the water jars from a large rain puddle. They had just started to walk again when Virat stopped still. "The first of the landlord's men," he breathed. "Coming toward us."

"Run, *Appa*, run!" Ashish screamed.

Virat took Ashish's hand. "We will be strong," he said. "Whatever happens, we must be strong."

But as the horse came closer, Virat puzzled over what appeared to be a billow of light blue fabric at its side. And the single person walking beside the horse wasn't wearing a *mundu* at all, but a *sari*—a *sari* of pure white. Virat blinked his eyes and stared, trying to make sense of it.

Ashish broke loose from his father's grip and ran toward the approaching rider.

"Go away!" he screamed. "Go away and leave my *appa* alone!"

✍❧

"We must be leaving them to themselves," Darshina warned when she saw the three up ahead. "They being Travelers. Nothing more than travelers."

"I don't know," Abigail said. She wrinkled her brow and shaded her eyes. "They look to be in distress."

"Many Indians are being in the way of distress," Darshina said. "We be doing best to leave them to themselves."

But Abigail could not. She slipped off the back of the horse and walked toward the screaming little boy.

"Please, I want to help you!" Abigail called out.

Ashish stopped still. "It is the pale English lady, *Appa*. She won't catch us. She won't hurt us."

✍❧

Virat fell to his knees before Abigail. His words poured out, rapid and urgent—and totally unintelligible to her.

"They thought we were being the landlord's men coming to catch them," Darshina translated.

"We shall take them back to the clinic," Abigail said. "They can stay with us and be safe."

In the distance, a great commotion of birds suddenly flew up into the air and flapped away. Virat stared at the spot. A dark shadow moved up the path.

"Tell the English lady we have no time!" he cried. "Tell her the landlord's men will attack us all. Go! Carry our boy away with you. We will lead the hunters in the other direction!"

Abigail looked uncertainly from Virat to the moving shadow.

"Go now!" Virat ordered. "Before it is too late . . . for all of us!"

Darshina picked up Ashish and handed him up to Abigail.

"No, *Appa!*" Ashish cried. "Don't leave me!"

"Hurry!" Virat insisted. Latha wailed behind him.

Abigail turned the horse and raced away with Ashish, leaving Darshina to walk back to the clinic alone.

"What have we done?" Latha cried. "Oh, what have we done?"

Virat reached out a shaky hand and touched her muddy arm. Soft as butter, it was to him. Despite all, still soft as butter to him. "You are a good wife, Latha," he said. "You are a good mother."

## 31

*O*ver here!”

An earthenware pot, half buried in the mud—one that had slipped from the load on Virat's back. A Sudra picked it up and held it high.

“The trail toward the mountains!” Boban Joseph ordered. “Move!”

Two sets of larger footprints and one very small set that had not been erased by the rain. Boban Joseph rode right over them without noticing, but the Sudras did not.

“Over here! A scatter of sticks, Master!” Yes, remnants of a make-shift shelter, hastily tossed apart.

“They came this way,” a Sudra called to Boban Joseph, “but they're changing direction!”

“Follow them!” Boban Jospeh ordered. “Pick up the pace!”

A yogi at prayer would not answer questions, but he responded to Boban Joseph's threats with a nod and a quick gesture.

“This way, Master!” a searcher called, pointing to a muddy slide down the side of a long, slippery slope.

Riding on horseback, with the twelve Sudras pointing out each twist and turn of the way, Boban Joseph had less and less trouble following the trail. An eager grin spread across his face. This would be a quick capture.

✒

"Shall we keep going?" Virat asked Latha. "Or shall we sit down and wait for what is certain to come?"

"Go!" Latha said. She lifted off her headload and threw it to the ground. "We will not make it easy for them."

Boban Joseph lashed at the horse with his switch, the same one he used on the bullocks that pulled his father's cart. Whooping like a triumphant warrior, he galloped toward the runaways. True to their word, Virat and Latha did not make it easy. But they could not outrun a horse.

"There!" Boban Joseph called as he caught sight of Virat and Latha scrambling up a hillside. He slowed the horse. "Grab them! Now!"

When no one responded, he turned around in the saddle. The Sudras, though they were running as fast as they could, had fallen far behind the rider. "Hurry, you lazy louts!" Boban Joseph bellowed.

Strong men the Sudras might be, but they had been walking and running for hours. Of course they could not keep up with a horse. Still, rather than apprehend a weary man and his stumbling wife alone, Boban Joseph stopped the horse and waited for them.

"No, we will not make it easy for them," Virat whispered.

✒

Two more hours passed before the first Sudras grabbed Virat. They bound his wrists, then drew the rope around him and tied it tightly about his waist. The next ones caught Latha and bound her in the same way.

"The boy!" Boban Joseph demanded. "Where is he?"

Latha raised her voice in an agonized wail. "He is no more. A leopard carried him away."

Boban Joseph paused and looked uncertainly from her to her husband. "Where?" he demanded.

Virat pointed up the mountainside. "On the road, far up there. His blood still smears the road."

"Do you want us to search for him?" a Sudra asked.

"No," said Boban Joseph. "If they were foolish enough to leave him behind, he will not survive the night."

Boban Joseph, sitting tall and proud in the saddle, turned the horse toward the village and led the procession along at a goodly pace. Virat and Latha, their wrists firmly bound to their waists, struggled to keep up with him. But the Sudras would not allow them to slow down. Latha stumbled on the torn hem of her *sari* and fell against Virat. Moments later, she stumbled again. The third time, she tumbled to her knees.

"Slower!" Virat cried. But Boban Joseph ignored him.

Latha tried to lift her *sari* with her bound hands. Faltering, she slipped into a mud hole and fell flat. This time she refused to get up.

"Do what you want to me," she said. "I don't care."

In the end, Latha and Virat walked back to the village, but with only their hands tied, not with the rope around their waists. And they walked in front where they could set the pace. They rested when they were tired, and when they called for a drink, the Sudras gave them water. "Let them take their comfort now," Boban Joseph muttered. "When my father gets them, then they will suffer right enough."

But how could Mammen Samuel Varghese publicly whip this runaway family while so many outsiders still swelled the village? Two hundred wedding guests, all congratulating him and praising him as a generous and gracious landlord! No, he could not. So Mammen Samuel sent a messenger to meet the procession on the road and instruct his son to take them along the back pathway to the workers' settlement.

"It isn't fair!" Boban Joseph complained. "The entire village should see a great landlord mete out his punishment!"

Every laborer in the settlement knew the exact hour and minute that Virat and Latha returned. Some workers stood brazenly in the courtyard, staring and ridiculing the two as they passed by. Others crowded around Virat and Latha's hut to gawk more closely. But most hovered outside their own huts and whispered to one another:

"Cursed, that's what they are. Punished by the gods."

"Their son is dead, eaten by a great tiger, or maybe a leopard."

"Evil boy, that one!"

"It was Virat's fault for withholding a proper sacrifice."

"No, no, it was Latha's fault! Didn't you know she is the one with the evil eye . . . "

Virat and Latha, caked with mud and weary beyond endurance, paid the gossipers no mind.

Anup waited for them at their door. "See where your foolishness has gotten you," he lamented. "See what happens when you refuse to accept your *karma*."

Virat said nothing. His exhausted body hadn't the strength to argue.

"You should never have named your son Ashish. You called him Blessing so long that you started to believe it. Now see what has happened. Now you have no son at all. You have lived long enough to know the truth, Virat—no blessings ever come to us. Not to such as you and me."

Latha would have wept, except that she was too exhausted for tears.

That night Virat and Latha lay together on the bare dirt floor of their hut. They had no sleeping mats. They had no earthenware pots. Even their water jugs were gone. They still owned the drying rack for dead animals and the two containers they had left behind with spices and dried vegetables, but nothing else.

"It doesn't matter," Virat said. "We are here. And Ashish . . . our Ashish is in the hands of the English woman's God."

Mammen Samuel Varghese didn't like violence. He talked harshly and clung fast to his money and his slaves, but he wasn't one to raise the lash to another person. So it pleased him to have an excuse to forego the whippings he had threatened. He had his workers back, and their son, too small to work anyway, was dead and gone. Besides, Mammen Samuel's eldest son had once again proven himself to the villagers. Why should the landlord dampen the lighthearted mood that still prevailed with such a show of violence? Of course, there must be punishment, but it could wait until a more opportune time.

With a smug feeling of moral superiority, Mammen Samuel greeted Brahmin Keshavan when the Brahmin appeared at the steps of the veranda.

"Your daughter married well," the Brahmin said.

"Yes," agreed Mammen Samuel. "I have successfully combined two great Christian houses." (He couldn't resist emphasizing the fact that they were Christian.)

"The union should bring you much success, and even more wealth."

Mammen Samuel smiled proudly.

"And your Untouchables have been brought back to you, I understand. It would seem your good fortune knows no bounds."

"Thanks be to God for the prowess, talents, and bravery of my first son," Mammen Samuel said.

After that, the two men sat in silence. Mammen Samuel could not imagine why the Brahmin had come out of his way to offer such praise. As the silence stretched out, be began to fear a trick.

Finally Brahmin Keshavan repeated, "Your daughter has married well."

"Yes," Mammen Samuel agreed again, but this time with less enthusiasm. "I am pleased."

"Your fortune knows no bounds," the Brahmin said again.

Mammen Samuel's eyes narrowed. Not everything that sounded like a flattering remark turned out to be a true compliment. He braced himself for what was still to come.

"I am certain you will want to pay me my due for the blessings I pronounced over your daughter at her wedding," the Brahmin said. "And you want to give me my share for the *mantras* I said on behalf of the Sudras who brought your slaves back to you. You show yourself to be a wise and compassionate man. Therefore, I am certain you will want to respond in a way that is wise and compassionate."

"Pshaw!" Mammen Samuel spat. "What do you know? The highest of all castes, you call yourself, yet you Brahmins consider yourselves subject neither to the law nor to the responsibility of work. Beggars, that's what you are—all of you. I will not give you one rupee!"

The expression on Brahmin Keshavan's face did not change at all. "I see you do not understand the extent of my service to you," he said. "You do not realize that I protect you from the evils around you. You do not comprehend the degree to which I prevail upon the gods and goddesses to withhold their plagues from your house."

Mammen Samuel stood up abruptly. "You do nothing but pass judgment. That is a service I do not need." And he walked away.

"It is all *karma*," Anup said. "Your fortunes, both good and bad, are the will of the gods."

"I don't want to hear it," Virat told him.

"Your lot is better than that of many around you. You are not blind or lame or without a hand. You have not been cursed with four girls. You have a good wife. The master did not kill you."

Virat said nothing.

"Nothing in the world is truly of so much consequence," Anup said with a sigh. "Not even your son."

Virat glared at him. "I dared to go into the upper caste side of the village for my son. I wore a broom on my back and a cup over my mouth for my son. I sold myself and my wife to be slaves to the landlord for my son. My son is of the greatest consequence to me."

"Then pray to the gods to have mercy on him in his next life," Anup said.

"We prayed and we prayed for this life. We sacrificed to the gods and we did *puja*. But the gods did not help us."

"Then forget your son," Anup said. "Forget that Ashish ever lived."

## 32

Ashish stared down from his perch behind the big horse's neck and whispered, "Will it eat me?"

Since the child spoke Malayalam and Abigail knew only English, she couldn't understand the question. But she couldn't miss the fear in Ashish's trembling voice. So Abigail pulled the little one closer to her and held on to him tightly as she urged the horse forward.

The little boy shrank back against Abigail and whimpered. She longed to console him, to tell him he was not alone, to speak words that would ease his fears. But she could not. Just as she had not been able to speak comforting words when he had come to her the first time, beaten and gasping for breath. Back then she could best soothe him with caresses and lullabies.

Abigail hummed one of the songs she used to sing to Ashish. Immediately his little body relaxed a bit. Encouraged, Abigail sang,

"Jesus loves me! This I know, For the Bible tells me so. Little ones to Him belong; They are weak, but He is strong."

Ashish leaned into her, his whimpers quieted.

"Yes, Jesus loves me! Yes, Jesus loves me!
Yes, Jesus loves me! The Bible tells me so."

Abigail paused, but immediately Ashish clutched her hand and made humming sounds. So she sang the next verse, and then the chorus again. And the next verse, and the next one, and the next. By verse five, Ashish hummed along with her. By verse seven, he stumbled along pronouncing the words to the chorus:

"Yes, Jesus loves me! Yes, Jesus loves me!
Yes, Jesus loves me! The Bible tells me so."

*So sad that the child has no idea what he's singing*, Abigail thought.

Ashish, resting comfortably against her, kept on humming.

*✧*

"You inform me that you are going to the fields to collect herbs, but you return with a child," Dr. Moore said.

"But I only—"

"And not just any child, but the self-same young boy we previously treated and sent home in the care of his father and mother."

"The thing is—"

"The very same child whose presence here came close to bringing the authorities to our door—the same authorities, I might remind you, that have it in their power to close the doors of our mission medical clinic. You do understand the problem, Miss Davidson, do you not?"

"Ashish is a very intelligent child, Sir," Abigail said quickly before the doctor could interrupt her again.

"Oh?" Dr. Moore's eyebrows shot up.

"Merely riding back from the field with me, he learned the words to the chorus of *Jesus Loves Me*."

"I see. And what right, exactly, does that give you to once again remove this boy from the home of his father and mother?"

"Dr. Moore," Abigail said, "his father and mother are the ones who gave him to me. *Pressed* him into my care, I should say! They said the landlord's men were after them and they begged Darshina and me to take the boy away to safety and care for him."

Dr. Moore shook his head. Eight years it had taken him to build up the small chain of rural mission health clinics in South India, and not once in those eight years had he clashed with the native authorities. Only one more year, perhaps two at the outset. After that, he would certainly gain the soon-to-be-vacated appointment at the mission hospital in Calcutta. After a few years there, he could return to England, a man of prestige, honor, and enough wealth to keep him comfortable and happy for the remainder of his life. And he would still be young enough to find a pretty wife, too, and start a family of his own.

But only if he proved his ability to work in peace with the local people. Only if he caused no problems.

"If the boy cannot live with his parents, he should be moved to the mission orphanage for boys," the doctor stated. "The sooner that is accomplished, the better for everyone involved."

❦

"It isn't right!" Abigail fumed to Darshina. "Why should that fat old landlord always have his way?"

"Mammen Samuel Varghese is being from a most high upper caste," Darshina said. "Not Brahmin, but the high upper caste of kings. He is being extremely rich too. Indian people be respecting rich men. It be meaning they have the favor of the gods and goddesses with them. Rich men are being blessed with good *karma* because they are being good in their past lives. They be earning for themselves the right for being respected in this life."

"Even if they make slaves of their neighbors and hire people to chase them down and kill them?"

"Yes," Darshina said. "Even then. That, too, is being the right of rich men."

"What do you know!" Abigail said with a dismissive wave of her hand. "You are one of those rich upper caste people."

Darshina glared at the Englishwoman. "Every time you be speaking you be showing again how much you not be understanding. I am being a woman. Every woman in India be suffering under the laws of Manu, the lawgiver."

Abigail's pale cheeks blushed hot. How could she be so foolish! How could she challenge one who faced imprisonment for a lifetime simply because she refused to step into her husband's funeral fire? Oh, yes, she still needed to learn so very much!

"Please, Darshina," Abigail pleaded, "forgive the ignorance of my foolish words to you."

*❧*

At dawn, Latha got up from the floor. She poured the dried vegetables out of the first container and into the second container of spices, and she carried the empty first container to the well. It didn't hold much water, but she had no water jar.

She brought it back to the hut and gave Virat a drink. She also took a drink for herself. Again she carried the container to the well, refilling it so Virat would have water to wash the worst of the mud off himself. She took it back a third time to fetch water to wash herself. Virat tied his filthy *mundu* back around his waist and Latha put the muddy, torn *sari* back on her washed body. They had no other clothing to wear. Fortunately, Virat still had his *chaddar*. Before he abandoned his pack, he had pulled it off and wrapped it around his head.

Latha didn't start a cooking fire because she had nothing to cook. Virat said no word of complaint.

All day, they worked hard at the jobs to which they were assigned—Virat on his knees weeding with the women, and Latha carrying water with the young boys. In the evening, Latha filled the small pot with water for Virat and her to drink while she started a fire in the cook pit. Once again she filled the pot with water, but this time she put it over the fire. As the water heated, she sprinkled in a handful of dried vegetables and spices. Virat drank his share of the flavored water first and Latha drank up the rest.

"When will you distribute more rice?" Virat asked Anup.

"I did that the day after the wedding," Anup said. "I have none left for you. I'm sorry."

When Virat told Latha, she said, "I saw some weeds grow-ing beside the road. I can gather some of those to boil in the water."

"I will try to catch a lizard," Virat said. "Maybe even a rat, if I can."

As they lay down on the dirt floor, Latha said, "I'm glad Ashish is not here."

Virat wondered if he would be glad for anything ever again.

*

"Come, Ashish." Abigail took the boy's hand and urged him to follow her. She led him out of the surgery, where he had slept the night, and across the courtyard, where he had never been before. "I want you to meet someone."

At the far end of the courtyard, another boy hunched over a small garden, pouring water on a row of plants.

"Krishna, I brought a friend for you."

The boy set the water jug down and turned around. Ashish gasped at the sight of his face. The boy's mouth pulled tight into the shape of a circle and his nose flattened where it should have stuck out. His whole face looked puckered, like the skin around Ashish's mother's bad eye.

"What happened to you?" Ashish asked.

"I got burned," Krishna answered. Ashish had trouble understanding what the boy said because he couldn't bring his lips together to make the sound of the letter "b."

"Can't the pale English lady fix you?"

"She already did," Krishna said. "As much as she can. Now my face doesn't hurt any more the way is used to."

"Ashish is going to stay here for a while," Abigail said, and Krisna nodded.

"Can you understand what she says?" Ashish asked the boy.

"I couldn't at first, but now I can."

Krishna was small, but he was older than Ashish. How old he didn't know, but all his front teeth were big, unlike Ashish's, which were all still small. Krishna showed Ashish how to tend the vegetables—chilies and onions and eggplant and cucumbers. He taught him some English words and told him what *Jesus loves me* meant.

"Do you live here all the time?" Ashish asked Krishna.

"Yes," Krishna said. "But I'm going to go someplace else to school. I'm going to learn to read."

Ashish gasped. "Isn't that a sin?"

"No," Krishna said. "I already know my ABCs. And I can read easy words."

"Are you a Brahmin?"

"No, I'm a filthy Untouchable just like you. But I'm going to go to school anyway. Miss Abigail said so. She's the pale English lady, and she never tells a lie."

❧

The rice plants reached as high as Virat's waist. Their deep green color had begun to change to golden yellow, and the stalks to bend under the weight of the heavy rice heads. It was a precarious time for the rice. Fortunately, the monsoon season had already started to draw to a close. Even so, dark clouds gathered during the night and rain poured down so hard that no one could go to the fields to work in the morning.

"No one except you, Virat," Anup said. "Someone has to guard the growing rice in the paddy. You will do it today and throughout the night."

"I will stay in the field with you," Latha told her husband. Virat argued, but he could not dissuade her.

All day the rain poured down. At first, Virat and Latha walked back and forth through the rice paddy. Hour after hour after hour. When Virat found a high spot, they sat down, but as the rain continued to pour, the water rose and flooded over that spot, too. So they walked again, and continued to walk for most of the rest of the day. As night came and exhaustion overtook them, they sank down together in the muddy field, propped against each other back-to-back, and fell into a restless sleep.

Virat opened his eyes to see a star-studded sky. "Are you awake?" he whispered.

"Yes," Latha said.

"The rain stopped."

"Yes."

They sat together in the soggy paddy, watching the stars and breathing the fresh, clean air.

"You are a good wife," Virat said. "Thank you for that."

"You are a good husband," said Latha.

✍❤

"I was a bad boy in my last life," Ashish said as he spun Krishna's wooden top across the courtyard. "I wish I hadn't been."

"What did you do bad?" Krishna asked.

"I don't know. Do you know what you did that was bad?"

"No," Krishna said. He spun the top back to Ashish. "But I don't want to do it ever again."

"Me too."

Krishna grabbed the top and held onto it. "You know that song you like Miss Abigail to sing to you? The *Jesus Loves Me* song?"

Ashish wobbled his head "yes."

"One part says: Jesus loves me when I'm good, When I do the things I should,

Jesus loves me when I'm bad, Though it makes Him very sad."

"How can he love me when I'm bad?"

"I don't know, but he does," Krishna said. "That's a very good thing about Jesus."

In the morning, when the workers came out to the field again, Anup told Virat and Latha to go back to their hut. "You don't have to work today," he said.

When Latha entered the hut to get the small pot to fill with water, she gasped out loud. "Virat!" she called. "Come and look!"

Stacked along one wall was an entire set of new earthenware pots. Cooking pots and small pots and bowls. Even two large water pots.

"Where did they come from?" Latha asked. "Do you think the landlord is playing a trick on us?"

Virat picked up one of the water jars and ran his hand across it to inspect the quality of the workmanship. Fine, but not perfect. He turned it over and examined the patterns on the sides, then the markings on the bottom.

"Did Ranjun make it?"

"It is his marking," Virat said. "but it's not his work. These have to be from his sons. A gift from Ravi and Jinil."

"No, not from Ranjun's sons," Latha said. "They have to be a gift to us from Pooni's sons."

That day Virat and Latha filled their stomachs on rice and coconut and mangos.

"Where did you get such wonderful food?" Latha asked— but only after she had finished eating.

"The gods gave it to me," Virat said.

"You took the sacrifice food from the *puja*?"

"Look at us," Virat said. "All our good deeds have not appeased the gods' anger. Why should we starve trying to make them happy?"

Latha thought for a minute. "Let's go back and see what else is there," she said. "We will need something to eat tomorrow too."

## 33
## *September*

The rains passed, leaving the earth clean and fresh, and the days pleasantly cool. In the paddies, the tall rice ripened to a rich golden brown and drooped heavy with maturing heads. A time of peaceful serenity and refreshment before the approaching harvest. A time to hope for better days to come.

Not for Virat, though. And not for Latha.

"What do you think?" Latha whispered to her husband in the quiet of their hut. "Will we ever see our son again?"

Virat had no answer for her.

One evening, they came back from the fields and found two of their new earthenware pots standing in the middle of the dirt floor. One was filled with rice, the other with wheat. When Devi passed by on her way home from the master's garden that evening, she left an armload of vegetables at their door.

"I got used to being hungry," Virat said. "But I do prefer a full stomach."

One day, Jebar fell over and died in the field. His distraught wife lay on her sleeping mat, turned her face to the wall, and refused to be comforted. After five days, she also died. While everyone worked in the fields, Anup rolled up the old couple's sleeping mats and left them in Virat's hut.

When Latha went to the well for water, or took her grain to the grinding stone, the women no longer paid her any special mind. They had found more interesting things to gossip about.

"Time passes," Anup said to Virat. "Things are again the way they used to be."

But, of course, they were not. They were not at all the way they used to be.

One warm afternoon, when Boban Joseph came to test the ripeness of the rice, Saji Stephen crept away from his play yard and followed after his big brother. When Boban Joseph caught sight of Saji Stephen behind him, Boban Joseph ordered, "Go home right now! You know you are not allowed to be out here in the rice paddies."

Saji Stephen turned and ran. But as soon as Boban Joseph went back to his work, the little boy defiantly whispered to himself, "I will play in the paddies if I want to!" and scrambled into the high growth to hide.

The rice wasn't yet ready for harvest, so Boban Joseph told Anup to let the workers go back to their huts. "Tell them to rest. Soon their work days will be long and hard." But then Boban Joseph pointed to Virat. "Not him, though. He will be watchman in the field today and all night tonight."

After everyone else had left, as he searched for a place to settle down, Virat heard a rustling sound among the rice stalks. He jumped to attention and grabbed his knife from its sheath. For several moments all was still. Suddenly, the rustling started again, but closer now. Not a thief, for a thief would be stealthy and careful. A thief would quickly chop a swath from the edge of the crop and run. No, it must be a wild animal.

As Virat crouched down into a defensive pose, Saji Stephen stood up and stomped his way through the growth that came all the way up to his chest.

Virat stared at the spoiled, troublesome child of his tormentor, and his face hardened. Saji Stephen pulled off a handful of rice and tossed it into the air. Virat crept closer, gripping his knife tightly. The boy jumped up and down, trampling the rice into the ground—the very rice Latha had hunkered down in mud to plant—and Virat shook with fury. Slowly, silently, he crept closer to the boy.

Suddenly, Saji Stephen stopped. For a moment he stood perfectly still before his voice rose in a terrified shriek. Although Virat had moved in close, the boy still didn't see him. Saji Stephen's shriek melted into a shrill wail.

Virat shook his head. What was the matter with the stupid boy? Then he saw it. A huge cobra, hood flared wide, swayed back and forth in front of the child. It had its serpent eyes fixed directly on Saji Stephen.

Justice from the Lord Shiva. The gods had sent the cobra to avenge Ashish—to make things fair and set a wrong to right. A serpent to destroy the evil son of the oppressor who took away Virat's own blessing.

But all this lasted for only for a second. Virat leapt up and snatched Saji Stephen away from the cobra's reach. The terrified boy's wails turned to great heaving sobs as he clutched at Virat.

"You should not be here," Virat said to the child. "Come, I will take you to your home."

All the way across the fields and up the path, Saji Stephen clung to Virat. When they reached the edge of the garden,

Virat pried the child's hands from him and said, "Go to your mother. You are safe now."

As Saji Stephen ran for the safety of his veranda, Virat turned around and walked back to guard the rice paddy.

*

Nothing that happened in the village stayed a secret for long. Always, someone saw or heard, and always that someone told someone else who told another someone else who told someone else again, and soon the entire village buzzed with the gossip.

"You are certain the *chamar* saved you from the cobra?" Mammen Samuel asked his son. "Could it perhaps have been someone else?"

"Yes, the *chamar*," Saji Stephen answered.

"The one whose teeth stick out and who wears the faded yellow *chaddar* wrapped around his head?"

"Yes, yes!"

"The father of Ashish? Are you certain it was him?"

"Yes, *Appa*, I told you, yes!"

Mammen Samuel sent the boy to his mother. He swiped at his sweat-soaked face with his sleeve and sat down on his veranda, cross-legged on his fine Persian carpet. He had much to ponder. Slowly he rubbed his anxious, aching brow. The sun sank low and set, the sky grew dark and stars glimmered overhead, yet Mammen Samuel's spirit grew increasingly troubled.

"You are distressed."

Mammen Samuel looked up to see Brahmin Keshavan standing at the edge of his veranda. Mammen Samuel heaved a sigh of resignation and waved him in.

Brahmin Keshavan sat down on the other side of the Persian carpet. "You took away the *chamar's* son and he gave your son back to you. Is that not so?"

Mammen Samuel said nothing.

"That is a problem only to a Christian," the Brahmin pointed out. "Not only do you believe you must return good for good, but you believe you must return good for evil. Of course, that is not possible. You acted out your *dharma* and he acted out his. Nothing less and nothing more."

"Do not annoy me with your gibberish!" Mammen Samuel said with an irritated wave of his hand. "I am in no mood to listen to it."

"Perhaps I understand the situation better than you because I know what you do not know."

Mammen Samuel looked up cautiously. Brahmin Keshavan could be most shrewd and tricky.

"The son of Virat the *chamar*, the one they call Blessing—he is not dead."

"What?" Mammen Samuel demanded.

"No. He lives on to mock you."

Brahmin Keshavan's face remained flat and expressionless, the same as always, yet Mammen Samuel caught the slightest trace of a mocking smile.

"How do you know this?" Mammen Samuel demanded.

"Stinginess in my home village has forced me to take my services to distant villages," Brahmin Keshavan said. "One day's journey to the east, I said blessings at a wedding and poured *ghee* into the wedding fire. I stayed two nights before I started my journey back home. That's when I saw the boy."

"You *saw* him?" Mammen Samuel demanded. "And you can be certain it was the same boy?"

"Absolutely certain. He is right now in the care of the missionaries at the English Mission Medical Clinic."

Mammen Samuel's eyes narrowed. "Why are you telling this to me?"

"The English gave out medicines as they condemned my holy *mantras* and blessed amulets, yet I sat quietly by and did nothing. They preached a foreign religion to gullible and polluted people, yet I held my tongue. But now they dare to teach Untouchables to read and write. Such an action is strictly forbidden, yet they do it in front of my face. The boy who fouled our water is learning to read . . . in English!"

"You *saw* this?" Mammen Samuel demanded.

"With my own two eyes," Brahmin Keshavan said. "And you know the same truth I know, Mammen Varghese: unless so great a transgression draws a harsh penalty, men will never keep to their castes."

Mammen Samuel, his eyes set and his jaw clenched, sat in stony silence.

"*Karma* guided the Untouchable *chamar* to save the life of your son, and *karma* saved the life of the *chamar's* son from your fury. You owe the Untouchable not one thing. Nothing."

"*Karma, karma, karma!*" Mammen Samuel growled. "You think that's the answer to everything. But it is nothing more than a Hindu excuse to protect everyone from having to accept responsibility for their actions."

"I should think one such as you would rejoice to have such an excuse," Brahmin Keshavan said. "For without it, you must bear a greater weight of responsibility than any of us."

Rage simmered in Mammen Samuel's eyes. The Brahmin stood up and carefully smoothed his *mundu*. "It is you who must decide your actions. But I warn you—weigh your alternatives carefully and consider the consequences of each one. For each path does have consequences."

Although Hindus seldom spoke of heaven or hell, Mammen Samuel Varghese—since he was Christian—knew for certain that both existed. Brahmin Keshavan would say that nothing could truly be considered real except this present world and the World Spirit. He would say it is up to every person to work to perfect each incarnation as he evolved through the wheel of time. That when one finally attains perfection—as he most certainly would soon—a person's soul would be absorbed into the World Sprit and become as one with it.

That night Mammen Samuel tossed on his bed and sighed. Such a weary religion! How many gods did they have, anyway? When he asked this question of the Brahmin, Keshavan simply answered, "To try to count them would be more difficult than to count the stars in the sky."

Mammen Samuel did not close his eyes all night. With the first light of dawn, he got up from his bed and bellowed for Babu. "I want my cart made ready immediately. And I want Boban Joseph sitting on the bench, ready to travel! Not the bullock cart, either. I want the horse!"

*✐*

Boban Joseph was well acquainted with his father's foul moods, so he took particular care to steer the horse straight and not allow the cart to jostle any more than necessary. Mammen Samuel said little, which pleased Boban Joseph just fine. Even though he had been eagerly guessing as to the purpose of the trip all morning, he thought it best not to ask.

"When we get to the English clinic, stay in the cart unless I call for you," Mammen Samuel instructed.

They arrived before noon. Without getting up from the cart bench, Mammen Samuel bellowed, "I have come to get the boy Ashish!"

When no one answered his call, he bellowed still louder: "Give me what is mine! I have come for Ashish!"

Dr. Moore opened the door, Darshina beside him and Abigail watching from behind. "You are standing upon British property, Sir, and we Englishmen do not communicate by bellowing commands through walls," the doctor said. He waited for Darshina to translate before he continued: "Should you wish to communicate in a civilized manner, you may enter and sit with me. If that is not acceptable to you, please leave the premises immediately."

Mammen Samuel listened impatiently to Darshina's translation. Shaking with rage, he roared, "I am an important man in the village!"

In response to Darshina's translation, Dr. Moore said, "You well may be exactly that, but this is not your village. I am an important man on this compound, and I say you will behave in a civilized manner or you will leave."

Darshina stared at the doctor. "I cannot be telling such a thing to him!" she protested.

"Tell him!" Dr. Moore ordered. He never took his eyes off Mammen Samuel.

Bowing low, Darshina repeated the doctor's words.

"I will hire men to beat you until you are dead! I will tell them to burn your clinic to the ground! I will—"

The landlord got no further with his threats, for Dr. Moore turned, stepped inside, and closed the door. Mammen Samuel stood outside, raging and shouting his threats. The door remained shut. Mammen Samuel got down from the cart and pounded on the clinic door. No one answered. He bellowed threats and even called down curses on the clinic and on the doctor and on everyone who ever had stepped or ever would step over the threshold. Nothing changed, except that the hour grew later.

Finally exhausted, Mammen Samuel said, "I wish to communicate with you in a civilized manner."

Immediately, Dr. Moore opened the door. "Do come in," he said. "Would you care for a cup of tea?"

⚜

"You have the boy Ashish," Mammen Samuel stated.

With Darshina translating for both, Dr. Moore answered, "Yes, that is true. Ashish is here with us."

"I have come to get him. He belongs to me."

"We do not approve of owning other people's children," Dr. Moore said.

"That boy is my property, and I will have him!"

Dr. Moore resettled the spectacles on his nose, and uncrossed and recrossed his long legs. "You said that you, too, are a Christian man, did you not?"

"Yes," Mammen Samuel said warily. "I am a Christian from a long line of Christians, a descendant of a family that can trace its ancestry all the way back to the first Indian king to follow Saint Thomas, disciple of Jesus the Christ." After Darshina finished translating, Mammen Samuel added, "The same Saint Thomas who died a martyr's death in this country, you understand."

"In that case, Sir, why do you continue to cling to the Hindu belief of the inferiority of people due to caste?" Dr. Moore asked. "If you have rejected the pagan belief of repeated death and endless rebirth, how can you condemn a man—or a little boy, in the case of Ashish—for suffering from the Hindu condition of untouchability?"

Mammen Samuel stood up abruptly, his eyes flashing. "Do not dare to scold me as though I were a naughty school child! I am a Christian, but I am still Indian." He wagged his finger at the doctor and ordered, "You give me my boy! Now!"

"No, Sir," Dr. Moore said. "I shall not."

# 34

*W*here does all this food come from?" Ashish asked as he swirled his hand around the earthenware plate on the ground before him. He scooped up a handful of rice and vegetables and stuffed it into his mouth.

"The vegetables grow on our plants," Krishna said. He put only small bites into his mouth because his lips were too scarred to open wide. Even then, much of the food ended up on his face.

"I know that, but I mean where does the rice come from? I don't see any paddies or fields here."

"From the doctor. He buys the rice. All English people are rich."

"Richer than the landlord?"

"Richer than anyone in all of India," Krishna said. "The English people are the bosses of the world."

After Ashish put the last bite in his mouth he set to work plucking up the rice grains that stuck on the edges of his plate.

"I like those marks on your face," Ashish said. "My *amma* has marks like that on her eye."

"They aren't marks, they're scars, and I hate them." Krishna took another careful bite. "Did your *amma's* auntie throw boiling water in her face too?"

"I don't know. It's just the way she is."

The doctor, Abigail, and Darshina were all closed in the surgery, which the boys were forbidden to enter unless they were specifically invited in. The only person they could see was the squat cook.

"Stay away from her," Krishna had warned Ashish on his first day at the clinic. "She doesn't like little boys."

That was not an entirely true statement as it turned out. She just didn't like Krishna.

"Wash yourselves!" the cook ordered the boys. "You are a mess." She glanced at Krishna and muttered, "It would take the entire river to set that one to right."

"Who is in the surgery?" Ashish asked Krishna.

"Another woman sick with the fever."

"I want to see her," Ashish said.

"You cannot. If you try, the English doctor will be very angry with you and you will have to spend all day lying on your cot."

"I had a fever once," Ashish said. "The pox goddess gave it to me and she kissed my face."

"Pox is a different kind of fever," Krishna said. "This is malaria fever. It doesn't make holes all in your face like pox does."

✐

Krishna looked down at the drawing Ashish had scratched in the dirt. "What is it?" he asked.

"A tiger," Ashish said. "That's me in its mouth."

"What a silly picture! If a tiger got you in its mouth, it would tear you into little pieces and—"

Abigail, who had come up behind the boys, put her hand on Krishna's shoulder and said, "Come with me. It's time for your lessons." Krishna nodded his understanding. Abigail took Ashish's hand and brought him along, too, though the boy had no idea where they were going or what they would do.

Abigail found a shady spot under a tree and sat down with her back against the trunk. Krishna flopped down in front of her and sat cross-legged, so Ashish did the same. From her bag, Abigail pulled a stack of cards with brightly colored letters printed on them and spread them on the ground. One by one, as she pointed to the cards, Krishna called out the letter names: F . . . B . . . M . . . S . . . C . . . K . . . A . . . L . . .

They went over the cards again and again. After awhile Abigail smiled at Ashish and said, "Now you try." She pointed to the first card.

Ashish hesitated. He looked at Krishna.

"What is the name of this first letter?" Abigail urged.

Ashish whispered, "A."

"Very good!" Abigail cheered. "Very, very good!"

Ashish also knew B and C. And K and S.

"Extraordinarily good!" Abigail exclaimed.

Abigail put the cards away and took out a book with a picture of Jesus Christ on the cross. As she pointed out the words under the picture, Krishna haltingly read, "For God . . . so loved . . . the world . . ."

From then on, Ashish did lessons with Krishna and Miss Abigail every morning and again each afternoon. He enjoyed the lessons, but they also left him distraught.

"Is it a sin for us to learn to read letters?" he asked Krishna. "Will we be punished by the gods?"

Krishna shrugged. "I have already been punished by the gods. Now I can do anything I want."

✍❧

Dr. Moore shook his head. "This man's fingers are completely severed." The young man on the cot had walked into the clinic alone, his hand wrapped in a blood-soaked *chaddar*. "He will have to learn to get along without them," Dr. Moore said. "Wash and dress his hand, Miss Davidson."

Abigail's touch was tender, her words soft and kind. It certainly helped that she had learned to speak words of comfort and assurance in the local tongue. Darshina urged the man to stay on the cot in the surgery, to rest for a while longer, but he would not. He wrapped his stained *chaddar* around his head, folded his wounded hand together with his good one and bowed so as to properly show his gratitude, and left the clinic. Staggering slightly, he made his way down the road alone.

"These natives lack even the vestiges of good sense!" Dr. Moore groused. "That young man will be back soon. Or perhaps he will be dead."

Darshina's eyes flashed, but she held her peace.

"Ashish is a smart child," Abigail said as she piled the dirty cloths into a basin. "Already I can communicate with him rather well."

"Is that because he has picked up a bit of English, or because you are willing to learn Malayalam?" It sounded more like an accusation than a question.

Abigail, refusing to take it as anything but an honest question, answered, "His English is coming along well, mostly because of Krishna. But Ashish is also learning the alphabet, and he can even recognize a few English words in my book."

Dr. Moore busied himself cleaning up his physician's instruments.

"I think he should accompany Krishna to the mission school in Madras," Abigail ventured. Then, more to herself than to the doctor, "Though I would be most sorry to bid him farewell."

"That school is for orphans, Miss Davidson. Ashish is not an orphan."

"Well, he may as well be! His parents are always leaving him somewhere. And as for that evil landlord—the farther the child can be from him, the better!"

"We are here to treat the people's ills, not the ills of the people's society."

"I don't see that one goes without the other," Abigail insisted. She had much more to say, but Darshina shot her a warning look.

☙

Abigail opened the book with the picture of Jesus Christ on the cross. "Here, Ashish," she said. "Can you read the words?"

Ashish wrinkled his forehead and scrunched up his eyes. "F . . . f . . . for . . . God . . . so . . ."

"Loved," Abigail prompted.

"Loved . . . the . . ."

"World!" Krishna said. "Loved the world!"

"Yes," Abigail said. She closed the book and called for Darshina to come and translate. "Krishna, you have learned so much. I am extremely proud of you. You are also learning well, Ashish."

Ashish hung his head. "No, Miss. I cannot learn."

"Why, whatever do you mean? Darshina, ask him why he would say such a thing!"

"The fortune-teller told my *amma* that I am a stupid boy. I heard her tell it to my *appa*."

"No!" Abigail protested. "That is not true! You are a very smart boy. That's why I want you to go to the school in Madras with Krishna. You will learn to read and to write. And you'll learn many other wonderful things too."

"Is the school close to where the workers live?" Ashish asked. "Would I be near *Amma* and *Appa*?"

Abigail got down on her knees and gripped the boy's arms. "You must forget about them, Ashish. All that is behind you. It's past. You have a new life now, you and Krishna together. What do you think about that?"

Ashish had no idea what he thought about it. Never before had anyone asked him his opinion on anything. He stood still and stared at the pale English lady.

"Perhaps one day you might even be my own little boy, Ashish," Abigail said. "Maybe you could be my blessing."

Ashish stared at her uncomprehendingly.

"I would take care of you. You would be with me whenever you aren't in school," Abigail said.

School. Ashish did think about that. All day and all night he thought about it. As he filled his stomach with rice and vegetables, he thought about it. As he lay on his cot under a slowly spinning fan and listened to the chirrup of crickets, he thought about it. As he read the names of the brightly colored letters on Miss Abigail's cards and picked out words in her book, he thought about the school.

Maybe the hunters caught his *amma* and *appa*. It might be that his parents were already dead. They were very good people, and very brave, so they might already have been reborn into a higher caste. Maybe *Appa* was a king somewhere and

*Amma* a princess. Maybe they lived in a house with a veranda and a cow and had plenty of food to eat. Maybe they had forgotten all about him. Maybe they no longer remembered their Ashish—their blessing. It could be so.

Tears filled Ashish's eyes and ran down the sides of his face.

Or might his parents still miss him? Would it be possible for them to ever be happy if he was no longer beside them?

Softly Ashish sang:

"Jesus loves me! This I know. For the Bible tells me so.
Little ones to Him belong; They are weak, but He is strong.
Yes, Jesus loves me! Yes, Jesus loves me!
Yes, Jesus loves me! The Bible tells me so."

✍❤

"What ever is the matter?" Abigail asked Ashish. "Yesterday you read your letters and words so well, but today you won't even try. Do you feel all right? Are you sick?"

The boy raised his head high and said, "I am Ashish. I am a blessing. Always and forever, I must remember who I am."

Darshina translated his words.

"Yes, yes," Abigail said. "That is really quite lovely. But why will you not read?"

"I cannot go to school with Krishna."

"Why not?"

"Because I am my *appa* and *amma's* blessing. I cannot be their blessing if I am not with them. Please, Miss Abigail, I want to go home."

# 35

## *October*

*I* do not approve of this, Miss Davidson. Not in the least," Dr. Moore stated. "A far better plan would be for me to send a message to Landlord Varghese and have him bring a wagon to the clinic and collect the boy."

"No!" Abigail insisted. "I do not trust that man. Please, Sir, Darshina and I can take the boy to his parents."

"And if his parents are not to be found? What then?"

"Then we will bring him back with us and send him to the school in Madras with Krishna."

Dr. Moore's eyes narrowed. "And keep him for yourself?"

"And send him to the school in Madras. But only if his parents are not to be found."

Dr. Moore sighed in resignation. "Why do I try to discuss the matter? I see that your mind is already made up."

Abigail flashed a quick smile to Darshina.

"I will ask Tanal to drive you in the wagon and to see you safely back," the doctor said. "He knows how to find the land-lord's settlement."

Tanal, an Untouchable of the carpenter caste, was always willing to run errands for Dr. Moore. Back when the mission medical clinic was first established, when Dr. Moore and the Indian cook were the only ones there, Tanal had brought in his young son suffering from a viper bite on his leg. Dr. Moore treated the boy, and two days later, the child stood up from his bed, well enough to walk home with his father. Before they left the clinic, Tanal bowed low, his hands folded before his face. Through the cook, he told Dr. Moore, "My debt to you will never be repaid. I will remain your tireless servant forever."

And so he had.

When Abigail looked outside early the next morning, Tanal already sat waiting in the cart. He had fitted it with a bench long enough for Abigail and Darshina to sit comfortably side by side with Ashish between them.

Abigail smoothed down the folds of her demure light blue skirt and adjusted her long-sleeved top with the lace insets. Her favorite outfit, saved back for special occasions. She always wore it with a smart navy blue straw hat. (Riding on the make-shift bench in the back of the open cart, however, she did feel a bit of a fool.)

Beggars, beggars, beggars, all along the side of the road. Abigail had seen roadside beggars, of course, but never so many! Crippled or blind, men leaning on sticks and women balancing babies on their hips, maimed children of every age. Poverty and despair stretched out all along the roadside.

"Why so many beggars?" Abigail asked Darshina.

"It is the month of *Thulam*, the most religious month of the year. Everyone is more generous during *Thulam*, so more beggars sit with their hands out."

Sprinkled among the beggars were *sadhus*—holy men dressed in saffron-colored cloth, all with white ash on their bodies and their long hair wrapped up in buns on top of their heads. Each *sadhu* had a mark on his forehead, the sign of his specific sect. One stepped right up and walked alongside the cart holding out a coconut half-shell. Abigail pulled away, but Darshina dropped in a coin.

"Ashish, I have something to give to you," Abigail said. "It is a very great gift and I want you to carefully keep it always."

Ashish looked questioningly from the pale English lady to Darshina, so Darshina translated Abigail's words.

Abigail laid a large leather-bound Bible in the boy's small hands. "I know you can only read a few words of this now, but you are a smart boy. One day you will be able to read the entire book."

Darshina repeated the words in his language.

Dr. Moore, of course, had no idea Abigail intended to make such a huge gift to so small a child. If he had, he would have been furious. He would have stopped her, which is exactly why Abigail took such care to keep it from him. It was, after all, her own Bible. She could do with it as she pleased.

"Be very, very careful with it," Abigail said. "It's a holy book. It tells about Jesus who loves you."

Abigail Davidson had never before seen a landlord's settlement of laborer huts. The primitive conditions in which the workers lived shocked her. Such tiny shelters. So many ragged workers. Eyes so dark and curious, and all fixed on her. Tanal stopped the cart in the courtyard beside the well and spoke to Darshina.

"He will wait here for us," she told Abigail.

Darshina and Abigail climbed down with Ashish. The boy blinked around him at all the staring eyes. Clutching the gift from Abigail, he pushed his way toward his family's hut. Abigail and Darshina hurried after him.

Already word had gotten around, and Latha and Virat came running. Laughing and crying at the same time, they grabbed up their son and hugged him tight.

Abigail, feeling increasingly uncomfortable, busied herself rearranging her skirt and adjusting the hat, which was making her feel sillier by the moment. But Virat stepped forward and dropped to his knees in front of her. He touched his forehead to the ground and clasped her feet in his hands.

"*Nandi*," Virat said. "*Orupadu nandi.*"

"He said 'Thank you,'" Darshina told Abigail. "He said, 'Thank you very much.'"

At daybreak, Virat and Latha did not join the other workers. The door of their hut didn't open and no one lit a fire in their cooking pit.

"Let them be," Anup said. "They have earned a day together."

Latha and Virat lay on their sleeping mats with Ashish between them and breathed in the pure air of the holy month. Ashish told them of his adventures at the mission clinic, of Miss Abigail and the doctor and Darshina. He told them about the boy Krishna, with an entire face like *Amma's* eye, and how he would be going away to school. He told them that he knew some English words and that he could read the colored letters on Miss Abigail's cards.

"She showed you how to read words?" Virat exclaimed.

That old guilty fear began to rise up in Ashish again. "Only a few," the boy said. "Mostly just letters."

Virat sat up and reached for the book Ashish brought home. "If this is the *Veda*, we will all die," he said. "Our hands will be cut off for polluting the holy book, and we will be cut into pieces."

"No, *Appa*, this is a different holy book. This is the book of Jesus. And Jesus doesn't mind if we touch it or read it."

"Is this Jesus a god?" Latha asked.

"God is his father."

"I think I understand," Virat said. "Jesus is another of the many manifestations of the divine. That must be it."

"Come," Latha said. She took a small bag of colored powder from behind the rice sack and carried it outside. On the ground in front of their hut she used the powder to carefully draw an intricate design of circles and triangles. "This is a gift for your new god," she told Ashish. "This is a gift for Jesus."

"Will he see the picture?" Ashish asked. "Will he stop here?"

"Perhaps. That's what happened in the story of Lakshmi, the Goddess of Wealth. One Thursday night she visited a village very much like this one. All the village women decorated their houses to welcome her, especially the upper caste women. But the goddess decided that the house of an untouchable sweeper woman was the most beautiful of all, so that's the one she entered."

"Yes, yes," Virat said with an impatient wave of his hand. "That's a common old tale, but like all the other stories of the gods, it isn't true."

"I think this story about Jesus is true," Ashish said. "And I think he might stop here when he sees the picture."

"If any god exists, he has forgotten us," Virat said.

Latha shook her head. "I think you might be wrong, Husband."

Virat gave Latha a startled look. It was not in Latha's nature to argue against him. He knew he should correct her, but exactly how, he wasn't sure.

"We walked among tigers and leopards," Latha said. "We had no food left. The rains did their best to wash us away. We had no shelter . . . no place to sleep. Master Landlord vowed he would kill us. His hunters caught us in the field and led us back bound like common slaves. The Englishwoman carried Ashish away from us on the back of a horse, and she wanted to send him to their English school and make him into an English boy. And yet, here we are, all together and all well."

Ashish squeezed himself down between his mother and father.

"I think you are wrong, Husband," Latha said.

"Perhaps I am," Virat agreed. "Perhaps we are not completely forgotten."

## 36

*H*arvest!"

When the call finally came, the entire settlement rushed to work. Already the paddies had been drained dry. Already the last of the wheat had been cleaned away from the storage shed and the threshing floor swept smooth. Sharpened scythes lay ready for the men to grab up and carry out to the rice paddies.

"Harvest!"

The settlement rose before dawn and lit their cooking fires. Flames danced in front of every hut and porridge bubbled on every fire.

"I will go the field with you," Ashish begged.

"Of course you will not," Virat told him. "You are much too small."

"I could carry water to you."

"No, my son. The bigger boys will do that. You will stay here and gather firewood so we can cook when we get home, and you will tend to the chili plant by the house so it will grow tall and healthy."

"But Devi will come to take me to Saji Stephen! Please, *Appa*. I will work hard in the fields."

Latha hugged her son and said nothing.

Ashish watched the laborers leave. As soon as they were out of sight, he took his mother's water pots to the well to fill them, but the pot was too big to hold and at the same time get water into it. On his first try, he almost dropped the water jar. On his second, he missed the jar completely and poured water all over his clothes. He stomped his feet and cried a little, but then he drew more water to try again.

"I'll help you," Little Girl called. As usual, she had Baby in tow. Ashish had not talked to Little Girl since he returned from the English Mission Medical Clinic.

As Ashish held out the water jar, Little Girl filled it with a steady hand. Ashish wanted to talk to her, but he didn't know what to say. Everything seemed so different now.

"Are you going to hunt for firewood?" Little Girl asked.

"After I tend the chili plant."

"You should grow more vegetables than only that chili. My *appa* says you can have some of our plants if you want them."

Ashish shook his head. "Your *amma* would be angry with me if I took them."

Little Girl shrugged. "I know where you can find a lot of firewood," she said. "After you tend the chili, I'll show you."

When Sethu came in from the field, Lidya had the cooking fire hot and a pot of rice and vegetables bubbling on the fire. Nothing unusual about that. But the large store of firewood neatly stacked beside the door was most unusual.

"Ashish brought it for us," Lidya told her mother.

"What did you give him in exchange for it?" Sethu asked.

"He didn't want anything."

Sethu called, "Little Girl! Did you go to Ashish's hut today?"

Little Girl shrank back. "I saw him at the well. He needed water to tend the chili plant, but he couldn't fill the water jug. I helped him, that's all. I didn't do anything bad."

"Maybe this one time you did something good," Sethu said.

✑❧

Two days after Ashish returned home, Devi came to the door of his hut. "Master Landlord says you are to come with me," she said. "Saji Stephen calls for you."

Ashish started to tremble and his eyes filled with tears. He didn't move.

"We must hurry," Devi said.

Ashish wiped his hand across his face and snuffled his nose. "No," he said.

"What do you mean *no?* You must come with me. Master Landlord called for you."

"No! I will not go."

Virat put his hand on his son's shoulder. "I'm sorry, my son. The landlord is our master. When he calls, you must go."

"No," Ashish said, and this time he wasn't whimpering any more. "I will work in the fields with you, *Appa*. Or I will carry water. Or I will gather firewood and tend the chili plant. But I will not go back to Saji Stephen."

Now Devi started to cry. "Please, Ashish. Please! If I don't bring you with me, the master will have me beaten."

"You don't have to go either," Ashish said. "If master landlord hurts us, we will go to the pale English lady and tell her. She will make him stop."

Ashish didn't go to play with Saji Stephen. But Devi did go to work in the garden. She feared the landlord, but that's not why she went. She went because she feared her mother more.

Ashish stepped into the edge of the wooded undergrowth and gathered up all the twigs and branches his small arms could hold. He carried them back to his hut, but he had to drop them outside because a pile of dirt clods blocked the door, each clod attached to a different vegetable plant. Ashish picked up each of the plants and carried it to the side of the hut where the chili plant already grew high and heavy with chilies. He found the broken piece of pottery his mother used for digging and scraped out four new holes. In the first hole he put an eggplant, carefully packing dirt around the roots. Already tall, the plant had tiny eggplants growing on it. The second hole he made bigger and put in a cluster of onions. He had no idea what the other two plants were, but he planted them anyway in the other two holes. Ashish got the water jar that sat alongside the wall of the hut and carefully poured water on each plant, the way Krishna had taught him.

When Ashish stood up to admire his work, and to wipe his muddy hands on his clothes, he saw Little Girl watching him.

"Did you learn about growing vegetables at the mission clinic too?" she asked.

Ashish smiled and nodded.

While Virat sat on the ground outside his hut, enjoying the cool evening and eating his meal, he watched as a cluster of little boys chased one another around in circles. Anup walked over and sat down near him.

"I like to see little boys at play," Anup said.

Virat scooped up another bite of spicy rice and slurped it into his mouth. "Tell Sethu we appreciate the vegetable plants," He said. "Ashish planted them today."

Anup said nothing.

Ashish had been ready to run out and play with the other boys, but when he saw Anup, he sank into the corner and did his best to be invisible.

"Devi tells me Ashish would not go to the master landlord's house with her today," Anup said.

Virat swirled up another dripping bite and lifted it to his mouth.

"Your son belongs to the master landlord. Your entire family belongs to him."

Virat scooped his hand expertly around the bowl and into the edges in search of another bite.

"Look at you, Virat. After everything that happened, you are still alive. Most certainly the gods have smiled on you. But you cannot humiliate the master landlord by disobeying his commands and still hope to survive. To allow your son to behave in such a disgraceful manner is even worse."

"The English have taught my son their ways," Virat said. "The landlord should take the matter up with the English."

"He will not do that. He will take the matter out on you."

Virat focused his attention on the last few grains of rice.

"Ashish!" Anup called. "Come over here!"

Ashish jumped at the sound of his name coming from so important a man. Slowly, he stood up and moved toward Anup.

"Your mother and father are blessed to have a strong and intelligent son like you," Anup said to the boy. "When they are old, they will need you to look after them. And they will have you, too . . . unless Master Landlord sends you away. Then your *appa* and *amma* will have no one to look out for them. They might get sick and have no one to care for them. They might starve to death. And it will be your fault."

"No, no," Ashish said. "I will work in the fields for Master Landlord. I will work very hard."

"You can't work in the fields if the master has already sent you away. And you can't work as a *chamar* either, because no one will teach you the ways. Not the English, because they don't know."

"I want to be a good boy," Ashish whimpered.

"Tomorrow Devi will come to take you to Saji Stephen," Anup said. "What will you do?"

Ashish said nothing.

"Well?" Anup tapped his fingers impatiently. "What will you do when Devi comes for you tomorrow?"

Ashish looked at his *appa*, but Virat kept his eyes on his bowl.

"Come, come, boy! I'm asking you a question. When Devi comes for you tomorrow, what will you do?"

"I will go with her," Ashish whispered.

## 37

That evening, no one spoke of the morrow. But after dark, as Virat and Latha lay side by side on their sleeping mats, Virat said, "I do my best to stay clean. I try to be a good man, kind and fair to all people. Why must I be untouchable?"

Latha reached over to her husband. On her other side, Ashish wiggled and turned, the way he always did when he had trouble getting to sleep.

"Because it is the way," Latha said. "Because it is our *karma*."

"I no longer believe in *karma*," said Virat.

Ashish flopped over onto his back.

"Even if we were not untouchable, we would still belong to the landlord," Latha whispered.

Virat laid his fingers on his wife's arm. Then he reached over and caressed his son's black hair.

"We are what we are," he said.

Stars glimmered in the October sky like ten thousand tiny candle flames. A cool breeze blew over, and the entire settlement seemed to sigh with grateful relief.

And then, in the gentleness of the night, Ashish's small voice sang words in a foreign tongue:

"Jesus loves me! He who died, Heaven's gate to open wide;
He will wash away my sin. Let His little child come in."

"Is that an English song?" Latha asked her son.

"It's about the God in my holy book," Ashish said.

"What do the words mean?"

"That the holy God whose name is Jesus loves me and washes all my sins off of me. When I die, he will open the gate to heaven and let me walk right in."

"No, no," Virat said. "You must have made a mistake. Only Brahmins have a chance of going to heaven."

"The God Jesus didn't like that rule," Ashish said. "So he changed it."

For a long time, Virat lay awake, his eyes fixed on the twinking stars scattered across the heavens. Latha lay completely still at his side, and Ashish's sleep-breaths came soft and even.

"With morning light, Latha and I must go back to work in the fields," Virat whispered into the night. "Ashish must go again to Saji Stephen. We will all still be despised Untouchables. I cannot change any of that."

Beside him, Latha shifted in her sleep and Ashish moaned softly.

"Help us, gods," Virat prayed.

But he knew better. After all that had happened, he knew better.

"Please," Virat prayed again. "Help me, Jesus God!"

# Afterword to Readers

From the dawn of history, the area we now know as South India has been the home of the ancient Dravidian people. Short, dark-skinned, and broad-featured, they lived simple, agrarian lives in a bountiful land. For all they knew, their home was the entire world.

But, of course, it was not.

Almost four thousand years ago, a highly cultured race of tall, light-skinned people invaded the Indian subcontinent from the north. These newcomers had prospered in the Russian Steppes and around the Caspian Sea, but as they became more numerous they had split into different tribes, each searching for more pasture land. Over time, some groups moved toward Greece, some to Asia Minor, some to Iran. Some groups migrated to India.

*Aryan*, the groups moving into India called themselves, from the Sanskrit word for "noble." And when the newcomers looked out at the dark-skinned natives, they truly did feel noble—and superior.

Over the next hundreds of years, the Aryans pushed their way down the Ganga and Yamuna Rivers, farther and farther into the Dravidians' bucolic homeland. Dominant Aryan families proclaimed themselves priests and composed hymns to record their exploits and consolidate their power. Technologically more advanced, the invaders knew how to work with iron. They built heavy chariots with cruelly spoked wheels and used them to roar down on the hapless Dravidians, who fought back armed with wooden spears. Inevitably, the Aryans triumphed.

*Dasa*, the conquerors called the dark-skinned ones. Slaves. The subjugated ones were denounced as *Mlechas*—unholy. Both the *Mlechas* and the impure places they lived—*mlechadesas* —were forbidden to Aryans.

But proclamations and denunciations are never as powerful as the perceived word of a god, so the priest class declared itself demi-gods. They established their hymns as scripture— the *Vedas*—and from them fashioned the philosophy we know as Hinduism. The *Vedas* ordained a strict and unforgiving system of *varnas*—which is to say, castes.

According to the *Vedas*, the four castes were born from the creator god *Brahma*. The priests set themselves up as *Brahmins*, the highest caste, born from the mouth of the god. No physical labor could be required of them, only priestly duties. Kings and mighty warriors made up the second caste, *Kshatriyas*, said to have come from the arms of the god. The third caste, *Vaisyas*, were merchants and tradesmen, said to have issued from the god's midsection. Only a small number of privileged people belonged to these upper three castes.

The fourth caste, *Sudras*, were said to have come from the feet of the god. *Sudras* were farmers, laborers, and servants. Their duty was to serve the first three castes.

Below all these lay the conquered people. The polluted and unholy ones. Those outside the caste system. Outcastes. They did not come from the god *Brahma* at all, and therefore they were not at all human. They were sub-human. Un-born, they were called, meaning it would have been better for everyone had they never been born.

Thus, not only were the Dravidians conquered, they were condemned as sinners beyond hope—less valuable than the snakes and rats, animals, and stinging insects.

Ever flexible, Hinduism has an innate ability to expand and absorb pieces of many and varied religions and philosophies. Still, its three major tenets hold constant: caste, karma, and reincarnation. A person is born into a particular caste, or outside the castes, as a reward or punishment for the deeds of his or her past life. An upper caste person is free to reap the benefits of that exalted position. An Untouchable must endure the indignities and oppression without complaint—or face something much worse in the next reincarnation.

For 3,500 years, the oppressed descendants of India's ancient peoples have struggled to survive under the heel of the upper castes. Sometimes one of these descendants finds a special blessing in a most unlikely place.

The fight to protect that blessing can be a matter of life or death.

It might even lead to God.

# Glossary of Terms

**Amma:** Malayalam for mother.

**Anna:** An old Indian coin, worth one sixteenth of a rupee.

**Appa:** Malayalam for father.

**Avatar:** In the Hindu philosophy, a divine incarnation of a god.

**Betel nut:** A chew made of nuts and tobacco wrapped in the leaves of the betel plant.

**Bhaghwan:** This word means god in the Hindu understanding.

**Brahma:** *Creator god* of the Hindu *trinity*. The other two gods are Vishnu, the preserver, and Shiva, the destroyer. (Not to be confused with Brahmin. See below.)

**Brahmin:** The highest and most honored of the varnas, or castes, in Indian society. Brahmins are the Hindu priests and spiritual leaders. They put great and minute emphasis on ritual purity, and are forbidden from doing any manual labor. They make up approximately 5 percent of India's population. (Not to be confused with the god Brahma. See above.)

**Bhudevas:** In the Hindu philosophy, gods on earth.

**Caste:** Traditional Hindu society is divided into four main varnas, or hierarchical groups known as castes: Brahmins

(5 percent), Kshatriyas (5 percent), Vaishyas (5 percent), and Sudras (50 percent). Below this four-fold caste structure are the "outcastes"—now called Dalits—an oppressed people forced in all ways to occupy the lowest positions of this social order (25 percent). Also outside the caste system are the "tribals," the indigenous Indian peoples. Technically, Christians and Muslims are also outside the system, since caste is really part of the Hindu religious philosophy, though in actuality most outcaste Christians and Muslims remain mired in its oppression. These and people of other nationalities and religions make up the other 10 percent of the population. Each caste has its own group of occupations associated with it.

**Chaddar:** A long strip of cloth, half the size of a mundu, worn by men as a shawl or turban.

**Chakras:** The word chakra means "wheel" in Sanskrit. In the Hindu philosophy, each human body is believed to have seven chakras, or energy centers, that run in sequence from the top of the head to the pelvic area. It is believed that when Chakras are in harmony, the body is at peace. (Differing chakra counts may be the result of the associated "auras.")

**Chamar:** One of the many Untouchable occupational subcastes, this one being that of leather tanners.

**Chapati:** Round, flat baked bread, similar to unsweetened pancakes or tortillas.

**Cows, sacred:** In India, "Mother Cow" is respected and looked after. It is considered sacred, and to harm a cow is a great sin. It is likened to harming one's own mother. The cow is also associated with mythological stories that surround several Hindu deities, including Krishna, said to have been raised by the son of a milkman.

**Dharma:** A moral law, or righteousness. This can vary, person to person, caste to caste.

**Dowry:** Money and/or property required of the family of the bride by the family of the groom in order to secure a marriage. The amount varies, depending on the "value" of the bride, but it is crippling for many families of girls. Dowry is a major cause of the abandonment and even killing of female children.

**Ghee:** Butter, boiled and clarified. It is greatly prized, both as a food, and as a part of ritual worship and the preparation of food for gods and goddesses.

**Guru:** A teacher and spiritual guide.

**Jatak:** A horoscope prepared by a fortune-teller, astrologer, or Brahmin.

**Jati:** Each caste, or varna, is further divided into sub-classes, each representing a stratum in the strict hierarchy of Indian society. While there are only four castes, those are broken into thousands of jatis, as is the outcaste strata.

**Jogi:** Wandering singers and dancers who accomplish amazing physical feats, such as piercing their skin with lances, eating fire, snake charming, and firewalking. They claim to be fully invested with powers of control over the material universe.

**Kara:** A rich strip of edging that decorates a fine and expensive mundu.

**Karma:** The sum total of a person's actions that is believed to lead to his or her present fate. This major tenet of Hinduism easily brings about an atmosphere of fatalism which can lead to hopelessness.

**Kshatriyas:** The second of the varnas, or castes, in Indian society. Formerly the kings and soldier-warriors, they, like the Brahmins, are respected and privileged. Also like the Brahmins, they may be "twice-born." Many are in the military, and many others are successful business owners and landlords. Kashatriyas make up about 5 percent of the Indian population.

**Kurta:** A collarless Indian shirt.

**Malayalam:** The language spoken on the Malabar coast of South India.

**Mantra:** Sacred words and sounds used for rhythmic chanting.

**Manu:** Known as "the Hindu lawgiver," it is his writings in the Manusmriti that codified the strict caste rules. Manu reduced the Untouchables (now called Dalits) to a status worth less than animals. He subjected them to continual abuse, exploitation, submission, and oppression, and sealed it as judgment from the gods. These rules continue to bind Untouchables to degrading, "polluting" manual occupations, and to keep them firmly under the heel of the upper castes.

**Manusmriti:** The writings of Manu (though said to be authored by the god Brahma) that codified the caste system and sanctified it as religious institution.

**Mem:** Short for Memsahib. (See below.)

**Memsahib:** Respectful address for an Indian to use toward a white woman.

**Monsoon:** The July to September season of torrential rain and wind. While the rains bring relief from the suffocating heat, it can be a time of treacherous downpours and flooding.

**Mundu:** A piece of thin cotton, linen, or silk cloth, fifty inches wide and five yards long, worn by men as a lower garment. It can be an ankle-length "skirt" or tied up to more closely resemble shorts.

**Neem:** A common and appreciated tree in India. Every part of this wonderful tree is used for medicinal purposes—bark, roots, leaves, branches, flowers, fruit.

**Outcastes:** Now called Dalits, these are the people who fall outside and below India's caste system. They are forced to occupy the lowest position in the Indian social order. For many centuries they accepted their miserable lot as their justly deserved karma, a result of their own sins in a former life. More recently they have attempted to assert the rights afforded them when India gained independence from Britain. These attempts are often met with strong resistance from the upper castes, and the results can be horrendous: torture, rape, massacres, and other atrocities. The dominant castes have deliberately prevented the outcastes from rising to the level of equality by imposing on them impossible limits in every area of life, from occupation to dress to the very right to eat and drink. The social order has been constructed to keep them helpless and subservient. A conservative estimate of the number of "outcastes" is 25 percent of the Indian population.

**Paddy:** This can refer to a food, in which case it means rice with the husk still on. Or it can refer to the rice field—the paddy field.

**Palanquin:** A decorated litter, used by the well-to-do as a means of transportation during times of important occasions.

**Puja:** Worship or a sacrifice before an idol.

**Purdah:** Seclusion. To be "in purdah" is to live in seclusion, going out only occasionally and only when fully covered up.

**Purification:** A ritual washing to remove sin and/or pollution.

**Rupee:** The most commonly used Indian currency.

**Sadhu:** An Indian holy man. Often, sadhus dress in saffron-colored robes that set them apart as dedicated to sacred matters.

**Sahib:** An Englishman. Often times, one who is very important.

**Sari:** A thin garment, fifty inches wide and five to six yards long, worn by Indian women, wrapped around the body to form a dress.

**Sati:** The ancient Indian practice of burning a widow alive, along with her husband's body, on his funeral pyre. Less commonly, it refers to the act of burying her alive in her husband's grave. In 1829 the British government declared the practice illegal throughout India, punishable in criminal courts. But a proclamation does not quickly change societal or religious practices. To the minds of Hindus, sati was an act of honor, the sign of a pure and righteous woman. It was also one of the very few ways a woman could hope to gain entrance into heaven.

**Sacred thread:** A thin rope of cotton threads worn over the left shoulder by all initiated males of the Brahmin caste— and, though less frequently, by those in the second and third castes too.

**Sanskrit:** The ancient language of India, and the language of the Vedas. Now it is used almost exclusively by the Brahmin caste for religious purposes.

**Sudras:** The fourth of the varnas, or castes, in Indian society, supposedly created from the feet of the creator god, *Brahma*. Although they are still people of caste, they are of much lower status and privilege. They cannot be "twice-born." They are relegated to such jobs as laborers and farmers and servants. In fact, they are believed to have been created for the purpose of serving the higher castes. Sudras are not allowed to read, study, recite, or even to listen to the Vedas. The stated penalty for doing so is horrific maiming or death.

**Thulam:** Sacred month on the Malayalam calendar, corresponding to October through November.

**Twice-born:** Under the Hindu social system, this was a sacrament of initiation open to members of the three upper varnas, (castes)—Brahmins, Kshatriyas, and Vaishyas. Regarded as a second—or spiritual—birth, the ceremony (*upanayana*) earns male caste members with a sacred thread to be worn at all times next to the skin over the left shoulder and across the right hip. Women are not included, regardless of caste.

**Untouchable:** An outcaste, as determined by the laws of Manu. Depending on strata, and on the area of the country in which one lives, this could also mean a person is unseeable (meaning laying eyes on them is polluting). Not long ago, polluting a member of an upper caste, even with a shadow, a footprint, or a drop of spittle that may result from speaking or sneezing, was crime enough to result in drastic punishments. Virat's situation is modeled after the father of a present-day advocate for Dalit rights. This prominent man attended Oxford University and has a doctorate degree, yet he is often spat upon and insulted by poverty-stricken outcastes because of his low-caste birth. Even though his tormentors may live in poverty on the streets, they are of a higher strata than he in the Indian caste system.

**Vaisyas:** Members of the third varna, or caste, in Indian society. Businessmen and traders, they are also high caste and may be "twice-born," although their status is much less than the two higher varnas. Vaisyas make up approximately 5 percent of the Indian population.

**Vara:** Stranger.

**Vedas:** Ancient Hindu scriptures, written in archaic Sanskrit in the form of a collection of mantras and hymns of praise to various gods. Vedas means sacred, revealed knowledge. The four Vedas are: the Rig Veda, the Sama Veda, the Atharva Veda, and the Yajur Veda. The Yajur Veda is considered to be the oldest and most important. The foundation of the philosophy of Hinduism, the Vedas set forth the theological basis for the caste system.

**Veranda:** An external covered platform that sits at ground level of an Indian house. In Virat's day, most of a family's living took place on the veranda.

**Yogi:** Indian holy man.

# Discussion Questions

1. For most Westerners, India is a country shrouded in mystery. We think of elephants and tigers, beggars and snake charmers and spicy food, dancers in jangling ankle bells and holy men in saffron robes. When you started this book, what were some of the pictures you had of India? Have those pictures changed? In what way? What words would you use to describe the country?

2. When Western missionaries came to India, they brought medical treatments and the strange idea that education is appropriate for all, regardless of caste. They also brought the Bible and its message of a God who loves all people. What do the exchanges between Dr. Moore and Abigail Davidson tell us about the difficulty of ministering in a culture one doesn't really understand? What did Abigail do to help her grasp the Indian culture? To what extent do you think she was successful? If you could give her a bit of advice, what would it be?

3. How does the abiding Indian belief in karma—that the sum total of a person's actions determines his fate—affect efforts to change one's life? Throughout the book, we see various characters comment about their lives being punishment for sins of the past (Virat, Latha, Ashish, Little One, Anup). How does this differ from the Christian belief in Original Sin?

4. Several characters and situations in this book are adapted from real people and actual circumstances. Virat's humiliating trek to the landowner in the first chapters is one of these. Another is the practice of killing baby girls, as Sethu the midwife was paid to do. Yet another is the maiming of children to make them into more pitiful beggars (Latha's blinded eye). What effect

might an adherence to karma have on such things? What effect might a Christian belief system have? Would there be a difference? Why?

5. The story of Saint Thomas's work in India, while apocryphal, is widely accepted among Indians. The Varghese family takes pride in its deep Christian roots. Why would Dr. Moore downplay the validity of this? Why would that history bring the landlord, Mammen Samuel Varghese, such a level of pride? In what ways does Mammen Samuel compromise his beliefs? Why? Do we Western Christians compromise our own beliefs for the sake of fitting into and benefiting from our culture? In what ways?

6. Many people believe the caste system to be the most onerous element of Indian society. How does this strict system of social strata differ from the British class differentiations of the time? How does it differ from the haves and have-nots we see around the world? The caste system (*varnas*) is part and parcel of Hinduism, yet the practice deeply impacts Indian Christians and divides churches in that country. Why do you suppose this is so? (HINT: You will see more about this in book 2, *The Hope of Shridula*, and book 3, *The Faith of Divena*.)

7. Some would compare the plight of Indian Untouchables (called Dalits today) to that of African slaves in the American South in the 18th and 19th centuries. In what ways are such comparisons fair? In what ways do the two kinds of servitude differ? What lessons might Indians take from the place African Americans have achieved in today's society? What hope might they gain?

8. The majority of Christians in India come from the Untouchable (Dalit) strata of society. How might adhering to Christian teachings affect their way of life?

(HINT: We'll see how they affected Mohandas Gandhi when he walks through the pages of book 2, *The Hope of Shridula*.) How might the growth of Christianity among the Outcastes affect the upper castes?

9. Many people ask how factual the situation is in which Virat finds himself. The answer: terribly factual. Today, millions of people are enslaved as bonded laborers, most of them in India. The majority belong to the Untouchable Dalit caste. Like Virat, their enslavement comes about because of a loan from a moneylender. Laborers work long hours in fields or factories or rock quarries, seven days a week. They must accept the moneylender's meager shelter and food, and the cost is added to their bills at inflated prices. No matter how hard they work, the debt is never paid off. Some families are enslaved for generations. With this so familiar a plight, why do you suppose people still borrow from moneylenders? What options might they have?

10. The title of this book is *The Faith of Ashish*, yet we never see the fruition of the child Ashish's faith. Is this a realistic conclusion? (HINT: He comes back in book 2, *The Hope of Shridula*.) Why do you think the book has "faith" in its name?

The Blessings in India saga continues with *The Hope of Shridula*, which will be published in Spring 2012. Here's a sample of the next book of this enthralling series.

❧

# 1

## May 1946

The last of the straggling laborers hefted massive bundles of grain onto their weary heads and started down the path toward the storage shed. Only twelve-year-old Shridula remained in the field. Frantically she raced up and down the rows, searching through the maze of harvested wheat stalks.

Each time a group of women left, the girl tried to go with them, her nervous fear rising. Each time Dinkar stopped her. The first time she had tried to slip in with the old women at the end of the line, the overseer ordered, "Shridula! Search for any water jars left in the fields." Of course, she found none. She knew she wouldn't. What water boy would be fool enough to leave a jar behind?

By the time the girl finished her search, twilight shrouded the empty field in dark shadows. Shridula hurried to grab up the last bundle of grain. Its stalk tie had been knocked undone and wheat spilled out across the ground. Quickly tucking the tie back together, Shridula struggled to balance the bundle up on her head. It shifted . . . and sagged . . . and sank down to her shoulders.

Shridula was not used to managing so unwieldy a head load. In truth, she wasn't used to working in the field at all. Her father made certain of that. This month was an exception, though, for it was the month of the first harvest. That meant everyone spent long days in the sweltering fields—including Shridula.

The girl, slight for her twelve years, possessed a haunting loveliness. Her black hair curled around her face in a most intriguing way that accented her piercing charcoal eyes. Stepping carefully, she picked her way out of the field and onto the path. Far up ahead, she could barely make out the form of the slowest woman. If she hurried, she still might be able to catch up with her. The thought of walking the path alone sent a shudder through the girl.

Shridula tried to hurry, but she could not. With each step, her awkward burden slipped further down toward her shoulders. She could hardly see through the stalks of grain that hung over her eyes.

"Please, allow me to lend you a hand."

Shridula caught her breath. How well she knew that voice! It was Master Landlord, Boban Joseph Varghese.

Afraid to lift her head, Shridula peeked out from under the mass of grain stalks. Master Landlord, fat and puffy-faced, stood on the other side of the thorn fence, ankle-deep in the stubbly remains of the wheat field. His old-man eyes fastened on her.

Shridula reached up with both hands and grabbed at the bundle on her head.

"Do not struggle with the load," Boban Joseph said, his voice as slippery-smooth as melted butter. "The women can retie it tomorrow. Let them carry it to the storehouse on their own worn-out old heads."

A shiver of dread ran through Shridula's thin body. She must be careful. Oh, she must be so very careful!

⁂

All day long, as fast as the women could carry bundles of grain from the fields, Ashish had gathered them up. He separated the bundles and propped the sheaves upright side-by-side in the storage shed. Everything must be done just right or the grain wouldn't dry properly. One after another after another after another, Ashish stacked the grain sheaves. By the time the last woman brought in the last bundle, by the time he stood the last of the sheaves upright, by the time he closed the shed door and squeezed the padlock shut, then kicked a rock against the door for good measure and headed back to his hut, the orange shards of sunset had already disappeared from the sky.

A welcoming glow from Zia's cooking fire beckoned to Ashish. He watched as his wife grabbed out a measure of spices and sprinkled them into the boiling rice pot. But this night something wasn't right. This night Zia worked alone.

"Where is Shridula?" Ashish asked his wife.

Zia bent low over the fire and gave the pot such a hard stir it almost tipped over.

"She has not yet returned from the fields," Zia said in a voice soft and even. But after so many years together, Ashish wasn't fooled.

The glow of firelight danced across Zia's features and cast the furrows of her brow into dark shadows. Ashish ran a gnarled hand over the deep crevices of his own aging face. He yanked up his *mundu*—his long, skirt-like garment—and pulled it high under his protruding ribs, untying the ends and retying them more tightly.

"She should not have to walk alone," he said. "I will go back." Ashish spoke with exaggerated nonchalance. He would remain calm for Zia's sake.

✑

"All night!" Ashish said to his daughter when she came in at first light. He spoke in a low voice, but it hung heavy with rebuke. "Gone from your home the entire night!"

Overhead, Ashish's giant *neem* tree reached its branches out to offer welcome shelter from the early morning sun. Twenty-eight years earlier, on the day of his wedding, Ashish had planted that tree. Back then, it was no more than a struggling sprout. Yet even as he placed it in the ground, he had talked to Zia of the refreshing breezes that would one day rustle through its dark green leaves. He promised her showers of sweetly fragrant blossoms to carpet the barren packed dirt around their hut.

But no breeze pushed its way through this morning's sweltering stillness, and the relentless sun had long since scorched away the last of the white blossoms. Still, the tree was true to its promise. Its great leaves sheltered Ashish's distraught daughter from curious eyes.

Zia stared at the disheveled girl: *sari* torn, smudged face, wheat clinging to her untidy hair. Zia stared, but said nothing.

"Master Landlord told me I must go with him." Shridula trembled and her eyes filled with tears. "I said no, but he said I had to obey him because he owns me. Because he owns all of us, so we must all do whatever he says."

"Please, Daughter, stay away from Master Landlord," Ashish pleaded.

"I did, *Appa!*" Shridula struggled to fight back tears. "I dropped the bundle of grain off my head and ran away from him, just as you told me to. He tried to catch me, but I ran into the field and sneaked into the storage shed the way you showed me and hid there. All night, I hid in the wheat shocks."

"That new landlord!" Zia clucked her tongue and shook her head. "He is worse than the old one ever was!"

Zia reached over to brush the grain from her daughter's hair, but Shridula pushed her mother's hand away. Her dark eyes flashed with defiance. "Someday I will leave here!" she announced. "I will not stay a slave to the landlord!"

*✍*

Boban Joseph was indeed worse than his father. Mammen Samuel Varghese had been an arrogant man, a heartless land-owner with little mercy for the hapless Untouchables unfortu-nate enough to be caught up in his money-lending schemes.

Yet Mammen Samuel took great pride in his family's deep Christian roots—he could trace his ancestry all the way back to the first century and the Apostle Thomas. He also clung tightly to the fringes of Hinduism. The duality served him well. It promoted his status and power, yet it also fattened his purse. Even so, Mammen Samuel Varghese had not been a happy man. He seethed continually over the sea of wrongs committed against him, some real and others conjured up in his mind.

Still, it had always been Mammen Samuel's habit to think matters out thoroughly. In every situation, he first considered the circumstances in which he found himself, then measured each potential action and carefully weighed its consequence. It's what he had done when he lent Ashish's father the hand-ful of rupees that led to his family's enslavement. Only after such consideration would Mammen Samuel make a decision. His son Boban Joseph did no such thing.

Do you have questions or comments?
Would you like to learn more about author
Kay Marshall Strom?

Visit her at her website www.kaystrom.com
and on www.GraceInAfrica.com

You are also welcome to join in the discussions on her blog:
http://kaystrom.wordpress.com

Abingdon Press has many great fiction books and authors
you are sure to enjoy.

Sign up for their fiction newsletter at
www.AbindgonPress.com
You will see what's new on the horizon, and much more—
interviews with authors, tips for starting a reading group,
ways to connect with other fiction readers . . .
even the opportunity to comment on this book!